Praise for
Women Outside the Walls

"Not {as we say here in the UK} quite like the home life of our dear young Queen, but rich in character and place. A good read."
--*Ann Purser,*
Author of the Lois Meade Mysteries

Praise for
TRISHA SUGAREK

"It's an astonishing work *{Ten Minutes to Curtain}* that finds a way to say so much with so little. A perpetual battle ground for issues of trust and mistrust, laughter and misery, overwhelming loss and astounding triumph."
--*BookReview.com*

"*Butterflies and Bullets*" comes off splendidly. These truncated pieces of life feel like literary snapshots…. The collection feels utterly whole… Sugarek keeps everything in a minimalist range, lending focus to intimate moments and her style reveals that every place is connected."
--*BookReview.com*

"Her style is appealing for the wit and unexpected twist of the exchanges."
--*Educators in Argentina*

"Trisha's poetry had me hooked from the very first with *Joy Filled Canine*. Dog-lovers will recognize the essence of dog at once. The joy, living for the day. `brandy eyes alight` - that's it, in three words.. *Song of Agony* - a bullet straight to the heart. A short tale of desperation, and again, pared down to a distillation of pain. There's where Trisha Sugarek's considerable talent lies.
--*Ann Purser, British Author*

Also by
TRISHA SUGAREK

<u>Poetry</u>

"Butterflies and Bullets"
" Haiku Poetry " with Sumi-E Artwork

<u>Plays</u>

"Ten Minutes to Curtain, Vol. II" A Collection of short plays
for the young Actor
"Cook County Justice"
"Scent of Magnolia"
"The Guyer Girls"
"Emma and the Lost Unicorn"
"Stanley the Stalwart Dragon"
"The Exciting Exploits of an Effervescent Elf"
"Women Outside the Walls"
"NEXT! A Hollywood Tale"
"Sins of the Mother"
"Possession is Nine Tenths"

<u>Juvenile Fiction</u>

The Fabled Forest Series
"Stanley the Stalwart Dragon"
"The Exciting Exploits of an Effervescent Elf"

WOMEN OUTSIDE

the

WALLS

Trisha Sugarek

Cover Design by Lori Smaltz

ISBN #9781453715017

1. Female friendship-Fiction. 2. Prison life-Fiction. 3. Women struggles-Fiction.
4. Chicago-Fiction.   5. Life change events-Fiction. 6. Hostage negotiations-Fiction.
7. Contemporary women-Fiction.

FIRST PAPERBACK EDITION
10 9 8 7 6 5 4 3 2 1

Dedication

To the women who wait......

AUTHOR'S NOTE

A few years ago I visited a state prison for men in Illinois. My first time ever, doing research for one of my plays. I was visiting a confessed murderer, Bill, and writing his story. *Cook County Justice* was about an innocent man who, at that time, had served fifty years. I sat in the reception area, very nervous and scared; much like Kitty in the beginning of this story.

I was deeply moved by the nameless women around me who come to visit their men. One woman told me that she was visiting her son and had been coming once a month and every holiday for thirteen years. During another time in her life she had faithfully visited her husband for fifteen years while he served time. Many of the children I saw had spent their growing up years in a visiting room behind bars.

The process that I write about [and went through] is accurate in this story. Most notable about the visiting room was the frustration, anger and fear. The air was thick with rage and disappointment emanating from inmates and their families.

There seemed to be two types of prisoners; ones like Bill who were 'keep your head down, don't make any waves, and speak in a monotone voice' kind. And the other type who were aggressive 'in your face' bullies and troublemakers who were always running a hustle.

As I sat there interviewing 'my murderer' I was struck on a visceral level about how these women coped year after year. How did they come to be here? Was it a simple matter of choosing the wrong men? Did they grow up with the same dreams most women have about living with a good husband and raising wonderful children? As I sat there I wondered; where did it all go so terribly wrong?

TS

ACKNOWLEDGEMENTS

Thanks to my friend, Shirley K. who has walked the walk and lived it all. Shirley kept my story true and shared her life with me as one of the women outside the walls.

Thanks to Bill Heirens, a confessed murderer [Cook County Justice], whom I visited in prison. Bill unwittingly introduced me to the women who were seated in the waiting room one rainy Sunday morning. Briefly, for a few hours, I was one of those women who waited to visit a man in prison.

Thanks to the characters in this book. I started with an idea and they took me along on their journey.

Thank you to the professional negotiators, who will remain anonymous. They generously advised me on hostage situations and negotiations. Please forgive me for the dramatic license that I took while writing this story.

And finally a heartfelt thank you to my readers who, over the years, have given me the encouragement to continue to tell my stories.

Trisha Sugarek

WOMEN OUTSIDE

the

WALLS

A Novel

~Prologue~

Reno, Nevada
1992

Scorching, desert sun soaked into the roof of the mobile homes, the aluminum so old and weathered that there was no reflection. Heat shimmered off the trailers, the rusted out cars parked in the weeds, and even the dirt. An abandoned tricycle laid on its side, the red paint worn away and one wheel missing.

A young girl bolted out the front door of one of the older trailers and scrambled down the four wooden steps to the road.

"You get back here, ya little bitch!" a male voice bellowed from inside.

The girl sauntered down the street between other mobile homes just like hers. A jaunty baseball cap shielded her face from the blinding light. Her sandals flapped on the hot pavement. She wore pristine white short shorts and a pink sleeveless blouse tied off at the waist.

As far as the eye could see were rust streaked, silver trailers with faded trim, red dirt and black sticky pavement with not a shrub or a flower in sight. This was her life and she couldn't *wait* to get out.

The few damp tendrils that had escaped her hat sparkled with fire where the sun touched them. Even though Alma had just turned sixteen, her body had blossomed into that of a full grown beautiful woman. As she walked away she muttered to herself.

It'll be a cold day in you-know-where before I take orders from one of Mom's boyfriends. How can she stand them? Ugh! You'll never catch me settling for some low life boyfriend. I don't take guff off nobody. Especially not from some lousy, drunken, pig of a step-father, or 'uncle' or whatever the heck Mom's calling this one.

Alma was concentrating on where she was going and what her future might hold when a deep voice called out.

"Hey, Lady Bug! Where you off to in such a hurry?"

Alma's head snapped up and when she recognized the voice calling from behind a screen door, a smile lit up her face. She slowed her angry march as she came up to the door of the neighboring trailer, accenting the sway of her hips.

"Hey, Charlie!" Alma purred. "Just goin' for a stroll; wanna come along?"

"Sure, lemme get my beer." the man replied as he stepped back into his door and almost instantly reappeared. He joined Alma in the middle of the street and they began to walk. The man was in his early twenties, and what he lacked in height, he made up for in physique.

He was unbelievably handsome, with shaggy, light brown hair that just touched the collar of his shirt. His cobalt blue eyes, with silver flecks, sparkled when he looked at her. As they walked down the middle of the road, Alma's smile had slowly faded and she appeared deep in thought.

"Whas' up? You're awful serious today."

"It's nothin'." Alma said."Come on now, tell Charlie what's buggin' ya," he replied.

"It's just that creep my Mom's got livin' with us.
What a loser!" Once Alma started the floodgates
seemed to open. Charlie was her best friend and always
listened, *really* listened to her.

"He lays around all day drinkin' beer while she goes
out to work. Then when she comes home he claims he
was out lookin' for a job. She has a few beers with him
and then the arguing begins. I don't know why she
keeps pickin' these losers." She sighed.

"She moves one of 'em in, pays the bills, and
supports the bum. In the end it's always the same; they
fight every night and finally he smacks her around and
she kicks 'im to the curb. I am *never* gonna' have a boy
friend like that! I've got plans, big plans, believe you
me!"

Charlie stopped in the road and Alma walked a few
steps before she realized he wasn't beside her anymore.
She stopped and looked around.

"What?" she asked.

"He's not botherin' you, is he?"

"What'd ya mean?"

"He's not touchin' ya?"

"Ha! That'll be the day! Just let 'im try somethin'
like that! I'll kill him!"

"You sure?" Charlie insisted.

"Wha'd you care?" she asked.

Charlie scowled at her. "I thought we were friends,
Alma. Friends look out for friends."

"Well, thanks, but you don't need to worry. He
wouldn't dare try anything like that. Besides, he's not
my type."

"Oh, really? And what would be your type be, at the
wise ol' age of fifteen?" Charlie laughed.

"Sixteen!" she corrected him. "Last week and you

know it. Anyway, my type is none of your beeswax."

"Okay, okay, don't get your knickers…." Charlie cleared his throat realizing what he had been about to say. *I've got no right to refer to a young girl's knickers in any context.* "Ah….I mean…don't get all mad and everything. I was just wondering."

He paused, thinking about her turning sixteen. "So…how does that old saying go? 'Sweet sixteen and never been kissed.' Would that describe you?"

Alma blushed at how close Charlie was to the truth. *Why does he only see a child when he looks at me? What I want is for him to realize that I'm a woman now and that* he's *my type. How can I convince him of that when he's with Cassandra?* She wondered to herself. *How can I compete with a tall, willowy blonde waitress who works a real job at the diner? I have to* do *something.*

As they walked along, Alma took off her cap and shook out her hair. Reddish gold flared to life as the sun's rays found her hair. She smirked sideways at Charlie "You volunteering to be the first?" she asked.

"*Me?!* No way. In case you haven't noticed, kiddo, you're jail bait."

It's now or never. Alma decided. *This is a perfect opportunity to get my first kiss and if I play it right, it could be with Charlie.*

"'Cause if you are, volunteering that is, I wouldn't mind if it was you."

Alma buried her face in the fall of her long hair. She was dying of embarrassment. *What if he turns me down? I'll lock myself in my bedroom and never come out.*

They had walked past the mobile home park and out into the desert. The sun was cradled in the saddle of the distant mountains and everything was turning a soft purplish pink. Charlie took her hand and led her off the road and into the shade of a mesquite tree. With his hand, he playfully dusted off a large flat rock.

"Sit." He ordered. "Okay, here's the deal, Alma. We're friends. I hope you know I would never hurt you. So, I'm gonna tell you a few home truths. Don't be in such a danged hurry to get your first kiss or… anything. You got lots of time. Be choosey. Don't go with the first guy who asks you. And whatever you do, don't sell yourself short or cheap."

"Jeez, forget it! I don't want your danged old kiss. I was just seein' if you would."

Charlie scowled down at her. "You know I'm with Cassandra for however long it lasts and I'm a one-woman-at-a-time kinda guy."

Tears glistened in Alma's eyes. "Are you sayin' that I'm cheap?"

"God, no! I was just sayin' slow down."

"Oh." Alma thought that over. She looked up at Charlie through her long, brown eyelashes.

"You never gave me a birthday present, Charlie."

Alma's lightning change of subjects had Charlie scrambling to catch up with her. "Well, I've been busy with work and all…"

Alma's eyes flashed with mischief. "So, now I know what I want from you for my birthday."

"And what's that?" Charlie asked.

"My first kiss, from you…"

"Goddamnit! Alma, haven't you been listening to a word I've been sayin'?"

Alma stood up. "Yes I have. But that doesn't change the fact that I'm now sixteen, have never been kissed and you owe me a birthday present.

Besides I feel safe with you."

"Alma, don't ask that of me. It's not right. I'm twenty-three and you're just a kid. I'm old enough to be your…" He fumbled for an example of a family member.

"Older cousin? Older '*kissin*' cousin?" Alma grinned up into his face. "Come on, Charlie. I want my first to be from someone I lo…*like*… Who's a friend and who has some experience. You do have experience, don'cha?"

"Knock it off, Bug. A'course I got experience. But the problem is, you don't. I would feel like a perv."

Alma decided she had to take matters into her own hands. Before Charlie knew what she was about to do, she grabbed his shirt front and mashed her body against his. Wrapping her arms around his neck she rose up on the tips of her toes and put her lips against his, not certain what to do next. His lips were so soft and warm she thought her bones would melt.

There was an instant when the world stood still for both of them. Then Charlie's arm encircled Alma's waist and his other hand cradled the back of her head. He broke away an inch and looked into her eyes which had darkened from their usual coppery hue to a rich brandy color.

I am so going to regret this, Charlie thought. *This is exactly what I have been trying to stay away from… she's just a kid, for Chrissakes.*

Groaning, he bent down and kissed her mouth softly. Alma made a purring sound in the back of her throat. Charlie lightly licked her bottom lip with the tip of his tongue. Her lips opened on a sigh. Need flooded Alma's innocent body. A growl emitted from Charlie's chest as his tongue played with hers.

My God, some dark recess of Charlie's brain still worked, this *is so wrong. Why does this feel like it's my first kiss? My heart feels too big for my chest and other parts of me are swiftly getting out of control. What the hell...? Space...lots of space between me and this young goddess is what I need.* He kissed her gently once more, then taking her firmly by her arms, set her away from him.

"There ya go, Bug, your first kiss."

He laughed to cover the storm of emotions that were bubbling up inside him. *What was going on here? This is just a kid, a girl, never in a million years is she right for me.* He laughed again.

Alma flinched at Charlie's laugh. *My first kiss ever and it's more exciting than anything I've ever fantasized about and he stands there laughing? I won't cry, I won't! At least not in front of him.*

She flipped her hair back. "Yep! And not half bad for an *old* guy," she retorted. "Thanks, Charlie."

Alma whirled around and ran down the road as if she was being chased by devils. Tears streamed down her face as she sobbed out her hurt. *I'm in love for the first time and he laughs?*

"Hey, Alma, wait a sec," Charlie yelled after her. "What the hell just happened?" he muttered to himself.

Alma ran all the way back to her trailer, pounded up the steps and through the front door.

As she stumbled down the hallway a drunken voice followed her.

"Hey, baby, get your Daddy a beer, would ya?"

"Fuck off!" Alma yelled back as she slammed her bedroom door and threw herself onto her bed in a torrent of tears.

* * * *

A week later Alma still felt humiliated about '*the kiss*'. She made certain that she avoided Charlie and never went outside when he was home from work. It was seven o'clock in the evening and she knew Charlie was working the night shift at the plant.

Alma peeked out the front curtains. *Chances are pretty good that I won't run into him and if I don't get out of the house,* Alma thought, *I'll surely go crazy. It's probably safe enough to walk down to the laundry room. Even though it's across the street from Cassandra and Charlie's trailer,* she reassured herself, *Charlie's at work by now.*

She stripped the sheets off her bed and gathered up the dirty clothes lying around and tossed them into a basket. Her mother's loser boyfriend sprawled in a lounger, snoring in front of the television.

Alma went to the tiny kitchen and took down the jar of quarters from the cabinet and stuffed a handful into her pocket. She walked through the living room and out the front door. She purposely let the screen door slam.

"Huh? Wha?" the boyfriend jerked out of his chair.

The desert sun was setting and the temperature had dropped so it was a pleasant walk in spite of the heavy basket of dirty clothes she carried. Alma opened the door to the laundry room and backed through it with the large basket held tightly in front of her.

As she turned around she realized that the room was not empty. Big as life, there was Cassandra cramming clothes into a machine.

Isn't this just great? Alma thought, *can't I catch a break, just once?*

"Hi." Alma said.

"Hi." Cassandra said, not looking at Alma.

"How're things?" Alma asked.

Maybe she'll say something about Charlie.

Cassandra turned around and Alma saw that her eyes were puffy, her nose was red, and her skin was all blotchy.

"Hey, what's wrong?" Alma asked.

"Nothin'!" Cassandra snapped. "Mind your own business."

"Okay, sor-rey. I was just askin'. You don't have to bite my head off."

Alma began loading clothes into two machines and angrily fed quarters into the slots.

Cassandra looked over. "Look, kid, I'm sorry, okay?" Cassandra sniffled. "It's just something you wouldn't understand."

"Guy trouble, huh? You and Charlie have a fight or somethin'?" Alma asked, jealousy smeared all over her words.

Cassandra collapsed on a bench and began to cry. "He's gone," she whispered.

"What?" Alma said.

"He left me. Said he won't be back. I thought…" She began to cry harder. "I thought we had somethin'."

"What do you mean, 'gone'?" Alma's voice was too loud but she couldn't seem to help it.

"What don't ya understand about the word 'gone', kid? Adios, vamoosed, vanished. Get it?" Cassandra cried. "He told me he couldn't hang around anymore. Told me it was great while it lasted. Basically, the bastard kissed me off!" Cassandra replied.

Alma stared at Cassandra for a few seconds, set her basket down carefully on top of the washing machine. She turned, and walked out the door of the laundry. In a daze, she walked down the road. *Charlie was gone? Without telling me he was going? Why? We're friends.*

How could he do this and not tell me? How could he leave and not take me with him?

She stumbled back to the trailer and up the stairs to the front door. As she entered the living room her mother's boyfriend was awake and slugging down another beer.

With a loud belch, he gazed up at Alma. "Hey, kid, there's a letter for you. I think I put it here some- where." He patted his dirty wife beater undershirt as if the letter was lurking somewhere between his hairy chest and the large stomach that hung over his belt buckle.

He looked around and then laughed. "Oh, yeah, here it is. Guess I was usin' it for a coaster last night." He sheepishly lifted his beer can off an envelope and wiped it against his T-shirt where the can had left a wet ring.

"Oops, sorry 'bout that."

"Gemme that!" Alma snatched the envelope out of his hand.

"Jesus, you don't have to get so pissy," he said.

Alma rushed down the hall to her bedroom.

The letter had to be from Charlie. No one wrote to her. She slammed her door shut, locked it and crawled onto her bed. The envelope had only her name across the front; no return name or address and no stamp. She carefully tore the end off and unfolded the single sheet.

She quickly read the signature at the bottom. She smiled. *It was from Charlie! He hadn't forgotten me totally.*

'Ladybug,

I'll be gone when you read this. Gotta go, kid. <u>Your</u> first kiss was more than I bargained for and it would be a big mistake for me to hang around.'

Unshed tears filled her eyes, Alma read on.

```
'I'm not comin' back and it would be
better if you forgot about me. I'm sure
gonna try to forget about you and that
kiss.
    Take care of yourself and remember
what I said, about bein' choosey.

Your friend always, Charlie'
```

Alma read it again and then a third time. She didn't know whether to cry or laugh. *The kiss meant as much to Charlie as it had to me. He loves me. But, he's gone. It doesn't make any sense. Why did he leave? It's because I'm a kid and he's older. But, doesn't he know that I don't care about that*

"Oh, Charlie, how could you?" she sobbed, tears streaming down her face. She curled into a small ball with the letter clutched to her chest. He was gone and her heart was broken.

Chapter 1

Statesville Prison
Illinois-2011

Kitty

"Mother must be spinning in her grave," Kitty muttered, as her chauffeur drove up the long driveway to the main entrance of Weston State Prison.

"The daughter of a daughter of the American Revolution visiting her husband in prison. My mother would die of shame, except that she's already gone. Thank God she didn't live to see this day."

The tall, distinguished black man, with salt and pepper hair, who drove for Kitty Lancaster, glanced into the rear view mirror.

"Excuse me, Ms. Lancaster, Ma'am?" I didn't catch that."

"Nothing, Beasley. Just drop me at the front door, if you would, and then go and park the car," Kitty replied.

"Yes'm."

Kitty opened her purse and took out a Tiffany makeup mirror and checked that her perfect hair was perfect and that her flawless makeup was flawless. She was not beautiful in the classic sense but she was often referred to as handsome. Her hair, a deep auburn, was styled twice a week. Her personal trainer made certain that she kept fit and trim. Preferring the French designers, her couture clothes were Chanel and conservative.

Gathering her furs about her Kitty shivered as the

shiny black town car pulled up to the front steps of the cold, granite building. It wasn't particularly cold outside but still she trembled when she thought about what she was required to do today.

This was the administration building of the Illinois State Correctional Facility for Men. She had been directed to this place by her attorney for her first visit with her incarcerated husband.

Beasley exited the car, trotted around and opened the rear door for her. Kitty stepped out and stared at the heavy doors where an armed guard stood just inside.

"Ma'am?" Beasley asked. "Are you sure?"

Kitty was silent. As much as she loved her husband, Edward, she wasn't certain she could do this. She could just imagine the filth, the criminals and the potential violence that awaited her.

"Ma'am?" Beasley repeated.

"What?" Kitty snapped out of her reverie. "Oh, yes Beasley, thank you, I'll be quite all right." Kitty straightened her posture and with chin held high, she walked up the steps and through the doors.

The first thing she noticed was the smell and all the other women that waited in the lobby. It reminded her of a DMV office with the uncomfortable chairs and benches. The same smell of old cigarettes and Pine Sol. Along the back wall was a counter manned by a woman in a correctional officer's uniform. Unrelieved black trousers and tie with a shirt that must have been white and crisp at some point. Her hair was short and frizzy.

She was talking on the telephone and ignored Kitty. Kitty walked to the counter amidst snickers and mumblings from the other women waiting and watching her. Still talking into the phone the woman guard pushed a clipboard over in front of Kitty. Kitty ignored it, tapped her manicured fingernails on the counter and stared at the woman,. With a beleaguered sigh Anne spoke into the telephone.

"Hang on a sec." She covered the receiver with one hand and shoved the clipboard closer to Kitty. "Sign in, please."

Anne turned back to the phone and continued telling her friend "...so I go over there to the garage and the mechanic says...."

"Excuse me." Kitty interrupted.

"Hold on *again,"* snapped Anne. "Sign in and then go have a seat."

Anne took a closer look at the woman standing in front of her. "You haven't been here before, hav'ya?" Anne turned back to the phone, "Gotta go, I'll talk at ya later. Yeah, see ya at Smitty's at seven."

Anne hung up the phone and turned to the back wall, gathered several sheets of paper and then turned back to Kitty.

"You'll need to fill these out. After you're finished, bring 'em back to me and sign in here. Be certain to write in the full name of the inmate you are visiting. Who are you here for?"

"Edward Lancaster," Kitty replied.

"He must be new; doesn't ring a bell right off. Okay, fill these out, and bring them back to the counter."

"My dear woman, I don't believe you know who I am."

"I'm guessing, Mrs. Edward Lancaster?" Anne said.

"Yes, Mrs. Edward Lancaster, the second, to be exact and I'm here to visit my husband. Now! I don't see any reason for all these forms. Completely unnecessary," Kitty sniffed.

She'd used that tone with board members on down to

head waiters and it had always gotten her whatever she wanted But oddly it didn't seem to be working with this five-foot two, one hundred-ten pound, frizzy haired prison guard. She could hear the other women behind her, twittering and murmuring about her interaction with the officer.

I might as well have a bull's-eye painted on my back, Kitty thought. *If looks could kill that blousy redhead's scorn is literally burning a hole in my silk blouse.* Kitty sighed. *Oh well, these women are of no concern to me. Just get on with it, Katherine;* she admonished herself as she turned back at the sound of Anne's voice.

"These forms are *completely necessary*, if you want to see your husband today," Anne said, staring Kitty down until she blinked.

"Well, really!" Kitty gathered up the forms and stepped aside. She took a gold pen from her purse and began to fill them out. "I had no idea there would be such a fuss," she muttered.

Chapter 2

Alma and Chelsea

Red lipstick half way to her mouth, Alma watched the drama at the front counter. Her daughter, Chelsea, elbowed her.

"She's a virgin, huh Alma?" whispered Chelsea. A teenager, wise beyond her fifteen years, Chelsea was a pretty adolescent now, but it was evident that she would be a stunning beauty as she matured. Her strawberry-blond hair, falling to the middle of her back, was natural and her green eyes were made even larger with expert make up. Her torso was concealed in a large man's dress shirt and her legs were encased in Slim-Jim jeans. Her designer high-tops were untied.

Alma laughed. "Oh yeah, a virgin and a rich one to boot. What the heck was she thinkin', comin' here dressed like she was shopping on Fifth Avenue?" Alma looked down at herself distracted by the contrast of her clothing.

"How does this blouse look, Chels? Do you think your father is gonna like it?" Alma fished inside her blouse to fix a bra strap; then cupped her breasts and did a little jiggle to create more cleavage.

"Jesus, do ya gotta do that in public?" Chelsea said.

"Hey. Watch the swearing!" She looked across the room. "Wonder who 'her highness' is here to see. From the looks a'her she could'a sent her maid for this job."

Alma stood and did a pirouette. She was lovely in spite of the heavy makeup. Her bright red hair was piled on top of her head with messy tendrils framing her heart-shaped face. Expressive green eyes sparkled as she asked, "How 'bout these jeans? Too tight, ya think?"

Chelsea was about to answer when the officer's voice rang out, "For Baldwin! You can go in now."

"Tie your shoes, baby," Alma told Chelsea.

Poking her fingers into the mess of red hair on top of her head, Alma adjusted a few well placed strands and with a sensual roll of her hips she crossed the room and waited at the heavy steel portal.

Chelsea hurriedly tied her shoelaces and ran to catch up with her mother. The door silently slid open and the two women walked into a small glass enclosed space, facing another heavy door. The door closed with a whisper behind them.

"I hate this part," said Chelsea.

"I know, honey. It takes just a minute and we'll be outta here," reassured Alma. The door in front of Alma and Chelsea opened as if Alma had uttered '*Sesame*'.

"There. See? Not so bad," said Alma.

"I still feel like I'm buried or drowning or something," Chelsea complained.

"I don't know where you got this fear of small, closed spaces. Ya didn't get it from me."

They walked into a large cafeteria style room with two dozen tables and chairs all bolted down. The linoleum floor was a sickly green and the chairs and tables were a faded orange. Alma sashayed up to a podium where another guard was seated.

"Hey, Brad honey, how's it hangin'?" Alma asked. Flirting with the young handsome guard was so much fun. Guaranteed he'd blush in five seconds. "Ya got a....table for me, handsome?" She purred.

Here it comes, watch for it... Alma thought to herself. *Three, two, one...Voila! The kid doesn't know whether he's on foot or horseback when I'm around,* she gloated. *He's probably not too much older than Chels and brand spanking new with the department of corrections. He's so cute, all embarrassed and shy around me.* She gloated. *Like most men he laps it up like a puppy.*

"Yes, Ma'am, Mrs. Gaynor. Table three."

"Brad, honey, don't call me 'ma'am'. It makes me feel so old and I'm just a couple of years older than you," Alma laughed and walked away.

"Oh, brother," Chelsea muttered.

"Hi Chelsea," Brad blushed an even brighter red.

"Yeah, whatever," replied Chelsea.

Alma made her way slowly to her assigned table, making certain that every man in the room had a good view. She basked in the low cat whistles and groans as she walked by.

"Here's our table, Chels," she told her daughter, making certain that her husky, sexy voice carried to the men nearby. Chelsea slouched into her chair, across from her mother.

"God, Alma, do you have to be such a spectacle every time we come here? Daddy would be really mad if he saw how you act."

"There's nothin' wrong with taking care of yourself and being proud that *others* appreciate it," Alma said. "You could take some lessons. Look how you're dressed. You're never gonna get a boy friend lookin' like that. If I was your age again I'd be showin' it off, you can bet money on it."

"Yeah, well you're you and I'm me, thank God."
Chelsea sighed.

What was keeping Charlie, Alma wondered. *I'm
sure not used to men keeping me waiting...for anything.
I hate this place where men are the bosses. Except for a
few furtive looks at my boobies and butt, these guards
couldn't care less about the favors I can bestow.*

I've just been without a man too darn long, she
complained to herself. *Why did I have to fall for a guy
who gets himself sent to prison? I'm dyin' to get my
hands on Charlie, even if it is for only two minutes.
What a stupid rule! And it looks like I'll never get laid
again what with Charlie always getting write-ups. No
conjungle visits for me any time soon. God, I hated this
dump!*

"What's wrong, Alma?" asked Chelsea.

"What? Oh, nothin' baby. Just thinkin'."

"Sour thoughts." Chelsea observed. "Your face looks
like sour grapes. Careful it don't freeze that way."

Alma laughed. "You remember what I used to tell
you when you were a little girl, about your face
freezing?"

Alma kept an eye on the door and suddenly it opened
and Charlie walked in. "Ah, there he is," Alma said.

Charlie swaggered across the room, and gave the
guard only the slightest nod. Brad held up three fingers,
indicating Charlie's table assignment. The sleeves of his
shirt were rolled up showing off his muscular arms. His
jeans were tight and the well toned muscles of his thighs
were visible through the denim.

As he wove his way through the tables he
approached a black couple sitting quietly. He passed
their table and bumped the chair of the woman hard.

His voice dripped with sarcasm, "Pardon me,

Ma'am." Charlie glared at the black man sitting opposite her.

Joe Washington jumped to his feet, his hands curled into fists. He was six inches taller and fifty pounds heavier than him but that didn't matter to Charlie. He'd killed a man with his bare hands so Joe presented little threat.

Standing his ground, Charlie growled, "Go ahead, *Boy*. Come on, come and get some."

Hattie Washington lay her hand on her husband's arm, "No, Joe, don' do nothing. Please."

"It's Joe or Mr. Washington to the likes of you, cracker." Joe snarled. "You got a short memory 'bout what happened the last time you messed with me. You keep away from me and mine or you won't walk away next time."

"Baldwin, go sit down with your family," Brad called out.

Charlie ignored the guard. "Take your best shot," Charlie said. "Last time ya caught me by surprise, a lucky punch. Go on," he taunted. "I don't mind the 'hole' nearly as much as you do."

"Joe, please, sit down. It don' matter," Hattie pleaded.

As the two men faced off, Brad got up and started across the room. "Hey, you two, sit down. Baldwin, get over to your table, NOW!"

Joe sat down. Charlie turned to walk away and muttered under his breath, "This ain't over, Washington."

"Anytime, Baldwin, you just name it," Joe replied.

Charlie continued over to where Alma and Chelsea waited. Chelsea jumped to her feet and ran to meet her father.

"Daddy! I missed you!" She hugged her father close. "Who was that man? Why are you mad at him?"

"He's nobody, little girl. How's my baby been?" Charlie kissed the top of her head.

"Just fine, but I ain't your baby no more. I'm fifteen, you know!"

Charlie laughed. "When did 'ya get to be so old?"

"Oh, Daddy, you know I turned fifteen last summer. I'm almost sixteen."

"Stay fifteen, will ya? I'm not ready for you to grow up. Remember, you'll always be my 'baby' even when you're fifty and got no teeth."

"Eeew, gross!" She playfully punched his arm. "How ya been, Daddy?"

"Couldn't be peachier. Ya know this here country club is the lap of luxury." Charlie grinned at his daughter.

"You're so funny." Chelsea wrinkled her nose, "This ain't no country club that's for sure."

"Sure it is and after I say hello to your Ma, we'll go out to the swimming pool and have some drinks brought to us."

He looked across at Alma, his eyes eating her up like a starving man. He let go of his daughter and reached for Alma. "Goddamn, woman, you look good enough to eat. C'mere."

Alma rushed into Charlie's arms and they kissed deeply. Charlie's hands lowered to Alma's butt and he cupped her, pressing her to his body as close as possible.

Alma moaned into his mouth.

"Oh, Charlie, I missed ya so much. Give Mama some sugar," Alma sighed as she ground her hips into Charlie. In the haze of sensual heat they barely heard the pencil tapping on the podium as Brad signaled them to break it up.

"Alma," Chelsea said, "Break it up. Daddy's gonna get in trouble with the guard over there."

Reluctantly, Alma and Charlie pulled apart and Alma slowly licked her bottom lip with her tongue. As she walked to her chair Charlie's smoky, passion filled eyes never left her.

"God, Alma, it's been a long time since we...," he glanced at Chelsea, "...never mind. You know what I mean."

"I know baby. If you could just behave better we might get a shot at some conjungle time," Alma purred.

"You mean 'conjugal' don'cha, Alma?" Chelsea asked with a straight face.

"Huh?" Alma said.

"Hey, I thought I warned you about calling your Mama by her name. She's your Ma and you're not gonna call her Alma. Understood?

"Oh, Charlie, it's okay..." Alma said.

"No, it ain't neither," Charlie insisted.

"But, honey, it makes me feel so old when she calls me 'Ma'."

Charlie raised his voice, "Yur her mother, for Chrissakes. Tell her you're sorry, Chels."

"Sor...rey." Chelsea said begrudgingly.

"Sorry, what?" asked Charlie.

"Sorry, *Ma*. Jeez, Daddy, what's the big deal?" Alma interrupted, changing the subject.

"How ya been, honey?" She asked Charlie.

"OK, I guess. As good as it can be locked up in this hell hole. How 'bout you two? Are you doin' all right?"

"We've been just fine, sweetie. Haven't we, Chels?"

"Who's shirt you wearin', Chels?" Charlie asked his daughter.

"Yours, Daddy. It's okay, right? You're not using it and besides all the girls are wearing their Daddy's shirts this year."

"Of course it's okay, Doll. In fact help yourself to any of my shirts at home. When I blow this joint, I'm getting all new ones anyway."

"Can I have your purple shirt?" Chelsea asked.

"Don't know why yur askin' now; you been wearing it for months," Alma muttered.

Charlie grinned at Chelsea. "Sure you can. That ol' thing ain't gonna fit me now anyway." Charlie flexed his biceps. "I been workin' out every day, ya know."

In a honeyed voice that she had learned from her mother, Chelsea purred, "Thank you, Daddy."

She turned to Alma, eager for a little payback about the 'Ma/Alma' nonsense. She hated it when her Daddy found fault with her.

"Tell 'im what you been doin', *Ma*."

"I don't know what you're talkin' about Chels. And if you know what's good for you, you'll stay outta my business."

Charlie pulled a prison credit card out of his shirt pocket and handed it to Chelsea. "How 'bout you go get us some sodas?"

"Save that card for later, hon. I bought you a new one with fifty bucks on it."

Alma handed it to Chelsea."Use this one, Chels."

With a dirty look aimed at Alma, Chelsea took the proffered card. She turned back to her father and smiled, "Sure, Daddy. Any flavor okay?"

"Sure, baby, but remember I don't like that Dr.

Pepper crap. And none of that diet stuff. I want the high octane kind. It's as close to a beer as you can get in here."

Laughing, Chelsea rose and walked away.

Charlie sat very still and stared at Alma. Trying to cover her discomfort, she started talking fast.

"There a virgin outside." She mimicked a voice that she thought sophisticated women used. "Very hoity-toity. La-de-da! Fur coat and *everything!* She got real pissy with the visitor intake officer. Refused to fill out the forms like she was somethin' better than the rest of us."

Charlie continued to stare at Alma with a stone cold expression on his face.

"Whad' Chelsea mean...'tell 'im what ya been doin', Alma."

"Nothin' much, baby, really."

Charlie continued to look at her, not saying a word.

"Now, Charlie, don't get all mad okay?" Alma whined.

Charlie answered in a disingenuous tone. "Why would I get mad, Alma? What 'ya been doin'?"

"Nothin' much." Her voice dropped to a whisper. "I went back to work."

"I'm sorry, I couldn't have heard you correctly." Charlie's icy tone sent shivers up her spine. "Could you say that again? So that I can understand."

"I said I went back to work." She replied defiantly.

"That's great, doll, 'cause I know when you say, 'back to work' you couldn't mean strippin'. Right, Alma? You don't mean to say you're dancin' again."

"Now, baby, don't be that way. I had to."

"What the fuck do you mean, 'you had to'?"

"We needed the money."

"You promised, Alma. When Chels got into her teens you promised you'd stop. That was our deal after she was born. Or have you conveniently forgotten?"

"I tried, Charlie, really. But other kind'a jobs don't pay five hundred a night."

"I told you no more and I meant it! That's not something I want my daughter around. Why can't you work in an office or somethin'?"

"Cause I'm a exotic dancer, that's why. That's what I *do*."

"Yeah, sure you are. If that's what you want to call it."

"Well, I am. That's what you called me when you came back to Reno. You said I was the best dancer you ever seen. You tol' me that, Charlie." Alma whined.

"That was then. This is now. I don't want ya strippin' no more. We got a daughter we gotta think about. I got one thing in my life that's good and clean and sweet and that's Chelsea. I don't want my daughter around yur strippin', whorin' friends."

"You're so nasty, Charlie. Why ya gotta be that way?" Alma trailed her long, red fingernails up Charlie's forearm. "Don'cha love me no more?"

"Goddamn it, Alma. 'Course I still love ya. I guess I always will. But, I swear to Christ, sometimes you are as dumb as a box'a rocks."

"Baby, I had to start dancin' again. That's the only way I know how to make good money, ya know that. That old poot who manages the park was after me about the rent. Tol' me if I didn't get caught up he'd evict us and sell the trailer. Then where would Chelsea and I be? Besides that, Chels needs stuff."

"That's how you're gonna get it for her? By takin' your clothes off?" Charlie snarled.

"You can call it exotic dancin' but you and I both know what your customers expect." Charlie glared at her and gripped her arm. "You whorin' Alma?"

"Charlie...!"

The guard rapped the podium with his pencil and called out. "Baldwin! Take it down a couple of notches or your visiting time is over."

Charlie let go of Alma and sat back in his chair.

"I ain't whored a day in my life and you know it!" Alma cried. "Shame on you. I ain't turnin' tricks. You should know I got more respect for myself than that. I went back to work dancin'...jus' dancin'. We can't make it with you in here. And yur never gonna get out if ya keep gettin' into trouble." She peeked at him through her lashes.

"Please honey, ya know I can't do no other kind'a job and make that kind'a money."

Alma paused to see what Charlie would say. He sat there and stared at her. Alma reached into her pocket and brought out a pack of cards.

"I brung the cards, ya wanna' play some Gin?"

Chelsea walked up, her hands holding three soda cans. "We gonna' play cards? Can I play, Daddy?"

"Sure, baby. A nickel a point, okay?"

"Oh, Daddy, you know I ain't supposed to gamble. You always told me 'a lady don't gamble'."

Charlie laughed. "*not* suppose to' gamble, no such word as 'ain't. And what I said was, 'a lady never gambles with her own money."

He slapped the table and laughed at his own joke. "Deal the cards, Chels." He looked Alma in the eye, "We ain't through with this conversation, Alma."

Chapter 3

Alma ~ nineteen years ago

Alma sat on the steps of her trailer. Her elbows were resting on her knees and her chin was resting on her joined fists, *Well hell, what am I suppose to do now?* She wondered. *My money will run out in a month and the rent's due on the first.*

As she reviewed her options she watched Cassandra, Charlie's ex-whatever, walk up the road from the mail boxes. She appeared to be headed home. Alma ducked her head in the hopes that the woman would walk on by.

"Hi kid." Cassandra said as she neared Alma.

"Hi." Alma replied.

"How are things?"

"Okay." Alma said. She stared at the dirt at her feet and didn't look up.

"It sure is quiet around your place. Your Mama's boyfriend not at home?"

"No."

"Where's your mom, at work?"

"Uh...yeah." Alma said.

Cassandra could always spot it when someone was lying to her. She hadn't grown up with two younger sisters for nothing.

"Come on kid, what's goin' on, really?"

Alma looked up and stared at Cassandra weighing how much she might be able to trust the older woman.

"My Mom took off, *okay*!?"

"Took off where?"

"Somewhere in Arizona. She left a note and some cash and she's gone. She's not comin' back." Alma's chin wobbled on this last part.

"Holy cow! When did this happen?" Cassandra exclaimed.

"She's been gone about a week more or less."

"I knew there was a new guy but....well...what happened?" Cassandra asked.

Alma dug a wrinkled piece of paper out of her jeans.

"Here's the note, you're welcome to read it." She thrust the paper at Cassandra. "The new guy said I cramped his style."

Cassandra took the letter and sat down on the step next to Alma. She read the note out loud,

'Alma, baby, Bruce has got this great new job in Arizona or maybe it's New Mexico. Anyway, he wanted me to go with him. But, here's the bad news, kiddo. He says no kids, they cramp his style.

You're practically grown anyways so I know you'll do just fine. I'm leavin' this money for you until you get a job. The rent's paid up on this piece of shit until the end of the month.

I'll write when we get settled. Love, Mom'

"Nice, huh?" Alma's eyes filled with tears.

"Geez kid, that's tough. What kinda mother would leave her kid behind?"

"My kind obviously." Alma brushed a hand roughly across her eyes.

"What're ya gonna do?"

"I'll get by, don't you worry about that."

"How much money did she leave ya?"

"A hundred and fifty bucks plus what's in the quarter jar. I got a little money of my own."

"But the rent's two thirds of that and that's due in two weeks."

"I'll get a job. I can take care of myself!" Alma's voice was full of bravado.

"Well, if ya need anything between now and then, you know where I live."

"Okay."

Cassandra didn't know what else to say. She stood up and looked down at Alma. "Well, I gotta get changed and get to work. I'll talk at ya later."

Alma didn't answer. She had resumed checking out the dirt at her feet. Cassandra walked away, shaking her head.

* * * *

At ten o'clock the next morning Cassandra pounded on the door of Alma's trailer. When there was no answer she opened the screen door and checked the front door. It was unlocked. Cassandra opened it and stuck her head inside.

"Alma? Yoo-hoo, anybody home?"

Cassandra was surprised at how neat and clean everything was. The kid was definitely not a slob like her mother. She walked down the hallway toward the bedroom.

"Alma? You here?" She said as she opened the bedroom door.

Alma was sprawled across the bed sound asleep.

"ALMA!" Cassandra said in a loud voice. "Rise and shine!"

When there was no response Cassandra grabbed the covers and yanked them off Alma.

"Hey! Cut it out!" Alma reared up. She was dressed in an old ratty T-shirt that reached her knees.

"Get up. Why aren't you in school?" Cassandra asked.

"Didn't feel like it." Alma said.

"Get dressed and meet me in the other room in ten minutes. You can shower later. We got stuff to discuss."

"Who died and made you the boss?" Alma sneered.

Cassandra stood there and just stared at Alma.

Alma broke eye contact first. "Okay, okay, I'll be out in a minute."

Without another word Cassandra left the bedroom.

Muttering to herself Alma slipped on yesterday's jeans and, stripping off her night shirt, hurried into a sports bra and a fresh blouse. She stepped over to a mirror, picked up her hair brush and ran it through her long curls. *I don't know who this broad thinks she is bossin' me around. It's none of her business if I go to school or not. Geez, why doesn't she mind her own beeswax anyway?*

Alma sauntered down the hall and walked into the living room. Cassandra was at the kitchen sink filling a coffee pot with water.

"Where's the coffee?" she asked.

Alma slumped into the lounge chair. "We keep it in the freezer."

Cassandra retrieved the ground coffee from the freezer and put some scoops into the filter basket and flipped the switch on the coffee machine.

"I assume you drink coffee?" She asked Alma.

"God, yes. And I could really use some this morning, what with unexpected company and all."

"Save your sarcasm for someone else, little girl."Cassandra warned. "Why was the front door unlocked? Anybody could have waltzed in here."

"I guess I forgot to lock it. No big deal."

"Yeah, you say that until you find some creep walkin' in on ya."

"Nobody except you knows my Ma and Bruce are gone."

"Still."

"Okay! I'll be more careful in the future, okay?"

The smell of freshly brewed coffee started to fill the air. Cassandra opened a cupboard door looking for cups.

"Over the stove is the coffee mugs." Alma said.

'The coffee mugs are over the stove' Cassandra corrected her.

"Yeah, whatever."

Cassandra reached up and got down two mugs. One had a garish logo from a local casino stenciled on the side and the other one said, 'World's Greatest Mom'. Cassandra poured the hot steaming coffee into them and, carrying both mugs, walked to the dinette in the corner.

"Come over here and sit." She instructed Alma.

Alma sighed and got slowly to her feet. She walked over and slouched into one of the kitchen chairs.

"Ya want some milk for your coffee? I think it's still good." Alma waved her hand at the refrigerator.

"Naw, I like mine black. Thanks anyway."

"Yeah, me too. My Ma always said she liked her coffee and men the same way; 'hot and black'.

But she never dated black guys as far back as I can remember."

"It's just a jokey expression, Alma, and highly inappropriate to say to you."

"Whatever."

"You got a fresh mouth on you, ya know that?"

"So?"

"So if we're gonna be roommates, you're gonna have to watch your tone. I don't put up with fresh kids."

"Roommates?!" Alma exclaimed. "What're you talking about?"

"You can't stay here and be on your own. It's not safe. Hell, you can't even remember to lock the doors."

"It's none of your business what I do."

"Well, I'm makin' it my business. Here's the deal so listen carefully. You'll move in with me. I got two bedrooms and two bathrooms. There *will* be rules. You will not skip school." She paused. "What grade are you in anyway?"

"I'm a junior."

"You will finish school. You can't have any failing grades. You will have a reasonable curfew. Since I work at night sometimes you will be on a honor system. You will not lie to me, *ever*. If you break the rules you will be grounded. In exchange I pay the rent, food and clothes for you. If you want spending money you'll have to get a part time job. If you do get a job I expect you to save part of your pay."

Alma stared at Cassandra, in shock. *Why is this broad doin' this for me. I don't get it. She's gonna take me on?*

She can't ever find out how relieved I am. How much she's saving me.

"Well, what's it gonna be?" Cassandra asked.

"What if I say no?"

"Then I'm callin' child protective services and they'll put you in foster care until you turn eighteen."

"You wouldn't!"

"I would and will."

"Well, that's not much of a choice." Alma sulked. "You sure got a lotta rules."

"Oh that's just half of them. I'll make up more as we go along."

"I'm not goin' into foster care."

Cassandra stuck her hand out. "Okay, then, do we have a deal then, roomy?"

Alma stared at her hand. She tentatively took Cassandra's hand and shook it. "Yeah, I guess so."

"Try not to be so enthusiastic, will ya? Your obvious joy is gonna make me cry."

Alma gave Cassandra a tiny smile. "And you call me 'sarcastic'."

* * * *

Two days later Alma sat in the living room amidst a few boxes, all her clothes on hangers, and two suitcases. The trailer had come furnished so she didn't have to worry about getting rid of the old tattered furniture. She sat and thought about the last few days.

Cassandra had given their landlord notice that she, Alma, was vacating her trailer. She informed him that she would be moving in with Cassandra. She'd also met with Alma's school and explained that Alma would be living with her. That any school notices or correspondence should be sent directly to her. Since she had left the school with the impression that Cassandra was Alma's aunt hopefully CPS would not get involved.

I can't believe I am moving in with such a cool lady. Alma thought. *I gotta figure out a way to get her to lay off so many rules. Geez, school every single day? And she's got a smarter mouth than I do and that's sayin' somethin'.*

There was a knock on the door and almost immediately the door opened and Cassandra walked in.

"Hey, kid, you ready?"

"Yeah, let's blow this joint." Alma grinned at her.

"I parked my car out front so we can load these boxes and the suitcases into the trunk. We can lay your clothes on the back seat."

Alma picked up two handfuls of hangers while Cassandra picked up a box.

"What ya got in here? Bricks?"

"Some books, some other junk." Alma frowned. "But we can leave anything you don't want to be bothered with."

"I was just joking with ya, Alma. You can take anything you want. We got plenty of room over at my place."

"I can't believe you gave me the big bedroom." Alma said as they walked out to the car.

"Why not? Is all I do is sleep in there. Besides young girls have got a ton more stuff that I do." She laughed. "Believe it or not I was a 'young girl' once myself."

"You're not that old."

"Gee, thanks."

They trooped back into the trailer for the rest of Alma's things.

"Better take a last look around. See if you missed anything."

Alma stepped into the kitchen and opened the

cabinet door above the stove.

"I almost forgot the quarter jar." She shook the jar and the quarters jingled merrily.

Cassandra looked over Alma's head and spotted the mug with the "World's greatest..." on it.

"I think you should take this along." Cassandra said as she reached up and took down the mug.

Alma stared at the mug, "I don't care about that. It's just a stupid old mug that I bought my Mom on Mother's Day."

"Well, I'm taking it with us. I kinda like it."

"Whatever." Alma glanced away and pressed her fingers to her eyes.

Cassandra turned away to give Alma a minute. She opened a box and pushed the mug inside. She straightened up and glanced around the room.

"It's funny, you know, how life works out."

"What'd ya mean?" Alma asked.

"Well, here we are two girls on our own being roommates and all. And both of us had crushes on the same guy at the same time."

Alma gasped. *She knew I was in love with her boyfriend? How did she know?*

"You knew?! How did you know?"

"Baby-girl, Cassandra knows *everything* so you better be careful."

Alma stood and gazed at her in awe.

"Oh! That reminds me. Ever bussed tables?"

"Uh...no." *What's Cassandra up to now?* Alma wondered. *There's no keepin' up with this chick.*

"Well, you can learn. The diner lost their bus boy and dishwasher and I put in a word for you. It would be the evening shift three nights a week and weekends. No Sundays. What'd ya think?"

"Really? A real job like you have?" Alma asked.

"Yep. But here's the deal. Your grades can't drop *at all* and you can't quit the cheer squad. Curfew still applies."

"Everything's a 'deal' with you."

"Take it or leave it." Cassandra grinned at her.

"What's it pay?"

"Minimum wage."

"I'll take it!" Alma crowed.

Chapter 4

Kitty

Kitty stood ramrod straight and stared silently at Anne while she shuffled through the forms that Kitty had handed her. "Relationship to inmate?" Anne looked up.

"I believe that I've already provided that information," Kitty sniffed.

"Well, you missed it on the form," Anne said, waiting.

"Oh for heaven's sake! Wife! I'm Edward's wife."

Anne entered it on the form, 'Wife'. Okay, then. Remove all belts, jewelry, purse... *furs."* Anne sneered. *"*Coat, hat, gloves and hand them over."

Shocked, Kitty stared at Anne. "I most certainly will not remove my jewelry or my clothing!"

"You can't take any valuables in with you, lady, especially your jewelry or money. They'll be stored in a locker and you'll get a key. You can buy a debit card at the machine."

"I will not put my furs and jewelry into a locker," Kitty sniffed.

"Okay," Anne sighed. "Your call. But I gotta warn you, you won't be seeing your husband today."

"How dare you?" Kitty said.

"Your choice," Anne said as she turned away to continue with her work.

"But, but…" Kitty sputtered.

Taking pity on her, Anne turned back. "Sorry, but them's the rules for *everybody*."

"For heaven's sake, alright!" Kitty began to take off her coat and her belt. She removed a diamond broach from her dress and the matching earrings and tucked them into her purse. She laid everything on the counter. "Satisfied now?" she asked Anne.

"You forgot your watch."

Kitty removed her watch and put it into her purse. "This is from Tiffany's. I hope your lockers are safe."

"Safe as a vault," Anne laughed and gestured around the room. "After all, look where you are."

Anne gathered up all of Kitty's belongings, turned to the back wall and opened a locker, shoved it all in and slammed the door. She locked it and handed Kitty the key.

"Here's your key. Come with me, please."

Anne walked down the length of the counter and Kitty kept pace with her on the other side until they reached a small cubicle. Three sided, the front was open. Anne led the way in while giving Kitty instructions.

"Remove your shoes, turn around with your back to me and face that wall…."

"Excuse me!? Kitty interrupted.

"I said, remove your…" Anne began again.

"I heard what you *said*. I'll do no such thing! Who do you think you are?"

Anne sighed. "Look, this is my job. Don't make it so hard. Now remove your shoes, turn around and raise your arms."

Starting to turn Kitty asked, "What do you propose to do?"

"Search you."

Kitty whirled back around, staring at Anne.

"You most certainly will not search me!"

"Look. If you want to see your husband, you get searched. *Every time.* It's no big deal. What's it going to be? You're not the only visitor I gotta process, ya know." Anne's patience had finally run out. "For the last time, do as I say or go home."

Kitty and Anne stared at each other. Finally Kitty sagged in defeat and reaching down, she removed her boots. Slowly she turned and faced the wall.

"Raise your arms straight out, please," Anne directed.

Anne's hands skimmed Kitty's torso and felt around her waistband and then her bra.

"Is that really necessary?" Kitty fumed.

"Yeah, it really is." Anne chuckled. "You'd be amazed at the stuff I find in a woman's bra." She then reached down and inspected the inside of Kitty's boots.

"Nice shoes. You can put them back on now. We're all done. Go back out and have a seat. I'll call you when it's time to go in,"

Kitty stepped into her boots and walked back out into the reception area. Head held high, she refused to let anyone see her cry. *How did I end up here, on a beautiful Sunday morning, in a prison waiting to see my husband who's an inmate? Heaven help me! Just a few short months ago Edward and I would have been on our way to the country club for a leisurely brunch with friends.*

She still wasn't clear on how trading stocks could land Edward in prison. Their attorney had tried to explain it to her but it just didn't make any sense. *It was Edward's money he had been using; it wasn't like he stole from someone.* Kitty sat on the far end of a bench and waited, trying to ignore all the stares from the other women.

* * * *

Hattie had watched the rich lady from the moment she walked through the front doors. She knew that the lady had no idea what was going to happen to her. The humiliation, the shame, the fear a person feels in a place like this. And she hadn't even gotten inside yet. Oh, yes, she knew because this sheltered, polished woman was just like the ones Hattie worked for six days a week, scrubbing floors and toilets. Wealthy women surrounded by people who took care of them and answered to their every whim. She watched as Kitty left the cubicle and walked to the bench that Hattie sat on. But the rich lady was careful to sit at the far end, away from Hattie.

Hattie turned to her with a sympathetic smile, "You ain't been here before."

"No." Kitty didn't look at Hattie.

"Well, ya'll get used to it. Miss Anne there she a decent lady. She jus' doin' her job."

Kitty didn't reply but just stared straight ahead as Hattie continued. "All us gets searched. It's them rules, ya know?" Hattie pointed to the far wall where there appeared to be an ATM machine.

"That there machine gives you a credit card to take in wit' ya. Jus' put some money in it and you get credit. That way ya can use the pop machines or gets yo'self a snack inside. Then what I do if there's any extra left on it, I leaves the card wid' my Joe for after. Joe's my husband."

"Thank you but I shan't have any need for that," Kitty replied.

Just then Anne's voice called out. "For Washington, you can go in now."

Hattie rose and started across the room. She paused and turned back to Kitty.

"Al'righ then. I'll see ya'll in there."

Chapter 5

Hattie and Kitty

K itty did not respond but watched Hattie go to stand in front of a set of heavy doors. The black woman was tall and raw-boned but walked like African royalty. Her hair was tightly braided and then wrapped in a coronet on the top of her head. She wore an off-the-rack dress probably from Target and cheap faux-leather flats. She wasn't beautiful exactly but the word 'regal' popped into Kitty's mind.

How do these other women tolerate coming here? Kitty wondered. *The black woman, obviously blue collar, had spoken with empathy and resignation. I'm just so much better than these women,* Kitty thought to herself, *richer, better educated, bigger house, and God knew, better clothes, How did they do this year after year? All I want to do is run screaming from the building.*

She shivered as she watched the doors slip open and, in one swallow, seemed to consume the black woman.

As Hattie waited in the security pod that led to the visiting room, she marveled once again at the smell. *I never will get used to this smell. It's a combination of Pine Sol, fear, hatred and hopelessness. I can't do anything about the smell of fear and anger, but I could shore teach them cleaning crews a thing or two about cleanin'. Who used Pine Sol anymore?*

There are products out there that left a room fresh and sweet smellin'. She shrugged her shoulders and walked up to Brad at his desk.

"Mornin', Mr. Brad."

"How're ya doin', Ms. Washington?" the guard replied. "Pretty spring mornin' out there. Take table four. Joe's on his way down."

"Thank you, Mr. Brad." Hattie walked straight to her table and sat down.

Across the room was a door that bore a large sign with red lettering. 'Personnel and Inmates ONLY. NO ADMITTANCE by Unauthorized Persons.' While she watched the door for the first sight of her husband Hattie had often wondered why anyone, unauthorized or not, would want to enter that door.

The door suddenly swung open. *There! There he was.* Hattie got chill bumps just looking at him. *It don't matter that we been married seventeen years or that he has been in this awful place for two of 'em, I still get chill bumps when I sees my man. He's so big and strong, and handsome in a craggy kind'a way. I never gets weary of seeing that face carved outta black granite. Only the laugh lines at the corner of his eyes,* she observed, *save him from lookin' stern and scary. Lord Jesus, I don' know what I done to deserve this fine man, but every day I thank you for 'im.*

Grinning at her, Joe walked to the table. Hattie rose and they embraced for the maximum two minutes allowed in the rules.

"Hi, wife." Joe spoke in a deep, melodic voice.

"Ah, Joe, I sure has missed ya."

"Missed you too, Hattie-girl. Where are the kids? Didn't they come with you?" Joe asked.

"No, none'a dem could come today.

Dey just scattered to the wind like a bunch 'a dan-do-lion weeds." Hattie laughed up into his face.

"Ruby had cheerleadin' practice, and Stella wanted to go with her big sister. JJ's got the flu bug so he's stayin' wid' your Mama. Lamar...well you knows Lamar. He got his nose into that there computer way too much."

"I understand the kids got activities but..."

"But what, baby?"

Joe guided Hattie back to her chair and sat next to her. "Well, I only get to see them once a month. I miss 'em."

"I knows, honey-bun. I jus' can't get down here more than that. That ol' car getting' more cranky by the hour. And the price of 'dat gas-o-lean, Lordy, it's sumpin' fierce."

"I don't want you to try and come more often after you worked all week. It's too much. But it's hard when I miss a visit with my young'uns." There was pain in Joe's voice.

"I know, Joey-boy."

After a moment, Joe suddenly grinned. "Anyway, you was sayin', 'bout the kids. Lamar stayin' outta trouble?"

Hattie smiled and took his hand. "Now, don't ya go worrying 'bout 'dat chil'. He knows his Mama knows what's what. Besides, he don't have no time to be bad no mo'. I got his little butt so busy with the swimmin' at the YMCA and bowlin' in the junior league af'ta school, he fall right in'ta the bed at night, half dead."

Joe laughed and kissed Hattie's fingers. "That's my girl. How's his grades?"

"They's sneakin' up, in spite of Lamar. He be okay, Joe. I don' want ya ta worry. There ain't goin' be no more trouble with 'dat 'der Juvenile Hall business *ever* again."

"I can't help worryin', girl. It's too much for you by yourself."

"We doin' jus' fine, Joe. But, Lordy, those kids is growin' up in a hurry, ain't they?"

Chapter 6

Alma ~ seventeen years earlier

Alma sat in the dingy, smoke filled dressing room of the Pussy Cat Gentlemen's Club. The walls throbbed with the beat of the music as her friend, Sally, finished up her number. Alma could faintly hear the crowd's roar as Sal did her famous upside down splits on the pole.

As she rubbed her feet, she gazed into the cracked mirror above her dressing table. *One more dance,* she thought, *and I'm through for the night. God, my feet hurt like hell. Oh well, where else am I goin' make this kind'a money? If those drunken fools out front are dumb enough to stuff their hard earned cash into my g-string I'm smart enough to take it.*

"Five minutes, Alma!" a voice shouted behind the closed door leading to the stage.

"Yeah, okay," Alma hollered back.

Alma rose and adjusted her costume. She was dressed in a western theme; red leather with white fringe that fit her like a second skin, a white cowboy hat, and white boots. Her vibrant hair was braided and tied off with red bows.

She checked her six guns to make sure they had caps in them and stuffed them back into the low slung holsters at her waist. *It's all about the fantasy with these rubes.* She mused to herself. *The secret was to not take everything off. Leave a little mystery and they kept comin' back and givin' me their money, in the hopes that one day I'll take it all off.*

As she walked across the room Sally came through the door.

"Pretty good crowd out there for a Thursday night," she told Alma.

"Yeah, I could hear through the walls that they approved of your splits," Alma laughed.

Sally began taking money out of her costume. "Keep 'em happy, that's my motto."

Alma laughed over her shoulder as she walked out the door. She stood in the dark, at the bottom of the steps that led to the stage, waiting for her music cue. These few minutes, alone in the dark with the smell of the place all around her, was the only time she allowed herself to wonder how she ended up here.

I had such big plans a couple of years ago. Where did it all go? She mentally shook herself. *Okay, Alma, stop feelin' sorry for yourself and get on with it. Your savings is growin' and as soon as you got enough you'll be outta here.*

The theme music from 'Annie Get Your Gun' started and Alma ran up the stairs and burst through the curtains. Wild applause and yelling greeted her. She danced and swaggered around the stage like a Wild West rodeo star.

Slowly the red leather, fringed mini-skirt and halter top were stripped off. The red bows in her hair were always thrown out to the crowd as keepsakes. It was a trophy that some of the men would fight over. Now clad in nothing but a g-string and a tiny strip of fringed leather that covered her breasts Alma drew her six guns and bent over with her rump to the audience. This was the climax end of her routine and she relished the reaction she always received. She bent over and aimed her six shooters at the audience between her legs. The caps always made a loud crack.

The men who frequented the club on a regular basis anticipated this finale and showed their approval by throwing lots of money on to the stage. When new-comers realized the symbolism of the guns going off they quickly followed suit to show their appreciation.

Alma whirled around and fired the guns off again, then raised each barrel to her mouth and sucked suggestively on the end of the barrel. She winked at the men, sitting in the first row, and blew the smoke out at the cheering throng. She holstered the pistols, turned and sauntered off the stage.

Yelling, clapping, and wolf whistles followed her as she disappeared behind the curtains. Being one of the stars at the club, someone else would pick up her tips from the floor of the stage and deliver them backstage.

Alma walked into the dressing room, sank into her chair and pulled off her six inch heeled boots. She rubbed her feet and moaned. She stripped the eye lashes off her eyes and carefully placed them in their case. She began to cream the makeup off her face. She rose and stepped over to the sink and splashed her face with cold water. Drying her hands and face she took a silk robe off a hook and put it on, not bothering to tie the front.

A stage hand knocked on the door and stepped through with a wad of cash in one hand and an iced drink in the other. He crossed the room to Alma and set the money and the drink down in front of her.

"Thanks, Scotty," Alma said. "You're a sweetie."

He blushed and murmured, "Any time, Miss Alma. Lots of ice with your Coke, just the way you like it. It was a good night for you."

Alma took a twenty dollar bill out of the pile of money and gave it to him.

"Thanks, Miss Alma, but you know you don't have to tip me."

"Sure I do, sweetie." She laughed. "You're my number one guy, ain'cha?"

"Yes, Ma'am." Scotty backed away and dashed out the door.

Next to Alma, Sally wiped the last of her makeup off and eyed the pile of cash. "Someday, I'm gonna' make as much as you, Al. Soon as I learn your secret."

"It's all in what you *don't* take off, Sal." Alma laughed. "I keep tellin' you girls that."

"But Ernie makes us go down to skin, you know that." Sal replied.

"Not this girl he doesn't. He knows better than to tell me how to dance." Alma snorted.

Suddenly the back door to the alley flew open and banged against the back wall.

"Holy shit!" Sally jumped up, knocking her chair over.

"Alma! Alma Gaynor! What the fuck do you think you're doin'?" Charlie stood in the doorway and yelled.

Alma rose and faced the back door. Her face was ashen and her mouth opened but no words came out. *Can this really be Charlie standing here in front of me? Three long years with no word and here he was like he had been gone a week.*

Charlie stomped over to her and, none too gently, grabbed the gaping sides of her robe and pulled them closed.

"Cover yourself, for God's sake! You're gettin' outta here right now!" Charlie shouted.

"Alma, who is this guy? Should I call Ernie?" Sal asked.

Alma finally found her voice. "No, it's okay, Sal, he's an old friend. Can you give us a minute?"

Sally hesitated. "Sure, honey. If you think it's okay for me to leave."

Alma stood gazing up at Charlie's face. "Yeah, it okay, really."

Her friend grabbed her purse and left.

Charlie frowned at Alma. "Get dressed; we're leaving."

"Says who?" Alma said, flipping her long hair over her shoulder. "You're not the boss of me."

"Says me," Charlie shouted into her face. "You're leaving if I have to put you over my shoulder and carry ya outta here."

Alma shouted back. "Yeah? You just try it! I work here and you got no say in what I do." Her curiosity got the best of her. "How'd you find me anyway?"

"I was sittin' out front, you little idiot! Christ! I've never been so embarrassed in my life. There I sat with my buddies and out you prance naked as the day you were born! I almost clocked one of my friends for what he said when he saw you shoot off those ridiculous guns."

"I was not naked!"

Charlie went on as if she had not spoken. "What the hell are you doin' in a sleazy joint like this? My God, you're just a kid!"

"I am not! I'm nineteen and in Nevada that's way past legal. And for your information I am one of the stars of this 'sleazy joint' as you so colorfully put it.

Which, by the way, is untrue. The Pussy Cat is in the top three grossing clubs in Reno."

"My God, are you bragging?" Charlie said. "I won't tell you again, get dressed, we're getting outta here."

"We are not! You think you can waltz in here three years later and tell me what to do? You left without saying goodbye…" As Charlie opened his mouth to contradict her, she held up her hand to stop him. "….that letter doesn't count. You should have told me in person. Over three years, Charlie, all that time without a word from you. I didn't know whether you were alive or dead!" She stamped her foot. "You can just get lost!" Alma's eyes filled with tears.

Charlie glared at her. "You…you…" he sputtered. He had no words to tell her what it meant to see her again. How beautiful she had become, how sexy.

A man of action and few words, he let his heart lead him and he crushed her to him, capturing her mouth with his. Alma struggled for a few moments then melted into him, her arms snaking around his neck. After several minutes, Charlie raised his head to look into Alma's eyes.

"My God, I did my best to forget you, girl, tried to forget that first kiss. Then I get dragged here by my buddies and what happens? You come dancin' out on stage and throw a goddamn red ribbon right into my lap." Groaning, he lowered his head again and took her mouth in a deep, passion filled kiss.

After several moments, Alma ended the kiss, breathing heavily.

"Charlie, why did you go? Why did you leave me behind?" she asked.

Charlie gently wiped a tear from Alma's face and sucked it off the end of his finger.

"You were too young. I was too old. You were too innocent and I was…."

Alma pressed two fingers against his mouth.

"Shh. None of that matters now, does it? You're back." She thought a moment. "Why are you back? Why now?" she asked.

"My Mom," Charlie replied. "She's sick…bad sick."

"Yeah, I know."

"You do? How?"

"I been to see her a few times since you left. She's a nice lady. Too nice to never hear from her only son," Alma reprimanded him.

"I know but I'm back now. Are you finished here for tonight? Charlie asked. "Will you come with me? Are you hungry? Where do you live? Not still with your mother?"

"God, no, Ma took off with a new guy shortly after you left." Alma said.

"And she just left you here?" he said.

"Well, you know Mama-Dearest. The new guy said a teenage kid cramped his style. You know what my Ma always said, 'a hard man was good to find'," Alma laughed.

"So, where do you live?" Charlie asked.

"Not far from here. And yes, I'm starved." Alma's smoky, intense green eyes gazed up into Charlie's. "Buy me dinner, will ya Charlie?"

Chapter 7

Kitty

"Lancaster. You can go in now," Anne's voice rang out.

Kitty rose and tentatively walked over to the doors as she had seen the other women do before her. She stood in front of them waiting but nothing happened. Just as she was about to turn and ask Anne to push a button or something the door slid open silently.

Kitty walked into the small chamber and the door closed behind her. Three of the walls were glass and as she looked out Kitty realized that no one was looking at her. No one cared.

The exit door into the visiting area wasn't opening. She was trapped. She rushed to the second door and raised her fist to pound on it when it began to move and finally opened.

Kitty rushed out into a cafeteria type room and stopped abruptly. She now felt embarrassed that the small enclosure had frightened her so. She looked around at the families gathered there. They sat with their men who were all dressed identically in blue jeans and soft, faded denim shirts.

The children were subdued as if they knew by instinct that noisy or bad behavior would not be tolerated in this place. For the most part, the women looked sad, tired and over worked but seemed determined to keep up a brave front. The younger ones were dressed in levis and sweaters while the older women appeared to have come directly from church and were wearing their best Sunday dresses with sensible black, low heeled shoes.

Kitty felt like she had just arrived naked at an Inaugural Ball. *What was I thinking this morning when I decided to wear a Chanel suit and silk blouse?* She marveled at her own stupidity. *Well, nothing left to do but bluff my way through it.* Kitty walked toward an empty table when a deep voice stopped her.

"Ma'am, you have to check in with me first," Brad called out to her.

Kitty turned and changed her direction. When she reached the guard's podium she had recovered her haughty, privileged façade. "Good morning. I would like to see Edward Lancaster, please," Kitty said.

"Yes, Ma'am, table five is empty. I'll call up and let the inmate know he has a visitor."

Kitty winced at the word '*inmate*'. She would never get used to it. She thanked the young guard and walked carefully to a table in the center of the room with a large number '5' stenciled on the top. As she walked by the other families seated at their tables, conversations died as she passed by.

She saw the black woman who had spoken to her in the waiting area and suddenly felt like she had a friend in this foreign land called prison. Hattie caught her eye and Kitty smiled tentatively. She was answered with a huge smile from Hattie and a little wave. Kitty reached her assigned table and sat down to wait for Edward.

I can do this. Kitty lectured herself. *I survived Edward being arrested, the trial, the turning away of what I thought were our friends, the expression on her son and daughter's faces. I must do this. For Edward. For me.*

Staring straight ahead, Kitty sat bolt upright at the table while conversations, laughter, and a low hum of anger and curses washed over her like a flash flood. She was so frightened. She'd never been around people like this.

Frustration and rage poured off the inmates. *The despair of these women is palatable,* Kitty thought to herself. *They wear too much makeup and laugh too loud as if to compensate for the hopelessness of their lives. What's keeping Edward?* According to the large, battered clock on the far wall, she had been sitting here for thirty minutes,

Finally a door marked *'Inmates and Personnel Only"* opened and Edward walked in. Kitty stood up, her face glowing with pleasure and took a step forward. Edward frowned at her, freezing her in place. He stepped over to the podium and waited.

"Lancaster, ya got a visit, table five," the guard told him.

Without uttering a word, Edward turned and walked toward Kitty, weaving between tables, his face blank. He looked older to Kitty somehow and diminished. *What had happened to him in the few weeks since he had been sent here? Where had the intelligent, powerful, successful stock broker disappeared to?* Kitty wondered.

In his place, the man now walking toward her was a tentative, cautious creature; almost like prey running a gauntlet of predators. Kitty was shocked at her thoughts. *Where had that analogy come from? She was just being fanciful, it's this place.* Kitty assured herself.

Edward reached her and sat down across from the chair that Kitty had occupied.

"Hello, Edward." Kitty sat back down, her eyes never leaving his face. "How are you?"

She reached for his hands but he subtly moved them out of range.

"Hello, Kitty, have you been well?"

"I've been fine, dear. They wouldn't let me come sooner. They said that there was a 'settling in' period before family could visit."

Edward frowned. "I thought I made it abundantly clear on the telephone that I did not want you to visit me here...in this place."

"Oh, Edward, for heaven sake, how can I not visit? You're my husband."

"I don't want you to see me in here," Edward said. "I don't want you here. Don't you understand? I don't want you sullied by this place or these people."

"Edward, I'm your wife. I need to see you, to see that you are all right. You shouldn't be in here, we both know that. It's all been a horrible mistake."

"Nevertheless here I sit," Edward said bitterly.

"What you did with the information about the merger...well, if your partners hadn't persuaded you...I don't know... somehow it all went wrong," Kitty replied.

"And let us not forget that I was the most logical fall guy. The oldest, kids all grown, wife a pillar of the community," Edward said. "We were so certain with it being a first offense; I would get a mild slap on the wrist, a hefty fine and probation. Slam dunk, I believe Richard called it."

"I still don't quite understand it all.

Regardless, you're here and I want to see you. Please, Edward," Kitty said.

"You're going to come here every Sunday for the next five years? *You?* Suffer the humiliation of coming to a prison, knowing you will see your husband dressed in inmate-denim?" Edward scoffed. "Believe me, you don't see too many Seville Row suits in here."

"I am not humiliated. I want to visit you as much as they will allow me to," Kitty sighed.

"No Kitty, I won't have it. That's my final word."

"Edward, I have to know how you are, how you are being treated," Kitty pleaded.

"I'm fine. Don't worry."

"Is that a bruise above your eye? What happened?" Kitty reached out to touch it.

Edward flinched away. "Nothing, it's nothing. I accidently ran into the cell door."

"But, Edward…"

Edward raised his hand. "Kitty, enough! They treat me fairly. I'll call once in awhile. Go home."

"But I have news," Kitty exclaimed. "I got a call from our attorney. Richard says that he is about to file an appeal. He's confident that there were some irregularities with the way that the police executed the search warrant. And some discovery issues at trial. He's quite optimistic."

"I know." Edward sighed. "He came to visit me. But, Kitty, you're forgetting one thing. I'm guilty. I did use information illegally for profit." Edward stared intently into Kitty's eyes. "Now, go home."

"Are you seriously suggesting that I forget about you?"

"Yes. If you're still there when I get out…well, then we'll see.

I still think you should consider a divorce."

Kitty's eyes shone with tears. "*Divorce you?* You must be mad. You expect me to just walk away? Forget that you are incarcerated. Ignore you for the next five years. Forget you're still alive. You must think me a frivolous, disloyal woman, Edward."

"Go home, Kitty." Edward's voice was sad and tired. "Don't come back. I won't see you."

"I'll do no such thing," Kitty exclaimed.

Without another word, Edward rose from his chair and began to walk away.

"What about your son?" Kitty said to his back. "What about Daniel?"

Edward stumbled at the mention of his son. He turned back. "What about Danny?"

"He wants to see his father."

Edward walked back to the table and sat down. "Absolutely not!" He hissed. "I've already told him, I don't want him coming here."

"He's heartbroken that you won't see him, Edward. Why are you doing this?"

"What do you think would happen if his firm heard about his jail bird father? His career as an attorney would be over forever."

"Some things are more important, Edward. Our son realizes that. He wants, no, he *needs* to see you. Can't you understand that kind of love?"

"I love our children, Kitty. But I'm firm on this. Tell Danny I love him...but he is not to come here. I won't see him."

"And Elizabeth? What should I tell your daughter?" Kitty asked.

"Christ, Kitty."

"Your daughter is expecting our first grandchild.

What do I tell her? Lizzy needs you."

"You don't make this easy, Kit."

Kitty laid her hand on Edward's arm. "None of it is easy. But I'm the one who has to try and make some sense of it...for our children."

Edward and Kitty stared at each other for several minutes. Edward rose and walked away again.

"Go home." He said.

"Eddie...don't!" Kitty pleaded in a whisper.

The use of her nickname for him made him pause. *She's not called me that for many years,* Edward mused. *If only I could take Kit in my arms and comfort her, change what was happening, make her smile again. But I'm not even certain I can survive five years in here. Better that I create some distance between us, that way she and the children can continue their lives without me. Even though the thought of losing them rips my heart apart.* He turned back to his wife.

"I'm firm on this. Don't come back. I won't see you, Kitty. Goodbye."

Kitty rose from her chair. She called after him. "I'll be back. You can't stop me, Eddie."

Edward walked across the room to the door he had entered only a few minutes earlier. The guard buzzed the lock open and as Kitty watched, Edward opened the door and was gone.

Head held high, Kitty walked to the podium and said, "I'd like to leave now, please."

"Sure thing. Just go wait by the door," Brad said.

Kitty walked to the heavy doors just as they began to open and she walked through. As the doors closed the ones in front of her opened. She walked into the reception area, tears glistening in her eyes but her step never faltered.

Anne looked up from her paperwork. "Well! That was quick."

Kitty handed her the locker key. "I'd like my things now, please."

Anne took the key, unlocked the locker and gathered Kitty's personal items into her arms. She turned back to the counter. She hadn't missed the pain on Kitty's face or the tears she so carefully kept from falling.

"Look, it's always tough at first," She told Kitty. "Your man just needs some time to get used to being locked up and you seeing him in here,"

"I'm sure I don't know what you mean," Kitty answered.

"Okay, have it your way then. See you next time," Anne shoved Kitty's things across the counter.

"Yes, thank you." Kitty put on her fur coat and crammed her belt, gloves and hat into her purse. She hurried across the reception room and out the front doors. She stood, shivering and crying, as the big black town car pulled noiselessly up to the curb. Without waiting for Beasley to open the door for her, she scrambled into the back seat and slammed the car door.

"Take me home, please, Beasley," she whispered.

Frowning, the chauffeur looked in the rear view mirror, "You all right, Mrs. Lancaster, Ma'am?"

Kitty tried to swallow her sobs. "I want to go home."

Chapter 8

Alma ~ Seventeen Years earlier

Charlie held the car door open as Alma slipped into the leather seat. She breathed in the rich smell of the interior of a new car. The seats were a luxurious chocolate brown and soft as a cloud.

"Where'd ya get such a nice car, Charlie? Rob a bank?"

"Been working the off shore rigs the last three years. It's hard work but big money. Nothin' much out there to spend your money on. When you come ashore all you want is a long hot shower and lots of uninterrupted sleep." He looked over at her. "Where shall we eat?"

"If you like Italian, there's a great little place not far from here," Alma said.

"That works for me. I'll need directions."

"Turn right up at the light." Alma laughed. "A man who can ask for directions, be still my heart."

"You always did have a fresh mouth for a kid."

"If you still think of me as a kid, you can let me out at the next bus stop."

"Cool down. After your performance tonight I'm scarred for life and will never *ever* think of you as a kid again. Believe me."

"Turn here. It's in the next block. See there, on the left. And a parking spot right in front. What are the chances?"

Charlie parked at the curb across from the restaurant. He got out and started around the car but before he could open the passenger door, Alma bounced out and slammed the door.

"Hey! Let me get your door, okay? I'm kind'a old fashioned that way. And please don't slam the door. It's not my old beater pick-up."

Alma looked at him. She didn't really know him anymore. "Okay, sorry. I'm just used to doing things for myself."

As they crossed the street Charlie had his arm loosely around her waist. He leaned down and whispered in her ear, "I like doing things for a lady."

As Alma reached for the door of the restaurant, Charlie gently took her hand in his and opened the door for her.

"Oops, sorry. Guess I'm gonna have to get used to this." Alma smiled up into Charlie's eyes.

The hostess greeted them and showed them to a table. The dining room was lit by candlelight and, this late at night, was only half filled with other patrons. The waiter came by with two water glasses, sourdough bread and a saucer of oil with fresh pepper for dipping.

Charlie could hardly tear his eyes away from Alma.

"You're staring." Alma told him as she tore a chunk of bread off the loaf and sopped up the olive oil with it. "What are you thinking?"

"I was wondering how you could be even more beautiful than when you were a k....before."

Alma shrugged. "Must be all the good food, fresh air and early nights," she joked.

"Yeah, about that. Are you sure that's a good career choice for you, Alma?"

Alma frowned at him. "Are you certain you want to

go down that path? Criticizing my job?"

"No, I was just asking. Don't get all prickly on me."

"My job choices are none of your business, so if you want this dinner to go on, my job is off limits. Unless of course you want to compliment my dancin' then we can talk about it. Okay?"

"Yeah, sure." Charlie was relieved when the waiter approached.

"Ready to order, sir?" He asked Charlie.

"Alma? Do you know what you want?"

"Yes, please. I'll have the chicken parmesan, a small dinner salad, no dressing."

"And for you, sir?"

"Give me the same, but I'll have blue cheese dressing on the salad." Charlie told him.

"Very good sir. Wine with dinner?"

"Alma?" Charlie asked.

"Not for me but you go ahead. The water is all I'll need, thank you."

"Same here." Charlie told the waiter.

The waiter thanked them and went away. Charlie looked at Alma and the way the candlelight illuminated her fiery hair. She had removed her stage makeup and her face was clean and beautiful.

"You're staring at me again." Alma teased him.

"Well, get used to it. You are a sight for these sore eyes. God! I missed you every day."

Alma blushed. It seemed like she had waited her whole life for Charlie to say things like that to her.

"You did?" She whispered.

"Yes, every day. What about you? What did you do when your mother took off? You were what? Barely seventeen?"

Charlie lifted his water glass and took a drink.

"Yeah. She left me a little money so I wouldn't starve. And I lived with Cassandra the last year and a half of high school."

Charlie choked on his water. He pounded himself on his chest and sputtered. "*Cassandra?* my…..?"

"Yeah, *your ex,* Cassandra. Funny how things work out huh? Guy takes off on his girl, breaking two hearts, Cassandra's and mine if you're wondering, and the two jilted girls end up living together. We enjoyed dissing you for months."

"My God! You and Cassy lived together?"

"Cassandra's a nice woman and still a good friend. She lives in San Francisco now and we keep in touch with email. She was really there for me since I had nowhere else to go. And she made sure I stayed in school."

"I can't believe it."

"She was so amazing, taking me on. Making sure I had some structure which was a real novelty for me. She really made me toe the line." Alma laughed remembering those days.

"I don't know what to say." Charlie groaned.

"Nothing to say, all blood under the bridge. We ended up thinkin' it was very funny."

Funny? They found it funny? Charlie stared at Alma. He would never understand the way that women thought.

The waiter arrived at that moment with their entrees. As he served them he announced what he had brought them.

"Two chicken parmesans and two small salads. Dressing on the side. Anything else, sir?"

"No, nothing, thanks."

"Very good sir," the waiter said as he departed.

Alma giggled.

"What?" Charlie asked.

"Oh, nothin' I just think it's hilarious. Waiters always tell you what they brought you as if it's a big surprise. I've always wondered why they do that."

"Yeah, you're right." Charlie chuckled. "I never noticed before."

Alma attacked her chicken. "God, I'm always starved after I finish dancing!"

Charlie picked up his knife and fork and slowly cut his meat. "So, where do you live now?"

"I'll show you after dinner. You *are* taking me home, right?" Alma asked. "This chicken is so good. How's yours?"

"Um, fine."

"How's your Mom doing? I haven't gotten over to see her in a coupl'weeks." Alma asked.

"She's not so good. Her cancer came back so she's doing the chemo thing right now."

"I'm so sorry. I'll try to get over there next week to see her."

"She'd really like that, Alma. Do you hear anything from your mom?"

Alma laughed. "Yeah, a Christmas card when she remembers she's got a kid. But hey, I know what she's like so I guess I understand. She was never June Cleaver. One thing she did do and that's teach me about men."

"What about men?" Charlie raised his eyebrows.

"Most of 'em are losers so stay clear. And I get daily reminders on that lesson."

"How's that?"

"Charlie, baby, look at where I work," Alma laughed.

"Yeah, I'll bet you see the cream of the crop," Charlie replied.

"So tell me about your job. What's it like workin' on oil rigs in the middle of the Gulf."

"it's hard work, sometimes it's dangerous. Down time is boring with nothing to do but watch TV and old movies. No women around. Chow's really good."

"Are you out there for a long time?" Alma asked.

"No, it's usually three weeks on, one week off. They shuttle us to the mainland by helicopter."

"Pretty glamorous life from where I sit," Alma observed as she wiped up her plate with a piece of bread.

The remainder of the meal was spent in small talk and catching up. Charlie couldn't get over how Alma tucked into her food. She could put any roust-about on the rig to shame. Finally she sat back with a contented sigh.

"God! That was so good! I love the food here."

"Want some coffee? Dessert?" Charlie asked.

"I don't know where I'd put it. Thanks but no. I'm full. And sleepy. Time to put this hard working girl to bed."

Alma grinned at him. *Let Charlie make what he would of that! Oh my God, he's blushing.*

"Okay, so you ready?" Charlie asked. At Alma's nod, he signaled their waiter for the bill.

When it arrived, Charlie threw down five twenty dollar bills and stood up. As they both rose from the table Alma blurted out, "Charlie! You're leaving way too much."

"Don't worry 'bout it. I've waited tables before. The guy is probably living on tips."

With his hand cradling Alma's elbow he guided her through the restaurant to the door. A light rain had begun.

"Wait for me here. I'll get the car."

Alma laughed and ran into the street. "I won't melt, Charlie. Besides, I love the rain; we get so little of it."

And with that she dashed across the street to his car.

Would he ever figure this woman out? Charlie wondered. *Would he ever get tired of her joy in the simplest things?* He doubted it and that scared the life out of him.

Charlie ran across and unlocked the car. Rain drops glistened in Alma's hair under the street light. He opened her door and she slid in, grinning up at him like the girl he dreamed about too often.

"Okay, where's home?" Charlie asked as he sat in the driver's seat and started the car.

"Up three blocks and make a left." she said

It was quiet in the damp, night filled car. Charlie recognized the smell of the strawberry scented shampoo Alma always used. He was unexpectedly touched that it was the same smell he remembered from when she was a kid.

He had to swallow the sudden emotion clogging his throat. Of course he wouldn't say that out loud, her being so prickly about the word 'kid'. He was yanked back from the past and the way she smelled by Alma's voice.

"You see that light up there about six blocks? Turn right, I'm in the first block."

"Got it." Charlie smiled. For a girl, she gave excellent directions.

"You give good directions, for a girl."

"Ha. Ha. For a girl, I do a lot of things good."

"I'll just bet you do." Charlie replied.

"Stop here. We're home." Alma said.

They had stopped in front of a Spanish style stucco, two story apartment building shaped like a horse shoe. The tidy landscaping surrounded a small pool.

"Very nice. No trailer park for you, huh?" Charlie asked.

"No way. They remind me of my mother's many boyfriends and the smell of stale beer and old dirty carpet. Wanna come in?"

Charlie didn't answer as he exited the car and walked around to open Alma's door. She sat perfectly still and watched him.

When he opened her door she said, "I could really get used to the old world charm, Sir Lancelot."

"Sir who?" Charlie asked as he ushered her up the walk to her door.

"One of King Arthur's guys. Unfortunately he fell in love with Arthur's wife. It didn't end well. But he opened car doors for her," she laughed. "Well, here we are."

Alma dug around in her purse and brought out her keys. She turned to Charlie and gave him that grin that caused his insides to turn to jelly and repeated her earlier invitation. "Wanna come in?"

"I'd better not." *What I ought to do is run for the hills. That grin of hers is gonna be trouble, with a capital 'T'.*

"Scardy-cat," Alma teased.

Charlie put his hands on Alma's shoulders and leaned in. She raised her head to meet his lips and closed her eyes. Charlie pecked a chaste kiss on the tip of her nose and backed away.

"Can I pick you up tomorrow night from work?" he

asked.

"No." Alma's eyes were bright with mischief.

"Oh….well." Charlie didn't know whether to be relieved or disappointed.

"I have tomorrow off. So if you want we can spend the day together." She batted her eyelashes at him.

"Oh! Great! What time? How's ten tomorrow morning?"

"Horrible. I don't get out of bed until noon on my days off. How 'bout we compromise and say two?"

"Okay. I'll be here at two." Charlie started to back away. "Okay then. Goodnight. See you tomorrow." He stopped, staring at Alma.

"Goddamnit!" He rushed back to her, crushed her to his body and gave her a heart stopping kiss. He released her after several minutes, so abruptly that she almost stumbled.

"The last time you kissed me like that and pushed me away, I didn't see you for three years." Alma told him. "Make sure you show up tomorrow, Buster!"

Charlie laughed. "I promise. See you tomorrow." He ran down the path towards his car.

Alma watched him go and whispered, "See you tomorrow, my love."

Chapter 9

Hattie

Hattie had been watching Kitty and Edward as she visited with her husband. Something was surely wrong there and she was shocked when the white lady's man got up and left the visiting room after only a few minutes.

"Oh oh, did ya see 'dat? Um,um,um, da prouder dey is, the harder dey gonna fall," she told Joe.

Joe watched Edward go through the door. "Wonder why Eddie say he got no fam'bly? Fine lookin' wife an' all,"

"Ya know that white man, Joe?" asked Hattie.

"Yeah, he got assigned to my cell when he got here," Joe said. "Don' say much, he's a real loner. I asked 'em 'bout family; he say he don't got none. Oh well, a man's got a right to his privacy. He sure don' belong in here. That piece of trash over there givin' him a real hard time."

"Who is 'dat white man? Is it 'bout this Eddie that gots the bad blood goin' twixt ya'll?" She asked. "Ain't like ya ta' be fightin' wit' no white man."

Joe scowled. "That's Baldwin. He's in here for murder. He's a bully, always pushin' the little guys around. He's got it in for Lancaster."

"Dey's a lotta heartbreak waitin' to happen der'.''She watched Kitty's ramrod straight back as she walked through the doors to leave. "Poor little thang. If she gonna get through 'dis here hard time she gonna have'ta bend a little."

"That's white folks' trouble, Hattie-girl. No tellin' what is goin' on in their heads," Joe told her. "How long JJ been sick?"

"Kept him home from school on Friday. Ya know, throwin' up with a tem'ture. Your Mama say why don' she keep 'im so I don't miss my visit wit' you. He gonna be fine, jus' a little ol' flu bug."

"How's Mama?" Joe asked.

"She good. She say to give ya her love and she be seein' ya soon."

"And Ruby?"

Hattie grinned. "Oh 'dat Ruby. Mostly all 'A's' on her report card, cheerleadin', and now she gots to be editor of her school paper. Tha' girl truly amazes me!"

"She's a wonder, for sure," Joe beamed with pride. "But, don'cha think maybe she's bitin' off too much?"

"Ruby say she gots to carry these ex-tra-cur...curlick...shoot! Whas' that word? Ya know, extra things outside a' her studies to put on her collitch application papers. I got the best news; been savin' it for last. 'Bout Ruby."

"Spit it out, woman," Joe laughed. "Wha'cha waitin' on?"

"Ruby hear from some'a her collitch applications..."
"And?"

Hattie beamed at Joe and raising her hands, she ticked the list off on her fingers. "University of Illinois, Champaign, accepted. DePaul University, accepted. Full scholarships. Northwestern, wait list. UCLA, wait list. Ain't that just *grand*, Joey-boy?"
"That is truly wonderful, woman. I'm happy UCLA

is a wait list. With me in here, we surely could never afford to send her away to school."

"Lordy, ain't it so. But, 'member, UCLA's got the best marine biological department." Hattie said.

"We'll hav'ta see. We still got some time. Tha's the best news, for sure. Our girl's got her pick of schools …my, oh my. And how 'bout my baby-girl, Stella, she doin' okay?" Joe asked.

"That chile could charm the birds right outta them trees. She was real mixed up…wantin' so bad to see her Daddy today. But she wanted to be a big girl and go wid' her sister. I tol' her, 'Stella, baby, Daddy gonna unnerstand. Ya'll go on now and do whats you want."

"How 'bout you, wife? You doin' okay? Not workin' too hard?"

"I'm jus' fine, Joey. My regular customers keepin' the wolf away. Four houses clean by Tuesday night. People always callin' me, can I come do fer 'em? It's six days a week now and could be seven. Lordy, Lordy, dem white folk don' know how to clean and don' wanna learn," Hattie laughed.

"Ain't it so. But, I thought we agreed you was only gonna work four days a week."

"I knows we did, but dem chil'un is needin' so much all the time. Ruby's cheer outfit, and Stella, that chil' growin' like a little weed. She be needin' larger shoes, why it seems like every month. Lamar's medicines. JJ's shoes for basketball. Whewee! Those shoes alone cost over sixty dollars."

"I'm sorry, Hattie…"

"Now, Joey-boy we done been over 'dis. No need for ya to say 'sorry'. It workin' out jus' fine."

"Woman shouldn't hav'ta carry this by herself." Joe pounded the table with his fist.

"God damn it! I hate this! Me in here, you out there workin' so hard."

"Now, Joe, it's al'right. We makin' it. You settle down and act right, ya hear? Don't let no trouble find ya like that raggedy white boy over yonder. Those good behavior days keep pilin' up and those jail days, why they keeps goin' down. Didn't we say?"

"Yeah…" Joe knew she was talking good sense to him.

His Hattie had a wise and down-to-earth sense to things even though she only went to the tenth grade in school. She loved to count what she called 'the good behavior days' and the 'jail days' and marked a calendar until the day he got back home.

"You and me, Joey-boy, we keep countin'. Buildin' up those good days and watchin' those jail days disappear. Okay, baby?"

"Yeah, I know."

"Promise me ya won't be doin' nothin' to get those good days taken away," Hattie pleaded.

Joe grinned at her. "I promise. Don' ya be worryin' none 'bout that. How many days is it now, Hattie, 'fore I get shuck'a this place?"

"Three hun'red eighty-seven days, not countin' future good behavior days. Three days a month for behavin' yor'self, tha's thirty-seven. Subtract that from three hundred, eighty-seven, that three hundred, fifty days left. A'course, ya got that parole hearin' in two months. Ya could be getting' out early."

Hattie raised her hands to the ceiling. "Baby Jesus, hear this poor woman's prayers."

"Um, um, to this day I don't know how ya do that." Joe laughed. "Ya sure ya don' have a calculator hidden away somewheres?"

"No. No calculator…jus' in my head," Hattie laughed and tapped her forehead with her finger. "Ya know, Joe, I never did unnerstan' where all dis' here arithmetic comes from up here."

Joe laughed again and kissed her finger tips. "Woman, I don't think I told ya lately how much I love ya."

They stared into each other's eyes, confident in their love and devotion.

"I got a letter from Elgin on Thursday." Joe announced.

"That no good nigger!" Hattie exclaimed.

"Hortense Washington! What kinda talk is that?" Joe exclaimed.

"I don't care. He not worth a mou'f full'a warm spit!"

"Maybe not. He's made some mistakes, that's for sure. But he's still my brother, Hattie-girl."

"Runnin' away like that, leaving his big brother to get sent up in here? It ain't right, Joe, and you know it."

"Tha's true 'nuf. But you know there was no way I was gonna tell the cops who he was. Elgin would'a never made it in here."

Hattie scoffed. "And you makin' it? We makin' it?"

"Oh, Hattie, some time you a hard woman."

"If blamin' Elgin for our sorrow is being hard, I guess 'das what I am."

"I know you're right, but I jus' couldn't do it." Joe shook his head. "What good would'a it done? I still gonna be put here for drivin' the get-away car." He looked into her eyes. "He's my baby brother, Hattie."

"Well, your twenty-three year old 'baby-brother's' the one landed ya in 'dis here jail and nothin' goin' change 'dat! Back home, fam'bly don' do each other that'a way."

Angry tears filled Hattie's eyes. "Ya know yur sentence was harder than need be 'cause you never would give 'em up."

"Hattie...darlin'," Joe began.

"Uh-uh! Don't ya be 'Hattie-darlin' me. He lied to us, Joe. 'A ride' he say he be needin' from you. Oh yeah, a ride to a *stick up*. It al'mos' killed your Mama."

"Listen, baby, there ain't no need goin' over this again. I jus' wanted to tell you I got a letter is all. He's fine. He got a job. He's doin' good in Denver."

Hattie's voice dripped with sarcasm. "Oh, well then, tha's just fine then, Joe. I's so happy to hear tha' no good boy is doin' so well. Did he ask about me? How me and the kids is doin'?"

Joe's voice was soft and sad. "No Hattie he didn't. Ya know it would never be in that boy's mind to ask. Ya know Elgin...he gonna worry 'bout his'self and leave me 'ta worry 'bout the rest."

"Oh yeah, I knows Elgin. He go 'round thinkin' the world owns 'im somthin'. While my man, who done nothin' wrong is sittin' up here in dis' jail, for *years*."

Joe sat and said nothing more. He knew his wife... his love. She was quick to flare when an injustice had been done. But she was just as quick to let it go and resort back to her cheerful nature. He watched as the anger drained away in Hattie. She could never stay angry with Joe for long.

Hattie tried to keep her resentment against his brother buried deep. She knew how much Elgin's betrayal and desertion had cost her husband. She peeked at him, a tiny smile lurking at the corners of her mouth.

Joe grinned. "Come on, baby. I know ya got a bigger smile than that for me. Come on, give Joe one of them special Hattie smiles."

Hattie smile blossomed and her face became beautiful and young.

"That's my girl. That's the smile I fell head over heels for," Joe said.

"Oh, al'right. Wha' that baby brother of yours have to say for his'self?" Hattie asked.

"He likes Denver and he says he's keepin' on the straight'n nar'er. He's workin' at a loadin' dock and says his boss likes him. Says he's a hard worker. He even got his'self a little apartment. He stayin' outta trouble."

Hattie sighed. "Oh Joey-boy, I don' wanna fight. And I don't wish your brother any harm. But don' ask me to forgive him neither. He put ya in here and I jus' can't forget 'dat."

Joe lowered his head and taking her hand, kissed her fingers. He whispered. "I know, Hattie-girl, I know."

Chapter 10

Hattie ~ eighteen years earlier

"Mama!" Joe stood in the front room of the shotgun house where he had grown up and hollered toward a back room. "Ya'll ready? I got the car pulled up out front."

Ida Mae walked down the long hallway that connected all the rooms, poking a hat pin into her large straw hat. The brim was covered in pink peonies, the exact shade of her dress and shoes.

"Stop that yellin', Joe. I raised ya better than that." She walked up to him and cupped his face in her hands. "Lordy, when'ja get so tall and broad, boy? I hardly recognize my own son."

Joe hugged her tight and lifted her off the floor. "All that beef steak they feed me up north, Mama."

"Put me down this minute, boy. You not so big or old that your mama can't still whoop ya," she laughed. "Come on, we gonna be late for the sermon."

Joe turned and opened the screen door for his mother. He started to close the front door.

"Best leave it open, son, keeps the air movin' in there."

"Sure, Mama, but we're gonna be gone awhile. Ain't ya worried?"

"Shoot, boy, who's gonna steal from me? I ain't got nothin' that nobody wantin'. Leave it open so's we don't come back to a hot box. I got your favorites for Sunday dinner; fried chicken and mashed spuds, greens and home-made peach ice cream for dessert. Nothin' like a closed up house to spoil an appetite."

Ida Mae took her son's arm as they stepped off the porch. The paint was peeling down to bare wood and this was just one of the reasons Joe used up his vacation time to visit his mother. He had the back of the house painted already and would start painting again tomorrow. *I'll have to get some sandpaper for these railings,* he reminded himself.

"What color you want the porch and railings, Mama?"

"I've always been partial to a bright white, son. I wish ya'll wouldn't work so hard; this suppose to be yur vacation."

"Doin' for my Mama *is* a vacation, don' you worry none."

Arm in arm they walked to Ida Mae's car. The clean, waxed surface glistened a burgundy red in the hot Alabama sun.

"Shoot, Ma, I can't believe you still have this Chrysler."

"Whas' wrong with it?" she asked as her critical eye scanned the vehicle for fault.

"Nothin'. That's what's got me stumped. A nineteen-seventy-eight New Yorker Town car in mint condition." Joe said as he opened the passenger door for Ida Mae and helped her in. "You know you could sell this for twenty times what Daddy paid for it and buy yourself a littler car that's got better gas mileage and is not nineteen feet long."

"What was good enough for your father is good enough for me. 'Sides what I want with one of them plastic, oriental toy cars? This here automobile can fit in five of my best friends when we goes to the outlet stores and lunch."

Joe walked around to the driver's door and got in. He hit all the buttons to roll up the windows.

As they pulled away from the house Ida Mae observed. "Ya 'membered what your Daddy taught you about lettin' the hot air out 'fore ya start that there air conditionin'."

"Some things ya just never forget, Mama."

"How 'bout the way to the church? Ya 'member that?"

"Yes, Ma'am." Joe laughed.

They drove a mile out of the little town of Clayhatchee and turned left onto an oyster-shell road. Childhood memories flooded Joe as the salty smell of the sun baked shells drifted in through the vents of the car. The car passed through patches of shade and sun and a family of deer, up ahead, paused in the middle of the road before bounding across a shallow ditch and into the trees beyond.

"Now, Joe, slow down so them shells don't jump up and nick the paint," Ida Mae scolded.

Joe laughed. "You sound just like Daddy, Mama. He hated this road and cussed it every Sunday. I'd sit in the back seat and wonder what Preacher Beauregard would think of all that cussin' right before church."

"Your Daddy was a God-fearin' man, Joe. But he was more afraid of wha' this devil road would do to his paint job."

They both laughed. "Slow down some more, baby, the road to the parkin' lot is jus' up here a bit."

"Yes, Ma'am." Joe slowed and turned right into the small parking lot next to a white-washed clapboard church. The lot was filled with pickups and cars and people were already gathered on the long covered porch of the building. Some sat on the steps leading up to the opened front doors.

Next to the church was a cemetery filled with very old, modest head stones. Some so old the names and dates could barely be read. A few newer, marble stones shone in the morning light. Joe parked the car and jumped out. He walked around and opened his mother's door.

"Watch out for that fancy hat of yours, Mama. We wouldn't want it to end up in the dust," he teased.

"You never mind about my hat, Joseph Ray. I been getting' me and my hat outta this car since before you was a twinkle in your Daddy's eye."

"Yes Ma'am. But I just love to hear you say it," he laughed and kissed her cheek.

"Oh, you! Cut out that nonsense and take me to church."

Joe and Ida Mae walked across the lot and as they approached the stairs they were greeted by many of Ida Mae's friends.

"My goodness, Ida Mae, this can't be your son, Joe," Rosalee exclaimed, grabbing Joe's hand. "Why my stars he's a full growed man."

Ben, Rosalee's husband, slapped Joe on the shoulder, "It surely is Joe, Rosalee. Might I remind you he's too young for the likes of you, a married woman."

Everyone laughed and Rosalee blushed. "Good to see you, Joe," Ben continued.

"Yes, sir, Mr. Ben. Good to see you again." Joe leaned down and kissed Rosalee's cheek. "How are ya, Miss Rosalee?"

Before she could answer, the single church bell began to ring calling the parishioners to service. Friends and neighbors began to file into the church. The deacons led the matriarchs to the front pews and helped them get settled. Joe was no exception and seated his mother with the other Church Mothers.

"Here's your Bible, Mama. I'll see you after."

"Thank you baby."

Joe stepped away and gazed at the older women seated in the pews. *They remind me of a garden bed full of flowers*, Joe mused. What he saw was pink, yellow, white, pale green and blue dresses. Most of their Sunday hats were in matching colors. They were so large that if one of them turned their head too quickly it would bump up against the hat next to them. *Some of these women have been sitting in the front pews of this church every Sunday for over fifty years,* Joe thought to himself. *And more than a few helped to raise me.* Some of the older ladies beamed smiles up at him.

Joe walked back up the aisle a few rows and sat down. The morning sun streamed through the stained glass of the windows and prisms of light bounced off the ceiling.

Just as the choir filed in followed by the preacher, Joe heard light footsteps coming down the aisle. He glanced up and was struck down by lightning.

His whole world slowed down until there was no one there except him and this vision walking toward him.

She was dressed quietly in a navy blue dress with a matching flirty little hat. *My God above who is this girl? Just how tall is she? Where did she come from? I wonder what her name is. I know,* Joe thought, *she is the mermaid Goddess, Mami Wata come to earth. Come to steal men's hearts.*

Joe had taken a course, just for laughs, in African mythology last winter. Mami Wata was described as the most beautiful woman imagined. Her beauty was so extreme it was supernatural. Her clothes were so new they seem to shine and more fashionable than any designer's. She possessed unimaginable wealth and dazzling jewelry.

Often she was shown with a snake coiled around her waist, its head resting between her breasts. Her hair was black and straight and her skin was light. *Except for the snake nestled between her breasts, shiny clothes and jewelry, this could be Mami Wata. A Goddess come to earth to become a mortal man's ruin.* Joe told himself. *My ruin. Oh, Lordy, save me now.* Joe prayed.

The vision walked on by, leaving a trail of gardenia scent that wrapped itself around Joe's fast beating heart. She paused in the aisle and took a moment to gaze at the crucifix that hung above the alter. Then excusing herself, she passed in front of others and sat down in the pew across from Joe.

She stared straight ahead with a small, mysterious smile on her face. The choir sang the opening hymn. The preacher spoke his sermon. The reading came from the Book of Genesis: thus the Lord sayeth something, and somebody was affrighted, and did not cling to his figment, or something.

The offering was collected. More hymns. It all went by in a blur for Joe.

He knew he was staring and couldn't help himself. He thought Mami Wata knew he was staring too, how could she not? She was after all a goddess.

Responding to his stare she glanced briefly towards him. Joe quickly looked down at his hymnal or Bible. He found himself blushing like a teenager.

Finally the service was over and Joe jumped up and rushed down the aisle to collect his mother.

Please don't let her leave before I can find out who she is. What if Mama doesn't know her? Joe worried all the way to the front. *Maybe Rosalee knows. What if she is just visitin'? What if she's gone before I can be introduced to her? Would the Gods really play with me that way?*

Joe reached his mother and they joined the congregation as they slowly made their way up the aisle to the doors. Joe thought he could see the jaunty, little navy hat with the single feather bobbing along way up in front of him.

"My stars, Joseph Ray, what's your hurry? You're about to run down the people in front of us. Slow down, for mercy's sakes."

"Mama, we gotta get outside before *she* leaves. You gotta tell me what her name is…"

"She who? What whose name is?" she demanded.

"Shhh," Joe whispered. "Folks are gonna hear you. Please. Can you hurry just a little?"

"Stop rushin' me. Everyone stays for the social after. There gonna be plenty of time to meet people."

Joe kept silent and watched the jaunty feather as it disappeared out the door. They finally reached the preacher who stood at the door greeting his parishioners.

"Preacher Durham, I'd like you to meet my son, Joseph Ray," Ida Mae said.

"Welcome, Joseph, we are surely glad you could worship with us." The preacher said as he shook Joe's hand.

"Thank you, sir, I enjoyed your sermon," Joe responded.

"I appreciate that, son. Miss Ida Mae, I'll see you at Wednesday's meeting, won't I?" the preacher asked.

"Yes you will, Preacher, I wouldn't miss it."

"Nice to meet you, sir," Joe said. "Come on, Ma, before all the sweet tea's gone."

Ida Mae laughed, "Boys never grow up when there's sweet tea to be had. See ya'll Wednesday, Preacher."

Joe took his mother's arm and hurried her down the steps and over to the tables set out in the grass.

"Joseph, stop draggin' me around," she exclaimed.

"Oh, no, she's gone," Joe whispered. He frantically looked around. "Quick, Ma, see if you can spot a little navy hat with a feather stickin' up."

" Ya mean like the one over there under the live oak tree?" she asked.

"Where?! Where?" Joe's head swiveled around. "Yes! That's her. Who is she, Ma? Do you know?"

"Why yes, that's Miss Clora's girl. Name's Hattie, I think. She been away, workin'."

"Introduce me, Mama, please. Do it before she gets away."

"My stars, child, what bug bit you?" She took a closer look at her son's face. "Oh, oh, I think them 'love bugs' must be hatchin'." Her merry laugh carried on the wind. Hattie glanced over when she heard it.

"Cut it out, Mama. Do I know Miss Clora? I don't remember her."

"That's cause you ain't never knowed her. Get me some sweet tea and a plate and we'll go over."

Joe groaned. "Can't we eat after I meet her?"

"Joseph Ray, you know a good sermon always makes me hungry and supper's a ways off. Now, get!"

"Yes, Mama. But while I get you a plate will you keep watch? Make sure they don't leave, okay?"

"Yes, yes, I'll be your 'lookout'. Better than that, I'll go over and have me a visit with Miss Clora and her girl while you get the food."

Joe kissed her cheek. "You're wonderful, Ma. Thank you."

Joe rushed over to the tables of food while Ida Mae sauntered over to the big oak tree. People had put out folding chairs and Clora and Hattie sat together in the shade. When Ida Mae walked nearer Clora looked up and smiled.

"Miss Ida, come visit with us a spell." Clora said. "Hattie girl, give Miss Ida Mae your seat."

"Why don't mind if I do, Clora." Ida Mae replied.

Hattie had risen and moved aside to allow Ida Mae to sit.

"Good mornin', Missus Washington."

"Good mornin', Hattie. That's just about the cutest hat I ever did see."

"Thank you, Ma'am."

"How'd you like the sermon, Clora? I think the new preacher is just what we needed."

"It was a good'un. These young people need to be reminded that material things are jus that....things!"

"Amen to that," Ida Mae replied.

"Speaking of young people," Clora continued, "who was that strappin' young man escortin' you this morning?"

"Tha's my son, Joseph."

"No! Tha' couldn't be skinny little Joey?"

"Sure 'nough." Ida Mae turned to Hattie.

"Are you home for good now, child?"

"Yes, my job was finished and they didn't keep me on."

"Oh, I'm sorry to hear that.

My son Joe is here on summer vacation visitin' me."

Clora smiled. "That must be very nice for you. Where's he live now, Ida?"

"Up yonder in Chicago. He got him a real good job after making 'master' mechanic. My youngest, Elgin, can't wait to graduate high school and move up there wit' him."

"So your son likes Chicago, Miss Ida Mae?" Hattie asked.

"As much as a body can like a big city, Hattie. He sure can't find a good payin' job like he got up there, 'round here."

Joe found a tray where he could fit four glasses of sweet tea and his mother's plate of food. He'd also fixed a second plate of finger-food for his Mama's friend and the 'goddess'. He carefully navigated the distance to the oak tree. He walked up to them just in time to hear his mother's comment about his job. *Oh, Lord, she's already braggin' on me. Mama, please don't make the Goddess think I'm full 'a myself,* he silently prayed.

"Here's your sweet tea, Mama," Joe announced. "And since I could see that you were visitin' with two lovely ladies I took the liberty of bringin' ya'll the same." Joe passed the glasses to the other women.

Ida Mae took the plate Joe offered her and daintily picked at the food.

"I thought ya'll might be a little hungry so I brought an extra plate for you and the young lady." Joe addressed Clora.

"Bless you; I was feelin' a mite peckish." Clora told him as she took the second plate. When Hattie took the glass from Joe their fingers brushed. A spark flashed between them and Hattie jumped in her chair, almost spilling the tea.

She blushed wildly and stared at her lap, brushing at a tiny stain on her skirt. Joe quickly handed her a paper napkin.

"Thank you," Hattie whispered.

"Clora, I'd like you to meet my son, Joseph Ray. Joe this is my friend, Miss Clora and her daughter, Miss Hattie."

Joe took Clora's hand and said, "Miss Clora, it's so nice to meet you." He turned to the 'goddess'. "Miss Hattie."

"Joseph, your mama has been tellin' us all about Chicago and your important job up there," Clora said.

"Well, Ma'am, I wouldn't call it 'important' exactly. I just got a promotion because I got my master mechanic's certificate, is all. It's a good company and work's regular."

"Well, my stars, that sounds important enough to me," Ida Mae bragged. "Joe, there's an empty chair there over by Rosalee and Ben. Why don't you bring it over and sit with us awhile."

"Yes, Ma'am." Joe walked over and snagged the chair.

"Sit here, Joseph, next to my Hattie," Clora directed.

"Yes, Ma'am." Joe said as he sat down by Hattie. "May I, Miss Hattie?"

"Yes, of course," Hattie murmured.

"Did you enjoy the sermon, Miss Hattie?" Joe asked.

"Yes."

"Do you live here in Clayhatchee, Miss Hattie?"
"Yes."

Lordy, the 'goddess' was so shy.

Both of us feelin' shy....this was gonna be an uphill battle, Joe thought.

"Oh, Clora, there's Miss Clairee." Ida Mae exclaimed. "Let's walk over and see if she's feelin' any better."

Clora rose from her chair and winked at Ida Mae. "Yes, let's do. You children have a nice visit. We'll be back in a bit."

"Joe, hold my plate for me, will you?"

"Yes, Ma'am."

Joe watched the two older women walk away arm in arm. *Sly old ladies, I know what you're up to Mama.* Joe grinned. The silence was getting louder and louder. It was evident that Hattie was not going to speak first.

"My mother said she thought you were away working in another town?" Joe asked.

"Yes."

"What sort of work do you do if I can ask?"

Hattie continued to stare down at her lap. "Cleanin' new residential construction sites, after they finish up with the buildin'."

"Oh, that sounds interestin'."

Hattie smiled. "It's a dirty job, but the pay was pretty good. And it was satisfyin' once ya got it clean."

"'Was'?" Joe asked.

"Yes, the subdivision was completed so they didn't keep us on."

"Oh."

"Thas' okay though. I got me a few houses to clean here and over in Coker. That way I can help my Mama out some." Hattie told him.

"Do you miss Chicago?"

"Not today." Joe looked at her meaningfully. "But it surely is a pretty city, sittin' there right next to a lake that goes on forever. And the people are real friendly for city folk."

Joe gazed over across the meadow. People were beginning to pack up the food and start towards their cars. *Silence again,* Joe thought. *She's gonna leave and I won't see her again unless I get a dose of some bravery goin' here and just plain ask her out.*

"Miss Hattie, I'm gonna be here another week or so before I have to go back to Chicago. I was wondering...um....could I?...."

"Yes, Joseph?" Hattie finally looked up, straight into Joe's eyes.

"I was wondering if I could see you again."

He couldn't look away. Her eyes were like pools of dark chocolate. Her lashes were the thickest, longest he'd ever seen. Her skin was glowing; creamy like coffee au lait. Dark, black coffee with lots of cream.

"Why, Joe, I would love to see you again."

The Goddess had spoken. She would love to see me again. Does life get any sweeter than this moment? Joe wondered.

"Okay, then. Can I take you to dinner tomorrow night?"

Suddenly Joe's mother was walking towards them.

"Joseph time to go," She called to him. "My chicken's gonna be all dried out if we don't get a move on, son,"

Joe groaned. Hattie hadn't answered him yet.

Hattie smiled into his eyes. "Yes."

'Yes?' Yes, what. Yes, it was time to go? Yes, the chicken was drying out? Yes, get a move on? WHAT?

"Yes?" he asked Hattie.

"Yes to dinner tomorrow. Seven?" Hattie asked.

"Yes! Wonderful." Joe grinned and jumped up. "See you at seven. Does my mother know where your mother lives?"

"Yes." Hattie rose and put out her hand to Joe.

Joe took her hand in both of his. "I'll see you then."

"See you then." Hattie blushed.

They stood there, Joe holding her hand, staring into each other's eyes. Joe's mother marched up.

"Let go a that girl, Joe and take me home. My chicken's gonna be ruint."

Joe reluctantly let go of Hattie's hand.

"Yes, Mama. Until tomorrow, Hattie."

"What 'bout tomorrow?" Ida Mae asked.

"Nothing, Mama."

"Goodbye, Miss Ida Mae."

"Goodbye, Hattie-girl. Tell your mama I'll see her soon."

"Yes, Ma'am, I surely will. Goodbye, Joe."

"See you tomorrow, Miss Hattie." Joe told her.

Chapter 11

Kitty and Hattie

The black town car purred up the road and parked in the visitor's parking lot. Kitty emerged from the driver's side, dressed very conservatively in khaki slacks, plain white blouse, jacket and loafers. The absence of jewelry was apparent and she only carried a small leather clutch for her keys and money.

The wind ruffled her hair as she hurried across the drive and up the steps to the door of the prison. As she entered the reception area the guard, Anne called out.

"Hi, Ms. Lancaster, how 'bout this early spring we're enjoying?"

Over the past few months since her disastrous first visit Kitty and the correctional officers had developed an easy manner with each other. Kitty went through the sign in and search process quietly. They in turn processed her quickly and with respect.

"Hello, Anne. It's a glorious day out there. The trees are actually budding out. Let's hope it stays this way and it's not just a March flirtation with nice weather."

"Another hard freeze would be tough on everything. How was the drive down?" Anne asked.

"Not too bad. Traffic was a little heavy until I got well this side of Chicago."

While they chatted Kitty tucked her watch into her purse and handed it over the counter to Anne.

"I think I'll keep my jacket, Anne. It's a little chilly in here this morning."

"Sure Mrs. L." Anne turned to a locker and put Kitty's things in. She turned with the key and handed it to Kitty. "Was there much construction on your drive here?" Anne asked.

"A short stretch. You know Illinois' highways, always a work in progress."

"I hate running into roadwork. They seem to do more leaning on their shovels than anything else."

Kitty laughed. "I know. I don't know how anything gets done. But, somebody's got to do it...the leaning I mean."

Anne chuckled. "OK, you ready?"

The two women walked to the cubicle and Anne's perfunctory search was quickly finished.

"All done. Pretty blouse, Mrs. L. Is it new?" Anne asked.

"Thank you. Yes, Elizabeth sent it to me from New York."

"How's she feeling?"

"Wonderful." Kitty said. "Her husband says she's glowing."

"My second was like that." Anne reflected. "But my first? Ugh! I was sick as a dog the first three months."

As they talked, Kitty and Anne walked back into the reception area.

"You can go right in." Anne told Kitty.

"Thanks, Anne."

Kitty turned toward the security door that led to the visiting room. Out of the corner of her eye she noticed Hattie Washington sitting alone.

"Anne, why is Mrs. Washington sitting there alone? Why isn't she in with her husband?"

"Don't know." Anne replied shaking her head. "I called her about ten minutes ago but she asked if she could sit for a few more minutes. She seemed a little upset so I let her be."

"I'll just check on her before I go in if that's all right."

"Sure. Let me know when you're ready." Anne said.

Kitty walked over to Hattie, whose head was down. She clutched a wadded up handkerchief in both hands.

"Mrs. Washington? Is something wrong?" Kitty asked.

Hattie looked up, her brown eyes swimming in tears. "Oh! Missus...it's you."

"You've been crying. What's wrong? Can I help?"

"No, no. I'm just bein' silly, is all." Tears spilled over and ran down Hattie's cheeks.

Kitty sat down next to Hattie. "Is there something I can do for you?"

"I'm just teary. I don' wanna trouble a fine 'lady' like yourself. Go on now and see your man."

Kitty picked up Hattie's hand and held it. "There's plenty of time for visiting. Please tell me, Mrs. Washington. Sometimes, just telling another woman helps."

"Oh, Missus Lancaster, I gots me this problem and I don't want to worry my Joe." Fresh tears scored her cheeks. "I was tryin' to stop these here waterworks 'fore I went in. I can't seem to stop my old eyes from leakin' every time I think on it."

"Whatever it is, I'm certain there's a solution. Tell me it's not one of your children?" Kitty asked.

"Oh no, Ma'am, they's all fine."

"You can tell me if you want to."

"I can't. You's this fine lady and all."

"Of course you can. But I may be intruding. You probably have friends or family at home that you can confide in."

"You ain't intrudin', Missus. I got Joe's Mama to talk to but I can't. Ya see, she's had her share of trouble what with her son bein' in here and all. And her youngest boy hidin' out in Colorado."

Hattie and Kitty sat silently for several minutes. Then as if a dam broke, Hattie began to speak in a low urgent voice.

"I got this here bump…ya know? And they done got them a sample and now they gots to cut it out…the bad part of my… breast." She whispered the word. "And I'm so scared I don't know what to do. I don' want to tell my Joe. I don't know how. And he'll be so worried and blame himself what with him being locked up in here."

"I know. Men blame themselves for anything that they can't control or fix. But, you have to tell him, Mrs. Washington. Think how he would feel if you went through this by yourself without telling him."

"I don't know how, Mrs. Lancaster. Thas' why I'm sittin' out here, trying to find the words."

"First of all, please call me Kitty. 'Mrs. Lancaster is so formal when we have so much in common."

Hattie's eyes went big and round. "We do? What in the world could we have in common, Missus?"

Kitty smiled and patted Hattie's hand. "I had something very similar about five years ago. I found a lump and had to go in for a biopsy. Then the doctors had to do a lumpectomy."

"Thas' the word, Miss Kitty! For the life of me

I can't 'member these ten dollar words." Hattie's
chuckle ended in a sob. "You went through the exact
same thang?"

"Yes, I did. The doctors found a small tumor and it
was questionable. They didn't want to leave it and then
it turn into a cancer later on."

"Ooo…that's what I'm afraid I gots…" Hattie
moaned.

"That's exactly why you must tell your Joe. Then
have the surgery as soon as you can, Mrs. Washington."

"Please call me Hattie, Miss Kitty."

"*Hattie.*" Kitty smiled again. "If the doctors are
concerned let them take it out."

"Did you lose much of your….breast?" Hattie hid
her face behind her hands. "Oh, it's so embarrassin',
talking about these private parts."

"It's all right, Hattie. We're two women who have
gone through child birth, the arrest and conviction of
our husbands, and now this. You don't need to feel
embarrassed with me," Kitty assured her. "And no,
they probably won't take any part of your breast. The
surgeon will cut a small incision in the skin and just
take the tumor. I have the smallest scar to show for the
whole thing. You'll see."

"Oh, sweet Jesus, was there much pain?"

"Surprisingly no. I was just a bit sore for a week or
two."

"Oh, Lordy."

"Hattie, it's very important that you have this taken
care of as soon as possible. Don't delay.
That's your best chance of a good outcome. I'm certain
that the doctors have told you this."

"What's a bunch of ol' men know about a woman's
parts?" Hattie scoffed. "Oh Miss Kitty, thank you so

much for talkin' wit' me. I feel so much better, me knowin' somebody has gone through dis' here trouble."

"You're very welcome. I'm happy to be of some help. Come now, dry those tears and let's go see our boys."

Kitty rose and taking Hattie's hand again led her over to the security doors.

Kitty called out. "Anne, we're ready to go in, please."

"Sure thing, Mrs. L." Anne said as she pressed the button to open the doors.

The two women walked through the set of doors and entered the visiting room. More than half the tables were already occupied. They crossed to the podium where Brad sat, once again on duty.

"Good mornin' Mr. Brad." Hattie said.

"Good mornin' ladies. How're you today?"

"How's your son's leg, Bradley?" Kitty asked.

"Much better, thanks. He'll be back on the soccer field before we know it."

"I'm so happy to hear that." Kitty replied.

"Disgusting how quickly they heal at that age." Brad laughed.

Kitty laughed. "Isn't it? If our leg were broken in two places it would take us months to recover. Bradley, would you be so kind as to call up and let our husbands know we're here?"

"Sure thing, Mrs. Lancaster." As Brad raised the telephone receiver to call, "Let's see, table three, Mrs. Lancaster. Mrs. Washington, you're table number four."

"Thank you, Bradley." Kitty said.

"Mr. Brad, do you think it would be all right if Mrs. Lancaster and I sit together 'til our men come on down?"

"No problem, Mrs. Washington. Just move to your assigned table when you're husbands get here."

"Thank you." Both women spoke at once and walked over to Hattie's table. Sitting down next to each other Kitty took Hattie's hand in hers.

"Hattie, I want you to promise me that you'll tell your Joe as soon as he comes down. He deserves to know so he can support you. Promise?"

"Yes, Miss Kitty, I promise."

The secured door for inmates to enter swung open and Joe walked into the room. He looked over and waved to Hattie. Brad called out to him, "Table four, Washington."

As Joe weaved his way through the other visitors, Kitty rose from the table.

"Tell him right away, Hattie. You'll feel better, I promise."

Joe reached them and Hattie rose for his kiss and hug.

"Hello, Mrs. Lancaster." Joe greeted her. "Does Eddie know you're here?"

"Nice to see you again Mr. Washington. Yes, I believe that Bradley has called up. If you will excuse me, have a nice visit."

"Thank you, Miss Kitty….for *everything*." Hattie said.

"See you next time, Hattie." Kitty said as she walked over to her assigned table and sat down.

Joe took Hattie's hand, "Sit down, woman, and tell me all the news from home. Where's the kids today?"

"I left 'em with Ruby."

"Okay, I guess. I sure do miss seeing 'em."

Hattie stared at her lap, unable to go on.

Joe squeezed her hand and lowered his head so he could see her face.

"Come on now, girl, nothin' as bad as that. Tell Joey what's the matter."

Hattie lifted her face, her eyes filled with tears.

"It's not one of the kids, is it?" Joe asked slightly alarmed by her tears.

"No, Joey, it's me." Tears spilled down Hattie's cheeks. "I got some news but I don' wanna worry you none."

"Well, spit it out woman. Whatever it is, we'll handle it."

"A couple months ago I was doin' that self examinin' thing all the magazines talk about ….."

"What exam thing, Hattie?"

Hattie made a circular motion in front of her chest with her hand. "You know…." She whispered. "…my boobies. And I felt a bump, right through my wash cloth."

Joe blanched. "My God, Hattie, you mean a 'lump'? In your breast?"

"Shhh! Joseph please, not so loud. Folks gonna hear us." She looked around to see if anyone was listening.

"Yes, a lump, a bump…anyway, I really didn't pay it no mind but I thought it was getting' bigger. So last week I went in'ta the clinic."

"Whad' they say?"

"Well now, here's the thing. They did a kind'a xray picture, a 'Mama-grafe' something and the doctor, he says, 'yep, there's somethin' there.' They cut me, Joe, and took like a little sample of it."

"You mean a biopsy?"

"Yeah, that's the word. Das' what they do."

"That's good, Hattie. That's what you needed to do.

Did they give you the results?"

"Yes, a couple days ago. They said they should take it out, the tumor. It's little and they said they want to be safer than sorrier."

"Okay, that's good." Joe said.

"But, thas what I needed to talk with you about, Joey. With no insurance, it's gonna cost lots a money. Even when they figure in what I make in a month, it's still more money than we gots."

"I don't care. Ya gotta catch these things quick like, Hattie. We got our savings. You go home and make an appointment right away, ya hear?"

Hattie frowned. "Now Joe, you know that savings is for the kids. I don' wanna be dippin' in'ta that."

"We'll make it up soon as I get outta here. You do what I say now. You call up tomorrow."

Chapter 12

Hattie ~ two years earlier

Hattie walked down the pathway to building number thirteen in the tenement. It was a village of twenty buildings all identical in color and squalor. She reflected on where her life had led her since leaving Clayhatchee, Alabama.

As long as I've lived here, Hattie thought to herself, *I wouldn't be able to find my own buildin' if it weren't for dat' large thirteen painted on all four sides. No matter which direction you come from, after getting off dat train, you can see dem' numbers. And dat cold, grey concrete each building was made of with them blind eyes for windows was downright spooky. Inside our apartment I hears the trains at all hours, as they thunder past. If there had been any grass growin' it had been trampled to death years ago.*

When I first come up north, I thought everybody would have a little shotgun house with a patch 'a garden in the back like back home, she mused. *Lordy, I do miss my little cottage with the green trim. But with my Joe's hours being cut in half there was no way we could afford it anymore. Oh well, no sense in dwellin' on what can't be changed. And I certainly don't want Joe to ever know I feel this way. He has enough to deal with; what with working two jobs to provide for me and the kids.* She sighed as she walked up the steps to the front door.

Hattie checked the mail box and pulled out coupon circulars and a couple of bills. Wearily she walked across the small lobby and into the elevator.

She tried her best to ignore the sticky floor and the graffiti on the walls. At least maintenance had finally fixed the light. She worked extra hours, cleaning for women who were too lazy or too busy to clean their own messes.

What was it about the rich? Couldn't they, at the very least, pick up 'dem wet towels and put dem in the hamper? Lord knew it was hard to get dat sour smell out of dem when they'd been lying on the floor for a couple of days or until I get der.

Exiting the elevator, she walked down the long dark hallway to number ten-twenty three and put her key in the lock. She couldn't wait to get her shoes off.

Stella, her youngest, pulled the door open.

"Mommy!" Stella threw herself into Hattie's arms. She yelled over her shoulder, "Mommy's home!"

"Hi baby-girl, how was your day?" Hattie asked.

"I made a paper book for you, Mommy, a real book with a pretty cover....ya wanna see it?" Stella said.

"I would love to see it, baby. Where's Ruby and your brothers?" asked Hattie.

"Ruby and Lamar is in the kitchen. We've been helpin' Ruby. And JJ's at the practice."

Stella skipped down the hallway in front of Hattie and turned into her bedroom. Hattie walked on to the kitchen at the back of the apartment.

"Something smells good," Hattie said as she entered.

Ruby stood at the stove. She was a mature sixteen year old with café latté skin and braided, black hair. Her best feature was her expressive almond shaped eyes.

"Hi Mom, I've got the gravy goin' and the water's hot for the noodles. I thought I'd get a start on dinner for you."

Hattie walked over to her daughter and kissed her cheek. "Aren't ya'll the sweetest? It smells real good, Ruby."

"It's out of a jar, but I threw in some chopped tomatoes and onions and some of that I-tal-yun sausage you bought. Hope it tastes okay," Ruby told her mother.

"Did your father call?" Hattie asked.

"No not yet. Is he workin' extra late?"

Hattie frowned. "He didn't say so this mornin'."

"Hi Mommy." Hattie's son, Lamar stood there with a fist full of silverware. "When's dinner gonna be ready, Ruby? I'm starved!" Lamar was tall and lanky with horn rimmed glasses and a tight Afro. He looked like a younger version of his father.

"I told ya already, it'll be ready when it's ready," Ruby told her brother. "You get on with setting the table or it's never gonna be ready. Now, Mommy, sit down there and get your shoes off. We got this under control."

"That sounds like a fine idea to me," Hattie sank into a kitchen chair and unlaced her white nurses shoes. She hated how big her feet looked in them. *Always remind me of two big white row boats when I looks down at my feet. But the support is jus' fine so I guess I don' care about them row boats at the end of my legs.*

Stella ran into the room holding a book in both hands. She was a lively child with a big bright smile. A dozen barrettes danced in her hair. She rushed up to Hattie and plunked herself into her Mother's lap.

"My stars, baby-girl, ya'll gettin' so big ya hardly fit

here in this tired old lap anymore. Wha'cha got there?" Hattie gave her daughter a squeeze.

"I made this for you, Mommy. See? It's a book without any writin' in it. I can't remember what the teacher called it. A something-book. You're supposed to put 'scraps' in it. But that don't sound right; why would you want to save scraps in a book? You already save 'em in the fridge or throw 'em in the alley for the cats." Stella's merry brown eyes gazed up at her mother. Hattie laughed and kissed her daughter.

"I think the teacher was talking about a scrapbook. And yes, you do save 'scraps' in it….scraps of memories and special times. Like the Mother's Day card you made for me, Stella"

Hattie caressed the front cover of the book decorated with kittens romping through some spring flowers.

"Now I have somewhere to keep it forever. In my scrapbook." Hattie hugged her. "Thank you darlin' I'll be cherishin' this forever."

Stella turned to her brother. "See, Lamar, Mommy does so like it. It's not a dumb idea like you said."

"Is too." mumbled Lamar.

"When's your brother comin' home, Ruby?" Hattie asked choosing to ignore the younger ones' squabble.

"He called earlier and said to go ahead and keep a plate warm for him. He didn't know what time he'd be home." Ruby poured the pasta from the colander into a large bowl. "Okay, this 'bout ready. Lamar, get the milk outta the fridge. What would you like to drink, Mommy?

"Oh just some water be fine." Hattie started to rise. "Here, I'll get it."

Stella jumped off Hattie's lap. "Stay there, Mommy, I'll get it."

She ran to the cupboard to get a glass down. Ruby was right behind her to help as the cupboard where the glasses were kept was too high for Stella to reach them.

"Be careful squirt," she told her.

Stella went to the sink and filled the glass. Then, holding it with both hands, she walked carefully back to Hattie's place and set it down.

"Thank you, darlin'. You're such a good helper." Hattie said.

In the meantime, Ruby had placed the big steaming bowls of pasta and sauce on the table. She took a bowl of salad out of the refrigerator and brought it to the table.

Lamar sat down and said, "'Bout time." and reached for the spoon sticking out of the pasta.

Hattie gently laid a hand on Lamar's arm. "Grace first, Lamar."

"Jeez, Ma, I'm starved!"

"Grace first," Hattie said in a firmer tone. "Let's bow our heads and give thanks. Heavenly Father, we thank you for what we are about to...."

The front door slammed and heavy footsteps could be heard starting down the hall.

Hattie called out. "JJ, we's all in the kitchen and you just in time for a hot dinner."

The prayer forgotten momentarily, Hattie looked toward the door leading into the kitchen.

Ruby rose and, crossing to the cupboards, reached for an extra dinner plate. She turned and began walking back to the table. Joe's younger brother Elgin, not JJ, stood in the doorway. Ruby stood frozen staring at her uncle, the plate slipping from her hands and shattering on the floor. Elgin's face was covered with blood, his clothing ripped and dirty. Stella began to cry.

"Cool. Ya been in a fight, Uncle Elgin?" Lamar asked.

Hattie jumped up, with a little scream, and rushed to Elgin, grabbing a dish towel from the counter.

"What on earth has happened to you, boy? Are you all right? Ruby, call 911! Stella, baby, stop your cryin', your uncle's gonna be okay."

"NO! No 911, no police!" Elgin cried.

Hattie pushed Elgin into a chair. "Sit down here, Elgie." Hattie said, using a childhood nickname.

Elgin flinched as she began cleaning his wound. There was a lot of blood but the only injury Hattie could find was a cut over his eye.

"Ruby-girl, get me a cool, wet rag."

Ruby brought her mother the dampened rag and Hattie continued to clean Elgin's face.

"What happened to ya? You fightin' again?" Hattie asked.

"No." Elgin winced as she cleaned the cut with some anticeptic.

"Well then, what happened to ya?"

"Got into a little bit of trouble. I gotta get outta here...out of town. Can I have some clean clothes, Hattie?" Elgin asked.

"Not unless ya'll tell me what's goin' on. You in what kind'a trouble, Elgin?" said Hattie.

Elgin was silent. How did he tell Hattie?

"Elgin, you best tell me what you been up to and you best tell me *right now*. Joe and me can probably fix it if you tell me the tru't." Elgin looked up into Hattie's eyes at the mention of Joe's name and dread filled her heart.

"Ruby, take Stella and Lamar and go watch some TV" Hattie told her children.

"But, Ma, I'm starving!" complained Lamar.

"Take your dinner plates with you. Go on now, hurry up. Load up those plates and go watch some T.V. And, Ruby, turn the sound up; I want to be able to hear it in here."

"Yes, Ma'am." Ruby replied. She knew that when the TV was turned up it was time for grown-up talk. Never, never had any of them ever questioned Hattie's rule.

Hattie got a bag of frozen peas out of the freezer and slapped it on Elgin's forehead where a goose egg was starting to rise. Lamar and Stella filled their plates and, followed by Ruby, they left the kitchen. In a moment, Hattie heard the television go on in the living room.

"Now, what's this all about?" Hattie asked Elgin.

"Oh, Hattie, yur' gonna kill me. I'm so sorry, but I know Joe's gonna be all right."

"*Joe?* What's he got to do with any of your shenanigans? Joe, he at work," Hattie insisted.

Elgin put his head in his hands and moaned. The kitchen was silent.

Hattie sighed. "You best tell me all of it Elgin."

Elgin raised his head, tears glistened in his eyes. "I asked Joe to pick me up after he got off work. Told him I needed a ride to the store. I was meetin' JC and Rat there. We was.....we was..."

"Go on, boy, spit it out," Hattie insisted.

"We was gonna rob it." Elgin hung his head.

"*WHAT!?*"

"We was gonna rob it but there must'a been a silent alarm 'cause all hell broke loose; cop cars pulled up out front and JC, Rat, and me, we barely made it outta the back door."

"We ran down an alley and jumped a fence and I fell on my face and almost got caught."

Hattie stared at him in horror. "Where's Joe?"

Elgin didn't answer and Hattie shook him by his arm.

"*WHAT HAPPENED TO MY JOE?*" She yelled.

"The cops got him." Elgin whispered.

"Oh, sweet Jesus, *NO!*"

"It'll be okay, Hattie. Joe didn't have nothin' to do with this. He'll tell the cops that. They'll let him go." Elgin explained.

"You don't know that, Elgin. How could you? Gettin' Joe involved in a *robbery*! He's your brother! He's got four chil'un to take care of."

"I know, Hattie, I know. I'm sorry."

"You sorry all right...sorry as you can be," Hattie's voice dripped with scorn. "Ya'll couldn't wait to get to the big city. We took you in. Gave ya bed n'board 'till you got yourself situated. Joe hep' you get a job. Not our fault if'n ya done lost it."

"I'm so sorry, Hattie." Elgin hung his head.

Hattie picked up his hand and slapped it on the bag of frozen peas on his head. She stepped to the hallway.

"Ruby! Come here please, right away."

Ruby's footsteps hurried down the hall and she entered the kitchen.

"Yes, Mama?"

"Get the first aid kit out from under the sink, Ruby. Put some peroxide on this here cut and a big Band-Aid. I have to go out for awhile. Give your uncle some'a Joe's clean clothes. And don't ask your uncle Elgin no questions," Hattie said and then turned to Elgin. "As for you, I want you outta my house in ten minutes."

"You is not to talk to my chil'un. Not a word about dis here mess. And Elgin, it breaks my ol' heart to say this, but don't come back."

Hattie sat in a chair, slipped on her shoes, quickly lacing them up, and rose.

"Ruby, you in charge like always, get the young un's to bed and when JJ come in you feed him. And tell him to stay at home. I'll be back soon as I can."

As Hattie rushed out of the kitchen to the front door, Ruby hollered, "But, Mom..."

"No 'buts' now girl, you do as I say. You keeps the chil'ren in the house, ya hear?" The front door slammed on Hattie's last words.

Chapter 13

Alma ~ seventeen years earlier

Alma rushed to answer the door the next day. She took a deep breath and blew her exhale into her palm, checking her breath. She opened the door and there he was. Tight, low rider jeans, a crisp, newly ironed shirt and that killer smile.

"Hi Charlie," she said as she unlatched the screened door.

Charlie stepped in and gave her a peck on the cheek. "Hello, beautiful. I see you got your beauty rest."

"Come on in. I cooked you some food. Are you hungry?"

"Yeah, I'm starved. I thought two o'clock would never come." He thrust a handful of Shasta daisies at her. "Um…these are for you."

"Oh, Charlie, they're my favorite. You remembered."

He frowned. "It's nothing."

"How come you're cranky? Did I do something wrong?"

"If being who you are and lookin' like you do is wrong, then, yeah, you did."

"Charlie, that's the most romantic thing anyone has ever said to me."

"It wasn't *supposed* to be romantic, you crazy woman! You're still too young for me, in spite of your job. I shouldn't start something I can't finish, especially with you."

Alma stepped into him and ran the back of her hand tenderly down his jaw line. "Who says it has to have a 'finish'?"

Charlie caught her hand and turning it over, kissed her palm. "God, woman, do you know what you do to me when you touch me?"

"I'd like to find out."

He stepped back. "Come on, let's get those posies into some water and you can show me what you cooked."

Alma gave him a knowing smile and turned to the kitchen. A low bar divided the kitchenette from the living room. The living room was done in shades of sand and white. A huge abstract painting in reds, yellows, blues and orange covered one wall.

"Nice room." Charlie said as he took it all in.

"Thank you. I love flea markets and garage sales. It's surprising what people will throw away."

"You've got quite the touch with somebody else's trash."

"Thanks again…I think."

"That didn't come out the way I meant it. You seem to have a knack with decoratin'." Charlie explained.

"I knew what you meant." She gave him a sexy smile.

Putting a wall, even if it was only a half wall, between him and Alma seemed like a good idea so he sat on the other side of the bar and watched her.

Alma reached up and opened a high cabinet door. Her midriff blouse pulled up and exposed lightly tanned skin and a peek of the lower curve of her breast. *My God, she's not wearing a bra.* Charlie sighed to himself.

"Honey, can you reach this vase for me please?" Alma said, turning and catching him transfixed on her body.

"Um...what?" Charlie stuttered. "Oh, yeah, sure." Charlie rose and walked around the bar. Alma didn't move as he started to reach up into the cabinet. There was nothing but a breath between their bodies. Alma watched the cords of muscle play in his neck. The top couple of buttons were undone on his shirt and dark blonde chest hair curled out.

Charlie brought the vase down and realized how close Alma was. He stood there frozen with the vase in one hand. Alma closed the inches between them and wrapped her arms around his neck. She slowly brought her lips up to his but instead of kissing him; she touched his bottom lip with her slick pink tongue. With the lightest touch she slowly caressed his mouth. He tasted of this morning's toothpaste, lemons and Charlie.

Unconsciously, Charlie let go of the vase and it landed on the counter with a loud smack. He encircled Alma with his arms. He opened his lips to her tongue and it darted in playfully to caress his.

Charlie groaned as he deepened their kiss. He was awash in sensation; the stroke of her tongue, the press of her body, the scent of her. She stood on her tiptoes to gain better access to his mouth.

He broke off the kiss then and trailed his lips down the column of her throat and buried his face in the juncture where her neck and shoulder met. He nipped the tender skin there and felt a shudder run through Alma's body. Her eyes were closed as she waited for his next caress. When it didn't come her eyes snapped open.

He looked into her passion glazed eyes. "Alma?"

"Baby, don't stop." Alma demanded.

He took her mouth again, consuming her. She plunged her hands into his heavy, soft hair. With a feminine knowledge as old as time she rocked her body against him. His hands crept up her sides, under the fabric of her blouse, until he was caressing the under sides of her breasts.

"More…" Alma purred.

Charlie shifted her body slightly to one side so that he could cup one breast. He held it gently and caressed the hard, beaded nipple with his thumb. Breaking the deep kiss, his mouth traveled down her neck, nibbling at her collar bone.

He lifted her breast gently and captured her nipple with his mouth through the fabric of her blouse. His tongue twirled around it as he suckled softly. Alma groaned again and rubbed her pelvis against him. She needed him closer, wanted to crawl inside his skin.

"Charlie….please."

"What, baby, what do you need?"

"I want…." she stuttered.

"Yeah, baby, tell me." Charlie groaned.

"I want you! I want *it*. I want everything." Alma sighed.

Charlie's hand moved down to Alma's butt and pulled her closer. She moaned her pleasure and frustration. His hand moved around to her most intimate place and cupped her between her legs.

"Is this what you want Alma?"

"Yes! yes, but…" Alma couldn't say it.

"What? Just tell me. I'm here for you, whatever you want."

Alma buried her face in his neck. "I want you naked. I want to see you…all of you." She whispered.

"Well, why didn't you say so?" Charlie laughed. "Which way is the bedroom?"

"Through there," Alma pointed over her shoulder to a door.

A second later Charlie had swept Alma into his arms like she weighed no more than a kitten.

"Wait!" she laughed.

"What?"

"I gotta turn off the stove."

Charlie bent down and fumbled with the dials on the stove.

"Here let me do it." Alma giggled. She deftly turned the switches off. "There, got it."

Charlie lost no time and strode over to the door. "Open it, baby."

Alma reached down and swung the door open. She hugged Charlie's neck with both arms and nibbled at his neck. He walked down a short hall and into the bedroom. The mini-blinds were half closed and slats of light lit the ceiling. A few candles burned around the room.

"Expecting company?" Charlie chuckled.

"A girl can dream, can't she?"

"Is that what you do? Dream about me?"

"Just every night, Charlie." Alma whispered.

Charlie laid Alma on the bed, half reclining against a half dozen pillows. He stepped back. Alma gaze was riveted on him.

"Do you want to take my clothes off or should I?" Charlie asked.

"You do it and I'll watch."

Charlie began to unbutton his shirt, exposing a tan expanse of chest. His flat nipples were a dusky pink surrounded by just the right amount of hair.

His stomach muscles and arms could have won contests. Alma's eyes widened with desire. One button was stubborn and Charlie popped it as he ripped the shirt off.

His hands went to his belt buckle which he released and he continued to the zipper of his jeans. He slipped off his sockless loafers and slid his pants down. Stepping out of them the only thing remaining was his Calvin shorts. They were black and form fitting.

Alma could no longer ignore the huge bulge that showed her just how much Charlie wanted her. Even though she had dreamed of this scene for years she was slightly afraid. *What if she did something wrong? What if he laughed at her? Oh, well, she had never been a coward in her life.*

"Stop!" she cried.

"Okay. What is it, doll?"

"I want to touch you…."

Charlie went utterly still. She thought for a moment, he would deny her. "Please…" she added.

Charlie walked over to the edge of the bed and stood before her. Alma got to her knees and walked over to him. She put her hands on his chest and traveled the contours. When she brushed his nipple he gasped.

"Did I hurt you?" She asked.

"God, no."

She smiled and wondered if her mouth on him, *there*, would give him the same pleasure as she felt. She leaned forward and licked his nipple. Her answer was in Charlie's groan of desire. She lapped his nipple and gently sucked at it.

"Alma, stop. You're drivin' me crazy. I can't control myself."

There was an unexpected exhilaration from taking

control and indulging her own pleasure. She nibbled up his chest and placed little kisses along his jaw line. Alma brought her hands up to his head and Charlie bent his head so that she could kiss him again.

As their kisses deepened, Alma's hand began to play in his chest hair and follow its path where it disappeared into his shorts. She broke their kiss and her mouth followed her hands. She slipped her fingers inside the waistband of his shorts and slowly pulled down. She was kissing the exposed skin when her mouth found a puckered scar. Alma stopped and looked. It was about four inches long and over an inch wide.

"Charlie, what happened?" She cried.

"Nothin' to worry about. A chain got away from me on the rig."

"Does it hurt?"

"No. It's just ugly, is all."

"I don't think so." She lowered her head and kissed the new, pink flesh.

She gently licked the wound with her tongue as her hand crept down to the hard ridge beneath his shorts.

"My God, Alma, you're gonna make me explode!" Charlie moaned.

Alma pulled his shorts down and Charlie's penis leapt free, long and thick.

"You're beautiful, you know that, Charlie?"

"You're crazy, ya know that, baby?" he mimicked her tone.

Alma wanted to kiss his penis. It looked and felt like velvet encasing steel. *What,* she wondered, *would he do if I kissed him there? Well, it appears that I* am *a coward after all 'cause as much as I want to I can't. What if he was shocked or thought I was a slut?*

Charlie pushed her back onto the bed and followed her down.

"Now it's my turn to see you...all of you." he murmured.

He took the edges of her top and started to lift it.

"Raise your arms, baby." Alma closed her eyes and raised her arms. She suddenly felt shy.

What a joke, she thought. *After being practically naked in front of hundreds of strange men for two years, I get a case of the virginal blushes with this man of all people? This man who has filled my dreams for far too long. Who's been the subject of every horny thought I've ever had.*

Her breasts felt a coolness as the top came off and she instinctually lowered her arms and tried to cover herself. Charlie gently took her hands and moved them aside.

"No, baby, let me see you. God, you are stunning." he breathed as he lowered his mouth and took one nipple into his mouth.

New pleasures shot through Alma and pooled below her stomach. Charlie moved to her other breast and kissed and teased it until her nipple was hard and extended.

He cupped her breast and moved his mouth down her belly, swirling his tongue in her belly button. His hands were busy at the button and zipper of her shorts and as he continued to kiss her stomach he slid them off and tossed them aside.

The small patch of fabric that covered her pubis was a silky peach color. A few reddish curls had escaped the sides.

Charlie moved down and kissed Alma behind her knee. She moaned and quivered with anticipation. He slowly kissed a path up the smooth, pale, skin of her inner thigh and suddenly she felt him blow a warm breath on the tiny fabric that covered her. Then his hot, wet tongue licked at the fabric. Alma bucked and gave a tiny scream.

"Easy, baby. Do you like that?" Charlie asked.

"Yes, but...." she moaned.

"Shhh.... Let me pleasure you."

Alma laid back and threaded her fingers through his hair. Charlie blew on the wet fabric and fiery chills shot up Alma's spine. He lapped at the fabric and thrust his tongue into the silk.

"Charlie, please...." Alma begged.

"What do you want, baby? You know what I want? I want to see you there. Taste you. Feel all of your heat. Will you let me?"

You're not a coward, Alma. You're not a coward. Alma repeated to herself. *It's what you have always wanted but didn't know it.*

"Yes." She answered.

Charlie groaned his pleasure. He licked and sucked at the fabric covering her as he slipped his fingers under the thin strings that held it in place. He pulled the thong down and away. He parted the folds of her sex and licked her, his tongue brushing the soft wet skin.

Alma gasped at the sensation, plunging her hands into his soft hair, not moving for fear that he would leave off what he was doing to her. His mouth was loving her in every way possible, his tongue stroking the moist heat of her.

She lifted her hips to him and he supported her with his hands as his tongue found the aching center of her being. His hot clever tongue stroked the bud until he could feel Alma give herself up to the soaring sensations. She pulled on his hair and cried out. He stopped for a long, unbearable moment. She squirmed as his firm grip held her still.

"Charlie, don't stop ...please...!"

He rewarded her by closing his lips around the tight swollen nub and he sucked harder. His wicked tongue licked faster and stroked deep inside her. He thrust one and then two fingers deep into her coaxing her closer and closer to a cliff that she hurtled toward.

His mouth and hands were everywhere as she tumbled over the edge and experienced pleasure like nothing she had ever known. Pulses of incredible sensations rode through her entire body. Charlie moved up her body and she could feel his hard, heavy sex pressed against her thigh.

He gently opened her thighs and settled between them. He kissed and stroked her breasts and murmured, "You're beautiful like this, Alma. So hot, so sexy, your taste drives me wild."

Alma squirmed beneath him. "Charlie... I want the rest...I want you...inside of me."

"Ah, baby, I thought you'd never ask." he replied as he raised himself up supporting his weight with his arm and with his other hand opened her thighs wider. He gazed into her face.

"Alma, honey, open your eyes. Look at me while I take you."

Alma opened her eyes and saw all the love and passion she could hope for in his eyes. He stroked her inner thigh and then guided himself to her wet, swollen entrance. She was so ready for him. He guided his penis so that it played at her opening, rubbing her clitoris with the tip of it. Slowly he entered her, reveling in the feelings she evoked in him. He withdrew and then

entered deeper this time. Kissing her, he withdrew
again and began to plunge deep inside her.

*What the fuck? What was wrong? There was
something stopping him, resisting.* Charlie froze and
rose up on his arms and stared down at Alma.

Reality dawned when he saw the mixture of passion
and fear of the unknown in her eyes.

"Jesus Christ! Alma! Are you a *virgin*?"

"So what if I am?" she demanded.

"Why didn't you tell me?"

"Because I knew you wouldn't take me to bed."

"You're damn right about that."

"Charlie, please don't stop. I want this. I want you."

"Damnit! Are you sure?" His eyes searched her
face. 'Cause we can't go back."

"I'm sure. I've been waiting for this…waiting for
you…for a long time."

"I don't want to hurt you but I can't help it. It's
gonna hurt the first time."

"You could never hurt me, Charlie."

She gently grasped his penis and, inexpertly, tried to
guide him to her. Charlie took her hand away and
brought it to his lips. He held it gently as he lowered
his head and kissed her sweetly. His penis found her
entrance like it was coming home. He gently pushed
himself into her.

He withdrew and the next time he went in deeper he
felt the tight barrier. Alma met his movement with a
buck which broke through and seated him fully inside
of her. He paused, waiting for her to adjust to him. He
looked down and saw two tears slide slowly down her
cheeks.

"Oh God, I've hurt you. I'm so sorry."

"No. I'm happy, Charlie, these are tears of

happiness. I've wanted you for so long." she sighed.

Charlie began to move slowly.

"Wrap your legs around me, doll."

He leaned down and began suckling her nipple until she was panting with passion. He moved more quickly then, deep, smooth strokes that brought her pleasure and erased the moment of pain. She lifted her hips to meet his thrusts.

He began to thrust deeper, faster and the tension between their two bodies began to climb.

"Charlie!" Alma cried.

"It's okay, baby, I'm here." He reached between them and found the nub of her sex with his finger. He rubbed it slowly.

"Charlie...I can't...it's too much...I..."

"Go with it, baby. I won't let you fall. Let yourself go."

And she did. Convulsing around him, driving him to his own climax. She milked him with her interior muscles, drawing every last drop of his essence into her. Still joined Charlie rolled with her until he was on his side, wrapping her in his warmth.

She curled into him like a sleepy little cat. Her breathing steadied and slowed. As he dropped into a satiated sleep he thought he heard her whisper.

"I love you."

* * *a month later* * *

The music thrummed through the walls of the dressing room. Muted laughter and an occasional happy shout could be heard from out front. Sally and Alma sat at their mirrors freshening their makeup for their next numbers.

"So I says to this guy, 'what makes you think I would go to the VIP room with you for twenty bucks?' Sally said. "You must got somethin' awful special there in your pants.

"Alma laughed. "There's nothin' *that* special."

"Tell me about it."

They were silent for a few moments concentrating on getting just the perfect 'smoky eye' applied and re-gluing a loose eyelash.

"Can I borrow your Pussy-Pink lip glitter? Sally asked.

"Sure. Here you go," Alma handed her the lipstick tube.

"So how's it goin' with what's-his-name?"

"Charlie. Yeah, it's really good. The only time we're not together is when I'm workin'. He's got a leave of absence from his job, 'cause of his mom bein' sick."

"How long is he gonna be around?"

"I hope forever." Alma sighed.

"Sounds pretty serious."

"Now don't you laugh, Sal. But, I'm so in love with him I can't see straight. I thought it was love when I was a kid and he broke my heart, but that doesn't even come close to what I feel now."

"How does he feel…about you?" asked Sally.

"I'm not sure. We haven't talked about it. I'm scared if I tell him how I really feel he'll run like a rabbit."

"Yeah, they're known to do that," Sally laughed.

"He acts like he cares. Brings me flowers, remembers little things that I like. When we….don't you dare laugh…when we make love, he is so tender I wanna' cry."

Sally stared at Alma. "'Make love?' You mean to tell me you finally lost your cherry? And you didn't even tell me. God! I'd given up on you. Thought you were going to be a virgin 'till you were forty."

Sally slapped Alma's shoulder and laughed hysterically. "God, I can't believe you finally gave it up!"

"It's not funny, Sal. I told you I was waiting for someone special. I just didn't tell you who it was."

"Well, I'm happy for you. Just make sure this fucker treats you...."

Sally stopped what she was about to say and watched amazed as Alma jumped up, knocking her chair over backwards, and ran for the toilet.

"Oh, God, oh god...." Alma cried as she dashed away.

Alma slammed the toilet seat up, sank to her knees and vomited noisily. The toilet was housed in a closet-sized room that barely allowed the door to be closed. Her feet stuck out of the partially closed door. She hugged the bowl and continued to dry heave, moaning loudly.

After a minute of shock, Sally followed her and held Alma's hair back. "Jeez, kid, what's wrong? You okay?"

Shaking, Alma got to her feet and wobbled back to her chair. Pulling it upright, she slumped into it.

"Yeah, I'm okay. I've had the flu since Tuesday. Thought I'd be all right by tonight. It comes and goes." Alma said.

"You sure ya got the flu?" Sally asked.

"Wha'd ya mean?"

"Ya got chills? Fever? Aches?"

"No...just throwin' up. Then I feel just fine 'till the

next time. Why?" Alma asked.

"When was your last period, Alma?"

"What!? I don't know. Four....no, five...Oh my God! Six weeks ago, I think. Where's a calendar?" Alma jumped up and immediately sat back down. "Yuk, I feel like shit."

"You could be preggers, is all I'm saying."

Alma's eyes went wide with shock. "No, that's not possible."

Did you use protection?" asked Sally.

"I am now. Pills. But that first weekend... well, we were kinda caught up in the moment. Oh, Sally," Alma groaned, "what am I gonna do?"

There was a sharp rap and Danny, the backstage hand, stuck his head around the corner of the door.

"Five minutes, Sal."

"Thanks, Danny." Sally turned back to Alma.

"What you're gonna do, after work, is go buy a home pregnancy test...hell, buy three to be sure. Go home and pee on them and *then* worry."

"What'll I tell Charlie? He's pickin' me up."

"Don't say a word to lover-boy. Not until you have to," Sally patted Alma's shoulder. "Gotta go entertain the drunks. Be back in a minute."

Sally checked her makeup one last time, grabbed a silver glittery boa and, with an exaggerated hip sway, walked out.

* * * *

Later that night Charlie lay on the bed with a remote in one hand and a beer in the other. He heard the toilet flush and set his beer on the night stand. Alma walked into the room wearing a sheer pink night gown with lace covering her breasts. One of her hands was hidden in the folds of the gown. Her face was devoid of makeup and Charlie marveled again at how beautiful she was.

He patted the edge of the bed. "Com'er, doll, I miss you."

Alma walked over and sat down. Charlie gently placed his hand on the back of her neck and pulled her in. He rained light kisses along the line of her mouth and Alma moaned. Regretfully, she pulled away.

"What is it, babe?" Charlie asked. "Not in the mood tonight?"

"Oh, Charlie, I'm always in the mood with you. It's just….well….like I need to talk to you, is all," Alma said.

"Well, don't look so scared, baby. What's up?"

Silently Alma raised her hand.

"What's this?" Charlie said as he took what looked like a tongue depressor from her. He turned it over and then saw the big pink plus sign in the window of the pregnancy test.

He looked from it to Alma's face.

"What the hell…. Is this a pregnancy test? You…?"

Alma silently nodded her head and watched Charlie's face. This was a turning point in her life. She loved him so much but somehow she couldn't tell him.

The moment she took all three tests and every one had a bright pink '+' sign she knew what she wanted. She wanted Charlie and she wanted this baby. She wanted a family, something she had never had and had always dreamed about.

"But I thought you said you was on the pill?" Charlie sputtered.

"I am, Charlie, *now*. I guess it happened that first weekend."

"My God." Charlie whispered.

The silence was so heavy Alma thought she would scream. *Please, God, let him be happy, let him say he wants to be a family with me and our baby.*

Charlie frowned. "What are you gonna do?"

And with those five little words Alma knew if she kept this baby she was on her own. Charlie asking her 'what are *you* was going to do'; not what are *we* going to do told her everything she needed to know.

"Well, I'm not keeping it for God's sake! What would I do with a kid?" Alma clinched her jaw to keep the tears back.

"Oh. Okay, then. 'Cause I'm not certain I'm ready for all that, ya know. Being a father? Jesus! It's never crossed my mind. And besides that I got a call from the rig today. If I want to keep my job I have to go back in a couple of days. Probably for about a month."

"Don't worry. This is not your problem. I'll take care of it." Alma said.

"Okay." Charlie jumped out of the bed and pulled his jeans on. Searching, he finally found his T-shirt on the floor. Pulling the shirt over his head he said, "Look, I'm gonna take off. I should get over to my mom's and see how she's doin'. See what she needs before I leave. I'll call you tomorrow."

"Sure, Charlie. I'll talk to you later." Alma reached for the remote and turned the television on. Blindly she stared at some inane sit-com as Charlie walked over and kissed her on the top of her head.

"See ya soon, Bug," he said and walked out the door.

Alma sat with tears streaming down her face and listened to his car start up and peel out. She sobbed once and the second sob came out as an animal in mortal pain. She threw the remote at the TV as hard as she could and collapsed onto the bed sobbing.

Chapter 14

Alma

"Gin!" Charlie hollered.

"Dang it, Daddy," Chelsea said. "Ya stuck me with a high count *again*." She counted her cards. "Ten, twenty, thirty, forty...fifty-five, Alma... uh, I mean '*Ma*'."

Charlie laughed. "Too bad, little girl. You and your Ma are outta your league. I am the Gin King! Your deal Alma."

Chelsea rose from her chair. "Don't deal 'til I get back, Alma."

"Hey!" Charlie said.

"Sor-rey. Ma, I gotta go to the can. Don't play 'til I get back, 'kay?"

"Okay, hon," Alma replied.

Chelsea walked off and Charlie turned to Alma. "The 'can'? I can guess where she got that from. She hangs around your job and listen to the way she talks! *'The can'*? For Chrissakes, Alma, don'cha teach her nothin'?"

Charlie glared at Alma as she continued to shuffle the cards.

"Well? Ya gonna tell me or not? Where ya strippin' at, huh?

"Now Charlie, don't get all mad, please. You'll get in'ta trouble again."

Charlie leaned in close, "Just tell me ya ain't workin' for that bastard, Rick. Say it, Alma. 'I ain't workin' for Rick.'"

Alma's eyes flashed, "Yes! All right? I'm back at the Paradise Lounge. Rick said…"

"Goddamn It!" Charlie hissed. "How could ya? Did ya forget what that fucker tried with Chelsea?" Charlie shook his head, "What the fuck's the matter with you?"

"I'm keeping Chels away…honest, Charlie. And I told Rick he had to behave himself."

"Ya told Rick he had to behave himself." Charlie sneered. "Well, that should take care of it then. What was I thinkin'? Jee-sus, Alma!"

"I laid down the law…" Alma explained.

"Yeah, I'll just bet you did…Key word being 'laid'!"

Alma ignored the sarcasm. "Besides Rick hired me at the same percentage as some of the girls that've been there a long time. He said 'no hard feelings'."

"'*No hard feelings*?'" Charlie hissed. "That's what that low life says after he molested my daughter?"

"Now, Charlie, he didn't exactly molest her, okay? It was just a kiss. She did kind'a have a crush on him, ya know."

Charlie ran his hands through his hair in frustration. "Christ-on-a-crutch! A real man doesn't take advantage of a kid who's got a crush on him. I gotta get outta here! I'm gonna kill that son of a bitch. Alma, you are not workin' there…you get your ass in there tomorrow and you quit, ya hear me? And tell him to stay the fuck away from my daughter."

"Yeah? And so what are we supposed to do for money, huh, Charlie?"

"*You* tell me! What?"

"There's plenty of jobs out there if you'd just get off

your butt and look!" Charlie said.

"I did look! I can't make the same kind'a dough. Ya keep tellin' me what I *ain't* supposed ta do..."

Charlie glared at Alma. "Shit!"

"Ya start fightin' in the joint... get yourself transferred out here to the middle of nowhere...I gotta leave my job in Reno, follow you. I can't strip, I can't bartend, I can't dance. I'm sick of you tellin' me what I *can't* do! Try tellin' me what I can do, why don'cha? What am I suppose to do with you in here another five to ten, minimum?" Alma's voice dwindled to a whine. "Why'd ya hav'ta to go and kill that guy, huh?"

"He had it comin', attackin' ya like that...besides, it was an accident," Charlie said. "Forget it! Here comes Chels. I don't wanna talk about it anymore."

Chelsea weaved her way through the tables until she reached Alma and Charlie.

"Did ya wait for me?" She took a closer look at her mother's face. "What's wrong? How come ya look funny, Ma? Come on, ya been fightin' again haven't ya?" Chelsea's eyes filled with tears. "I'm sorry, Ma, I'm sorry I told on ya. Please don't be mad at her, Daddy."

"It ain't nothin', sweetie. Don't you get all upset now." Alma reassured her daughter.

"I ain't mad at her, honey," Charlie said. "I'm mad at me for bein' in here is all. Listen, Chels, I want you to promise me somethin'. Will ya?"

"What is it, Daddy?" Chelsea asked.

"I want you to promise me that you'll stay away from the club where your Ma works."

"I want ya to stay far away from Rick. Will ya promise your old Dad?"

"Oh, Daddy," Chelsea replied. "I don't need to promise you that. I am *so* over Rick!"

Charlie laughed with relief. "Okay then! That's settled. Deal the cards, Alma."

Alma shuffled the cards once more and began to deal. "See, doll, nothin' to worry about. Chel's a good girl, ain't'cha, honey?"

Charlie sighed. "Just deal, will ya?"

Chapter 15

Alma ~ seventeen years earlier

Three months and I'm finally finished throwing up my toe nails every hour. What a relief to be over that part, Alma thought to herself. *And since Sal is the only one that even has a clue about my baby, I can still work.* Alma stretched and then snuggled down under the down quilt. *Wonder what Charlie's doin'.*

She had not heard from him after he almost ran from her apartment the night of the pregnancy test. The only word that she had had of him was through his mom whom Alma continued to visit every couple of weeks.

It's clear that he's not thinkin' about me. How could I fall for him all over again and let him break my heart a second time? She admonished herself. *When will you wise up, Alma?*

As if in answer, Alma felt a miniscule flutter under her heart. She lay perfectly still. *Oh my, there it was again, she* thought. *It's the baby, I know it is.*

"Hello, baby-girl," she whispered. "It's Mama. Don't you worry about a thing." She made slow circles on the slight bulge that was her tummy now. "We're going to do just fine, you and me."

As Alma threw back the covers she continued to talk to her baby.

"Speaking of us doing okay, Mama needs to get her tush in gear and get to work."

"The rent's not gonna get paid by itself."

An hour later Alma walked in the back door of the Pussy Cat. Sally and some of the other girls were chatting, smoking and laughing.

"Hey, Al, was'up?" Sally cried.

"Nothin'. What'd I miss?" Alma said.

"Just the usual shop talk."

Taking her makeup kit from her carry-all she tossed the bag on the floor. Alma sat at her dressing table and opened the box. She placed her foundation, blush, glitter, mascara, lipstick and brushes in a neat row. Opening a small tub she dipped her finger into the rich cream and began to rub conditioner into her skin.

All around her swirled chatter, laughter, and little screams but she didn't participate. Except for Sally, who was older than the rest, Alma thought the other girls were pretty silly. Their conversations consisted of what some rich customer had bought them for a little of their 'time'; the latest Frederick's of Hollywood catalog; and how sore their feet were. They didn't seem to have goals and dreams like she did. And the anticipation of the baby now removed her even further from their frivolous world.

Danny knocked and immediately poked his head in. "Hey, Louise, you're up."

Louise rose and headed for the door.

"Time to make the register ca-ching, ca-ching, ladies," she said as she walked out.

"God, I wish I had tits like hers," Sally exclaimed. "And they're real!"

"How do you know?" Alma asked.

Sally winked, "'Cause she let me feel them." The other girls screamed with mirth.

"Oh, that's just gross, Sally!" Alma told her.

Sally laughed. "I didn't say I liked it."

Alma playfully stuck her tongue out at Sally which made her laugh even harder.

Danny stuck his head in again. "Destiny, Amber, Epic, lap dances out front! Ernie says move your asses."

The other girls groaned as they got up and sauntered out. Alma continued to apply her makeup while Sally watched her.

"How're ya feelin', kid?"

Alma looked at her through the mirror. "Great, why?"

"Have you heard from him? The asshole?"

"Noooo…and don't call him that. He didn't ask for a baby or a family. What we had was just for kicks. I know that now." Alma replied.

"I still say you were nuts to keep it. What'd ya goin' do when you start to show? When you can't get into a costume anymore?"

"I've been savin' every dollar I can. We're gonna be all right."

"Does the assho….does *Charlie* know you didn't get an abortion?"

"Nope, it's none of his business." Fiercely Alma said. "*I'm* taking care of this baby…he's got no part in it."

"Five minutes, Alma," Danny called out with a sharp knock on the door.

"Okay, Danny, thanks," she replied.

* * * *

Later that night Alma and all the girls sat at their dressing tables creaming off their makeup and talking about the evening.

"Men are such pigs! Amber complained.

"What's new?" Louise asked.

"Pigs with money to spend." Epic corrected her.

"Gots to love the moola." Destiny said.

The last number was danced by Sally and she would be finished in a couple of minutes.

"Looks like *you* had a very good night, Alma," Epic observed.

Alma carefully counted her tips putting them in piles by denominations. "Yeah, pretty good."

"I just don't get it. She's never completely naked and they throw money at her for keeping her clothes on," Destiny said to Epic.

"I keep tellin' ya. Leave somethin' to the imagination; it turns 'em on more than if they see everything ya got." Alma explained.

"Yeah, but what 'bout Ernie?" asked Louise.

"Put your foot down. The more tips you get the bigger his take. Simple math." Alma laughed.

As Sally came through the door from the stage, Alma rose from her chair and began to take off her robe. She was in her bra and bikini panties, plain white and nothing fancy. She walked over to the clothes rack where all the girls hung their street clothes.

There was a knock at the back door.

"I'll get it," Sally said. She opened the door a crack and said in a low murmur, "What are *you* doing here? Get lost!"

She started to close the door.

"I'm not leavin'." A masculine voice murmured.

"Get your foot outta the goddamn door, asshole."

"Not until I see her." The voice replied.

Alma stood there frozen, half in and half out of her robe.

That can't be....Charlie's voice? She said to herself. But her heart told her different. *Not after all this time. I can't see him...I can't bear to talk to him again.* Her heart ached at the thought.

Sally's voice suddenly got louder. "Get lost, I said. She doesn't want to see you, much less hear anything you've got to say."

"Alma!" Charlie suddenly yelled from behind the door. "Please, give me five minutes. Alma!"

Alma turned deathly white and began to shake.

"You son-of-a-bitch, get outta here. I'm calling the bouncers if you don't get your foot the hell outta this door." Sally said.

"Sally, it's okay. Let him in. I want to get this over with one last time." Alma said.

Sally looked at Alma over her shoulder. "You sure, honey? You don't have to see him, ya know?"

"I'm sure. Let 'im in."

Sally reluctantly opened the door and there he was. *My God,* Alma thought. *He's more gorgeous than I remembered.*

Working out in the sun on the ocean had given Charlie a deep bronzed tan and lightened his hair putting golden streaks in that tangled with the light brown. His eyes seemed to reflect the blue of the sea. He had taken a couple of steps into the room and stood just staring at her.

"You want us girls to get lost, Alma?" Sally asked.

"No, Charlie's got nothin' more to say to me that you all can't hear," Alma replied. "Do you Charlie?"

Charlie looked around the room and realized that nobody was going anywhere.

"Alma baby, please. I made a terrible mistake,

leaving you like I did. It's just that with my mom being sick and you bein' pregnant….."

Everyone except Sally gasped at this news. Eyes big, the girls looked at each other.

Charlie continued as if no one else was in the room except the two of them.

"….I admit it, I ran. And have regretted it every day I've been gone. I shouldn't have left you alone to deal with the abortion and everything. I am so sorry. Please, please forgive me."

Alma stood perfectly still, her robe caught on one arm and shoulder, and smiled. She didn't answer and didn't move; she just stood there smiling.

They stood there for what seemed like forever to Alma. Charlie took in her body with his eyes like a man who was starving for life itself. He paused when his glance fell on her belly. It was slightly rounded above the line of her bikini underwear. *Christ, it's not like Alma to carry an ounce of extra weight,* Charlie thought to himself.

He glanced up and met Alma's eyes. He looked at her stomach again and back up to Alma. She stood there serenely smiling.

What the fuck? Charlie thought. *This just isn't possible. She had told him she didn't want a kid. She said she was terminating the pregnancy….hadn't she?* He tried to remember back to that awful night and what she had said before he bolted like the coward he was.

But, no, she hadn't actually said she was getting an abortion. She'd said…what? 'Not to worry, she would take care of it.'

Charlie looked into Alma's eyes once again and there it was: the truth. *My God, my baby is there hidden away in this wonderful woman whom I have always loved.*

Slowly he walked over to Alma, never breaking their eye contact. When he was a foot away, Alma calmly raised one hand to stop him from touching her. Charlie stood there looking at her and then he sank to his knees in front of her and, gently resting his hands on her waist, he buried his face in her tummy.

"My baby." His voice trembled. "Hello baby. It's your Daddy here."

Epic, Louise and Destiny all began to quietly blubber, tears running down their faces.

"This is just too romantic," Destiny sighed.

"They're gonna have a baby." Epic sighed.

Charlie looked up at Alma. "Why didn't you tell me? I'd have come home."

"You made your choice, Charlie, that night. We don't need you."

I've never seen this Alma, Charlie thought, s*o serene, so calm, so sure of herself. If I'm not careful, I'm going to lose her and the baby.*

"Alma, please I didn't know. Give me a chance to make it up to you....and our baby. Please."

Alma stared in amazement at the top of Charlie's head. *Could this really be my Charlie? Kneeling before me like some knight of old, humbling himself in front of all the girls. My tough, tell-it-like-it-is Charlie pleading for another chance.*
Begging to be a part of our lives..the baby's and mine.

"Al, you got to," Epic said.

"For sure."

" Say yes."

" Listen to him, Alma," the other girls echoed.

"You're a damn fool if you do," Sally told Alma.

"Who's to say he won't skip out again when it gets tough...and it will."

"Can you answer Sally?" Alma asked Charlie.

Charlie kissed Alma's belly and, talking to the soft rounded skin where his child lay in dark safety he said, "I can promise *you*, my sweet child, that I will never leave. I will always love you and your Mother. Always."

He looked up again. "I quit my job on the rig. I'm not leaving. Will you at least give me a chance to prove it to you?

Alma gently moved his hands away and stepped back.

"Maybe. You can call me tomorrow," She grinned. "But, I ain't promisin' nothin'."

Charlie stood up. He smiled at Alma. "That's all I'm asking." He looked around the room. Half the girls were sighing and the other half were laughing. Sally stood apart staring daggers at him.

"You better-by-God treat her right this time or you'll be walkin' funny for a month when I get through with you!" Sally warned him.

Charlie grinned at Sally. "Yes, ma'am."

He turned back to Alma. "How are you getting home?"

"With Sal. I'll talk to you tomorrow." Alma said.

Charlie walked back to the door. "Okay, then. I'll call you. Take care of yourself. Sally, don't keep her out too late."

"Humph! Back five minutes and already bossin' us around. Sally sniffed.

"You bet, I'm gonna be a Daddy."

"Good night, Charlie." Alma said.

Chapter 16

Hattie ~ eighteen years earlier

"Hattie, you know I gotta leave for Chicago this Friday." Joe said.

"I knows ya do. I'll be sorry to see ya go."

They sat together on an old plaid blanket from the trunk of Joe's mother's car. A lazy bayou snaked around a bend and the Spanish moss, hanging from the ancient oak trees, dipped its fingers into the murky waters. Somewhere close by a bull alligator barked.

Hattie nervously pleated the fabric of her sun dress. It was white with big yellow daisies on it. Her beautiful sculpted feet were bare where she had kicked off her low heeled sandals. During their time together Hattie had become less shy but was still very quiet. Especially when Joe got that serious tone to his voice.

"I've really enjoyed our time together." He told her.

"Me too, Joe." Hattie didn't look at him.

Hattie couldn't seem to say more even if she wanted to. Just the thought of Joe leaving made her heart ache and her throat close up with tears. They had spent every minute of the past week and a half together with the exception of the nights. Hattie had even helped Joe finish the painting on his mother's house just so that they could be together.

"I want to talk to you 'bout somethin'." Joe took both of Hattie's hands in his, stopping her nervous play with her skirt.

"Hattie, look at me, please."

Hattie turned her head and smiled sweetly.

"Hattie, I want you to know that I've fallen in love with you. I don't know how it happened so quick like, but I have."

Hattie sat there silently; a slow blush crept up her cheeks. "Do you think you might could love me?" Joe asked.

"Oh, Joe, a'course I love ya." Her eyes glowed with her love. "I don't want ya to leave. It's just about killin' me to see ya go."

"I wouldn't leave you for the world, ceptin' I got a real good job up in Chicago and I can't lose it." Joe explained to her. "I make three times what I'd make here if I stayed."

"I know." Hattie whispered.

"That's why I want to ask you somethin' real serious. And you don't have to answer right now; only think about it, okay?"

"What is it, Joey?"

"Would you come to Chicago if I sent for you?"

"Oh no, I couldn't!" Hattie ducked her head. "I'm not that kinda girl. I know them girls up north are prob'ly fast but I'm a church goin' kinda girl, Joe. You know that."

Joe laughed and kissed Hattie's knuckles. "Hattie-girl, I guess I got ahead of myself.....I meant would ya'll think about marryin' me and *then* come to Chicago if I sent for you?"

Hattie threw herself into Joe's arms and they fell back laughing onto the blanket. "Oh, Joey, I don't have to think 'bout nothin'. I want to marry you and I'd move to the moon if ya ask me to."

Joe kissed her gently and then pulled back to look into Hattie's eyes. He lowered his head and took her mouth again. His tongue played along her bottom lip until she opened for him. He plunged his tongue inside her mouth, teasing her tongue until she whimpered.

The sun shone down on the young lovers and the birds sang as if to celebrate their new found love. Several minutes pasted until Joe knew he had to stop before he spoiled the moment and her trust in him.

Reluctantly he pulled back, dug into the pocket of his jeans and pulled out a simple ring.

"My Mama gave me this to give to you if you should say 'yes'."

He showed Hattie the delicate ring set with a garnet and seed pearls.

"My Daddy gave this to her when they got engaged some sixty years ago."

"Oh Joe, it's so beautiful."

Joe helped her slip it on her ring finger.

"Look Hattie, it's a perfect fit, just like you and me."

Chapter 17

Hattie and Kitty

A month could seem like forever, thought Hattie, as she sat with Joe and savored every minute. *It's the soonest I could manage to get back here what with the kids' activities and keeping that clunker of a car runnin'. And, a' course, money is always a problem. Scarce as a hen's teeth.*

Hattie watched as Missus Lancaster went up to the guard to ask about her husband.

"Poor little thin'. Joe, what's the matter wid her man? Why don't he come down for his visit?"

"No tellin' what's in white folks' minds, Hattie-girl. Never you mind, he'll come when he's ready." Joe said.

Kitty waited until Officer Brad noticed her.

"Excuse me, but it appears that my husband didn't get the message that I'm here. Could you tell me how long ago you called up?" Kitty asked.

"I called up about an hour ago, Mrs. Lancaster. Let me call again. Maybe they couldn't find him or forgot to tell him…or something." Brad explained.

Why did she keep comin' to visit? Brad wondered, *everybody knew Lancaster wasn't gonna come down.*

"Thank you." Kitty said as she walked back to her table.

Hattie called out to Kitty as she passed by. "Miss Kitty, would you like to sit with me and my Joe while you waits for yours to come down?" she asked.

Kitty detoured around to Hattie and Joe's table. "Hello. How are you, Mr. Washington?" Kitty asked.

Joe stood. "Jus' fine, Mrs. Lancaster. How ya'll doin?"

"I'm well, thank you." Kitty said.

Hattie took a clean handkerchief from her pocket and dusted off the seat of an empty chair.

"Come and sit a spell," she told Kitty. "Your husband be down any minute now, I expect."

Kitty remained standing. "I don't want to intrude on your time together." She told them.

"You not intrudin', Missus." Joe said.

Kitty sat and leaned in closer to Joe. "Mr. Washington, I wanted to thank you personally for making Edward's time here easier."

Joe's smile lit up his face. "Ain't nothin' to thank me for, Missus. Eddie gonna do jus' fine, you'll see. You need to not give up on him."

"I hope you're right." Kitty turned to Hattie. "How are your children, Hattie?" Kitty asked.

"Jus' fine. I was jus' about to tell my Joe, here, what those young'uns been up to. Stella, she our youngest, she keeps me in stitches, thas' a fact!" Hattie laughed. "I was jus' about to say what my baby-girl did the other night."

Hattie turned to Joe. "So, I was fixin' supper for all of us and Ruby's helpin' me. The boys, they settin' the table. Well, all a sudden like, there in the do 'way stands our Stella. She got what look like all of Ruby's face makeup on."

"She wearin' my red dancin' dress and my best Sunday hat. You know the one, Joe, with the big cabbage roses on it. I swear that chile' got half my jewelry box hangin' 'round her neck. I says to her, 'Stella, who are you all dressed up to be?'

And she say, very lady-like 'n all, 'Why Miss Billie Holiday, o'course.' So I says, playing along like, 'Well, Miss Holiday, it's grand you could join us all this evenin'. Let me show you to yo' table."

"Oh Lord, that chile!" Laughing Joe turned to Kitty. "She been listenin' to her Granny's old 78 records of Miss Billie. Stella does love that music. And I guess my Mama knows 'bout every story there is when it comes to Lady Day."

"The imagination of children," laughed Kitty, "there's just no end to it."

"Oh, wait!" Hattie said. "You ain't heard the best part. That Stella, she sashayed in'ta my kitchen and set herself right down. Then she say to me, 'I believe that I'll have a large bourbon before my dinner, Miss Hattie...' and then..." Hattie laughed. "And then she looked up at me with those big ol' eyes of hers and says, 'What's a large bourbon, Mama?'"

Kitty and Joe joined Hattie in the laughter. The fact that they were all three parents and loved their children crossed all social-economical barriers. *Prison visiting rooms certainly leveled the playing field.* Kitty thought.

"She's a caution, Mrs. Lancaster," Joe told Kitty.

"Please, won't you call me Katherine? Or better yet, call me 'Kitty'. My friends all call me Kitty." she said.

Beaming Joe said, "And our friends call us Hattie and Joe, Miss Kitty."

"Well, Joe if you and Hattie will excuse me, I think I'll go and check on Edward again." Kitty looked around at the door again. "I cannot imagine what's keeping him."

"Jus' be patient with him, Miss Kitty. He'll come around, you'll see," Joe said.

"Oh, I know he will. He's just being silly," Kitty replied. "All this nonsense about me not coming here to visit him. Goodness, I'm his wife. Where else would I go?"

Chapter 18

Alma ~ five years earlier

Smoke swirled around the heads of the customers. Red and blue strobe lights danced a crazy pattern on the walls. The smell of old beer, sweat, and oddly, hairspray thickened the air. Theme music from 'Flash Dance' thrummed against the walls. Up on the stage, a spot light suddenly came on. Alma sat in a straight chair leaning back Her red hair fell down the back of the chair almost touching the floor. A single light bulb hung above her body. Amidst hoots and hollers, suddenly a shower of water splashed down and soaked her.

She turned in the chair and, spread eagle, gave her audience a sultry pout. She had on tiny, black shorts and a man's white shirt. Through the wet cloth her nipples were clearly visible. As she rose from the chair she swayed like a cobra mesmerized by the music.

She sank to the floor and crawled to the edge of the stage. She rose and danced to the music. She ripped her shirt open, buttons flying everywhere. She made a running leap onto the pole and slowly descended it. She stripped off the shirt and threw it away.

The men watching her went wild. She was wearing a nude colored bikini top under the shirt, which barely covered her nipples. Her breasts, naturally large were firm and high and beautiful enough to make a grown man cry. And a few of them did. As Alma continued her dance, Charlie sat at the back of the room at the bar.

Christ, he thought, *ten years I've been with her, had a kid with her, and she can still give me a boner just watching her bump and grind. All that dancin' made certain she didn't have an ounce of fat on her. No one would ever guess she'd had a kid. Not a mark on that incredible body and it's all mine.* Charlie glowed with pride as he watched his wife dance and tease her audience.

Alma was fast approaching the climax of her number. She had removed the tear-away black shorts and was down to a nude 'G-string', the tiny bikini bra, black, fishnet stockings and stiletto heels. Five and ten dollars bills were quickly tucked into her G-string as she gyrated around the edge of the stage.

She always spoke to her customers that tipped her, thanking them graciously. That was one of the things that the men watching her loved; that she recognized them as regulars and was so sweet to them.

She made a graceful, running jump at the pole, landed at the top, and hung on with her well muscled legs. Once her hands and arms had a grip on the pole with her torso held parallel, she widened her legs and slowly slid down the pole. Men were on their feet, whistling and hooting.

As Alma reached the floor she wrapped herself around the pole and rubbed it. She loved this part when she knew she was driving the men crazy. As she took one more swing around the pole a guy in the audience drunkenly tried to tuck a bill into her G-string as she went by. Instead, he hooked his finger in the spaghetti thin strap at her hip, and with the momentum of her movement, tore the G-string from her hips.

Alma gasped. She never got totally naked when she performed. In all her years of dancing, no patron had ever seen her like this.

The sexual tension quickly turned the men into a pack of lust- driven animals. They yelled obscenities and pounded their fists on the stage floor. As Alma scrambled to cover herself and make a graceful exit, a burly man who had been sitting in the corner in the shadows, rushed up onto the stage.

He charged Alma and grabbed her. Alma lost her balance and they both went down, the drunk on top of her. Spurred on by the men watching, he ripped away her bikini top.

"Drill 'er, Dude!" Someone in the crowd roared.

"Give 'er what she's been askin' for!"

"I'm next!"

"Fuck her lights out!"Another drunk yelled.

The man began to grope her and fumble with his zipper. She could feel his erection through his pants as he dry humped her.

My God, Alma's brain screamed at her, *I'm going to get raped right here, right now. Where the heck are the bouncers?* She struggled harder, kicking, scratching, and biting when the man who was attacking her was suddenly lifted away like he weighed nothing. *Thank Christ, management had made it to the stage,* Alma almost fainted with relief, a*nd not a minute too soon.*

But as she scrabbled away from her attacker it was Charlie's face she saw. Charlie knocked the man off the stage and as he crashed down amidst tables and chairs Charlie jumped on top of him. Alma stood there frozen watching Charlie's frenzied attack on the drunk. Holding the man by his shirt collar, he started pounding him with his fists. Lost in a red haze of fury Charlie continued to beat the drunk who had dared to touch Alma.

"You son-of'a-fuckin' bitch, you think you can grab my woman?" Charlie punctuated each word with his fist. "You think you can put your dirty fuckin' hands on my wife?"

The man's face was lost in a sea of blood as Charlie struck him again and again. The bouncers and Ernie, the owner, fought their way through the crowd.

"Let us through." They yelled as they shoved their way toward the stage.

"Get outta the way!"

"Okay, that's enough!" Ernie yelled at no one in particular. He glanced up at Alma.

"Go get dressed, Alma." She didn't move. "Go on now, get lost."

He and the bouncers pulled Charlie away from the now slack body of the man who had attacked Alma. Ernie leaned over the man for a few minutes and finally looked up.

"Call 911." He looked over at Charlie. "You'd better get outta here, Baldwin. The cops'll be right behind the EMT's."

Alma had rushed off stage and grabbed a robe. As she came back to check on Charlie she heard someone say, 'Somebody, call 911.'

"Charlie, do as Ernie says. Get outta here." Alma stood shivering as she spoke.

"Not without you, Babe," Charlie said.

"I'll just finish my shift and be right home…"

"The hell you will," Charlie glared at her.

"The hell you will, Alma," Ernie and Charlie had

spoken simultaneously. "Go get dressed and get on home. That's it for tonight," Ernie ordered.

Charlie jumped up on the stage and putting an arm around Alma, disappeared with her into the back dressing room. Most of the patrons started to head for the front door. They wanted to be long gone when the cops got there.

A few die-hards settled at the bar, wanting to see what happened next.

"Hey! Ernie!" one of the bouncers said as he leaned over the unconscious man. "This guy ain't comin' around. I think he's...dead."

Chapter 19

Alma

"For Chrissakes, Alma, ya gonna play or what?" Charlie scowled at her.

"Oops, sorry honey." Alma studied her hand, glanced at Charlie's discard and drew a card. She threw down a discard.

"What's so interestin' anyway?" he asked.

"Shh, keep your voice down." Alma sliced her eyes over toward Hattie and Joe's table. "Look at who's all chummy."

Charlie discarded. "Play, will ya?"

Taking Charlie's card, "Ol' Miss Rich-La-De-Da is back again to see her ol' man. Will ya look at 'em? Aunt Jemima and Miss Hoity-toity!"

"So what?"

Alma took his discard again, studied her cards a moment and placed a final suit down on the table. She discarded a final card and exclaimed, "Gin!"

"Goddamnit, Alma. You're really pissing me off. Gawkin' at everybody, yappin' about some old bag and you make gin all at the same time."

Alma smirked. "Sorry, hon." She picked up the pencil to record their scores. "How many, Charlie?"

He counted the cards left in his hand, "Ten, twenty, twenty-five."

"Ya got ninety-five to my forty. You're losin', Baby." Flirting with him she asked, "What'd I get if I win? Somethin' real nice and hard?"

Charlie grinned across the table at her. "Don't we wish? Deal, Alma, the game's not over 'till it's over. And pay attention, fer Chrissakes. Word's out that the old bag and her man are loaded. They're rollin' in it."

He sorted his new hand as he talked. "A lotta good all that money is doin' him in here. I'd sure like to find an angle so's I could get my hands on some of it."

Alma sorted her cards. "Now, Baby, don't do nothin' stupid, okay? You're never gonna get outta here."

"Don'cha worry, I'm getting' out. I'm just sayin', sure would be good to get a hold of some of that cash."

"Uh-huh…but I'm just sayin'." She resorted her cards.

"I still don't get it. How come Chelsea didn't come today?" he asked.

Alma shot him an unreadable look. "Uh I told ya hon, some of her friends was goin' to the mall and then to the movies. She asked could she skip this time and go with them. I didn't see no harm in her not comin'. She said to tell you she sent ya lots of hugs and kisses."

Charlie laid his cards down on the table. "Is it too much to expect to see my daughter once a week? Her friends and the movies are there all the time."

"These were new friends, Charlie, from the high school. She wanted to go real bad." Alma discarded and then saw that Charlie had stopped playing. "Don'cha wanna play no more, sweetie?"

"Did ya find a new job yet?" he asked, ignoring the cards.

"Baby, I keep lookin', really I do. But, what do I know besides dancin' and takin' my clothes off? Ya know we can't make it on welfare and me workin' some lousy minimum wage job."

"Ya could *try*, couldn'cha? I don't want Chelsea

around that club."

"You sure are crabby today, Charlie. Besides, Chels is sixteen now. She ain't around the club that much. She can stay by herself at home 'till I get off work." Alma sighed and laid down her cards. "Do ya wanna do something else, Baby?"

Charlie picked up his cards. "No, let's finish." He discarded.

Alma brightened. "Okay." She studied her hand and then took the whole pile of discarded cards.

"Jesus! Why don'cha take my cards too while you're at it?"

"I'm sorry, hon." Alma discarded.

"Forget it," Charlie replied as he picked up her card. "Just keep playin', will ya?"

* * * *

Across the room Kitty sat alone staring at the door that Edward would come through. It had been a half an hour since the young guard had called up. She rose and crossed over to the podium.

"Excuse me, Bradley, but did you have an opportunity to call up and remind my husband that I am here?"

Brad smiled. "I sure did, Mrs. Lancaster, right after you come in."

"Well, I can't imagine what's keeping him."

"He'll probably be done in a few....he probably just got hung up." Brad said.

Behind her, the door swung open and Kitty turned, smiling but it was Joe who entered.

He walked towards Brad and Kitty. "Mornin' Miss Kitty." he said.

"Good morning, Joe. Have you seen Edward?" she asked.

"No ma'am. Not since chow."

"Your wife's at table four, Washington." Brad said.

"Sure thing. Thanks." Joe said as he turned away.

"Thank you, Bradley." Kitty turned away to make her way back to her table.

As she followed in Joe's wake, Hattie waved to her.

"Miss Kitty," she called. "Why don't you set a spell with us?"

"That's very kind of you, Hattie, but I don't want to intrude. I'll see you after visiting hours. I'm certain Edward will be down in just a minute. Thank you anyway." Kitty crossed the room and sat down at her own table.

Hattie stood up as Joe approached her and they hugged each other tightly.

"How's my girl today?" Joe said as he kissed her.

"Hi husband. I'm jus' fine. How ya doin'?"

"Good, good. Where's the kids?"

"Left 'em at home. I didn't wanna worry 'em. What wid' my situation and all."

"So...what's the latest on your surgery?"

"Those doctors wanna do it right away."

"Thas' good. When ya goin' in?"

"Soon. I gots to have some time to get things organized. I gotta get a temporary woman to fill in for my ladies. The kids is all set, a'cours', your Mama will keep 'em."

"Don't go puttin' it off, Hattie. It's gotta be done quick before this thing gets ahead of the doctors."

"I know, Joey. I jus' needs me some time to get everythin' all worked out."

Hattie looked across to where Kitty was sitting.

"Did ya talk wid' Mr. Lancaster, Joe? Make him see some sense? I declare, he's breakin' that Miss Kitty's heart. Sitting there week after week, waitin' on 'im. Watchin' that door. Lordy, it's 'nough to make dis' ole woman cry."

"I talked to him, Hattie girl. But that man's full'a shame, right down to the bottom of his shoes. The idea of his wife or his children seein' him in here…well, it just about kills 'im."

"Poor thang. How's a man gonna survive 'dis here place wid 'out his woman?"

"I don't know." Joe kissed Hattie's hand. "I know one thing, for certain, I couldn't."

"Well, ya just keeps workin' on him, ya hear?"

* * * *

Several tables away, the slap of cards could be heard. Alma glanced over at Kitty.

"He never comes down. Don't she get it? And you call me stupid…that's just about the dumbest thing I've ever seen. Sitting there week after week, staring at that door."

"Will you mind your own beeswax and play? It's your turn," Charlie told her.

"All right, baby, don't get sore." Alma took Charlie's discard, rearranged her hand, put down several sets of cards and discarded her last one.

"J. I. N….Gin!" she exclaimed.

Charlie sat a moment in shock and then threw his cards down in disgust. "Je-sus H. Christ on a crutch! I'll be damned if I know where you learned to play cards like this."

"Sorry, hon." Alma crowed. "How many?"

Charlie picked his cards up and counted. "Twenty-five."

"Looks like I'm beating you *again*, Charlie."

"Just shut up and deal, will ya?"

Alma smiled at him and shuffled the cards. She spoke as she dealt the new hand. "Do ya think they're ever gonna give ya conjungle visits, baby?"

"Ya mean, 'conjugal' visits, Alma." he said. *How can she be so dumb one minute and so smart the next? I'll never understand women.*

Alma batted her eye lashes at Charlie. "Whatever they call it. A visit where we can be alone and you can take my clothes off....that kind'a visit."

Charlie took the last card of his newly dealt hand and stared without seeing it. He set the cards down on the table.

"I don't wanna play no more," he told Alma.

"Okay, hon. Wha'd ya wanna do?"

"I want you to tell me where the fuck Chelsea *really* is, thas' what I want. This is the second time she's missed our visit."

Keeping busy gathering up the cards, Alma didn't meet Charlie's eyes. A blush crept up her neck.

"I told ya, hon, she's out with her friends."

"Bull shit! She never misses visiting day much less two in a row."

"Well, she's growin' up. She's got other interests now, new friends, like I told ya."

Alma shuffled the cards, and slowly put them back into their case. Stalling, she picked up the score sheet and pencil and carefully placed them by the pack of cards. Charlie sat back and watched Alma, not moving and he didn't speak. He waited. Alma looked everywhere but at him.

"I know what ya told me, Alma. Why ya lyin' to me, huh?"

"I ain't lyin'."

"Yeah, you are too."

"Charlie...."

"What're ya hidin' from me? I can always tell 'cause ya won't look at me."

Charlie took her hand and started to squeeze it.

"Ow! God, Charlie, cut it out! I ain't lyin'. Ow! That hurts."

"Answer me, Alma. What's goin' on? Tell me or I swear to God I'll break your fingers."

"Stop it." She hissed. "The guard's gonna see. You'll get the hole, Charlie."

"I don't give a rat's ass who sees. You're keepin' somethin' from me." He put more pressure on Alma's fingers. "Now *what is it?!*"

"All right! All right, let go!" She snatched her hand away and cradled it in her lap. "God, I think ya broke somethin'."

"Shut up about your Goddamn hand and tell me... Fuck! It's Chelsea, ain't it?"

Alma's head snapped up from inspecting her hand.

"Is it? Tell me!" He insisted.

"Not before you promise me to keep your cool..." Alma cried.

"You better tell me and be damn quick about it!"

"Calm down and lower your voice, won'cha? Ya keep actin' up and gettin' time added onto your sentence, you're never gonna get outta here."

"Alma...if you know what's good for ya, you'll start talkin'."

"Okay!" She took a deep breath. "It is about Chels...but I don't want ya to worry... She's..."

"For Chrissakes, what?! She's what?"

Alma exhaled on her words. "She's... gone."

"Gone? Wha' the fuck!" Charlie yelled.

He quickly glanced at Brad and gave him a sickly grin. He immediately lowered his voice to a whisper.

"Gone where?"

"I don't know where." Alma looked down at her hands and then her eyes darted up to meet Charlie's. "I'm sorry, baby, I can't find her."

Charlie lowered his head into his hands and ran his fingers roughly through his hair. "Wha'd ya mean, ya can't find her? What in the sweet name of Jesus is goin' on?"

"That's what I'm tryin' to tell ya."

"When did all this happen?"

"About a week ago."

"A week! Fuck me!"

"She didn't come home... she was suppose to be in by eleven. I kept callin' from the club. Ya know, to check that she was home... sometimes she doesn't answer if she's listenin' to her music and it's turned up..." Alma's voice trailed off.

Charlie sat there watching Alma's face. "Go on. There's more, ain't there. What ain'cha tellin' me?"

"Well...it's Rick, he's not..." Alma rushed through the rest, trying to get it all said before Charlie could react.

"Rick hasn't been in to work...he's gone too...I think maybe he's with Chels."

Charlie laid his hands flat on the table to keep from grabbing Alma around her throat. He stared at her in disbelief.

"Sweet Jesus, Mary, Joseph. I'm going to kill you, Alma."

"Why? I didn't do nothin', Charlie. She's always goin' off somewhere."

"She's your daughter, for fuck's sake. You said you'd keep her away from that bastard. What kind of mother are you?"

"I did keep her away! Honest!"

"Yeah, right."

"I've been out lookin' for her." She assured him.

"Did you call the cops?

"Nooo…"

"Why the hell not?

" 'Cause if she's with Rick… well, then, she ain't really missing is she?"

"Je-sus Christ! You are un-be-lievable!"

"I mean, if she's just run off with him. I don't know, hon, I was afraid to go to the cops. That's why I waited to see you. I didn't know what else to do."

"You bitch! You're protectin' that bastard, Rick! Where is your brain? You stupid, fuckin' bitch!"

"Ya don't have to be so nasty, Charlie. Rick's not a bad man. He won't hurt her. I thought they'd come back. I really did. I'm sorry baby."

"Christ, Alma! She's fuckin' 15 years old! I gotta get away from you or I swear to God, I'm gonna kill you right here in front'a everybody."

"Sixteen, she's sixteen now." Alma said.

"Don't! Don't say another word." Charlie warned.

Charlie jumped up and paced to the soda machine, jammed the credits into it and practically ripped the can from the slot. He walked slowly back towards Alma and sat down.

"Okay." He took a deep breath. "Now, tell me everything, from the beginning. And I want the truth, Alma."

"Okay, okay. Jeez, ya act like I ain't worried too."

"Alma…"

"Chels told me she was goin' to the movies, that was…let's see…Thursday night. Not last Thursday but, you know, the one before that and…"

"Christ, Alma, get on with it would'cha."

"I am! Gimme a chance, will ya? Anyway, she gets all dolled up. I remember 'cause we had a fight about what she had on. She comes outta her bedroom and she's got this mini skirt on that barely covers her ass. I made her change. So we had a big blow up about that. She's all pissed at me 'cause I made her…"

Suddenly Alma had a light bulb moment. "Oh, Jeez, do ya think she was dressed like that… Oh, Jeez, she was meetin' Rick!"

"Ya think?" Charlie sneered.

"Well, I didn't know. Anyway, we had this fight about what she was wearin', and she leaves in a big huff! The movie was at seven. She was supposed to be in by eleven, but when has she ever been on time? So I don't get worried until around one o'clock…I kept callin' the house between my numbers. I got home 'bout three-thirty…I peeked in to check on her… I was so sure she'd be in bed, hon. But, she wasn't in her room. So, I lay on the couch, watchin' my TV shows. I figure I'm really gonna give it to her when she walks in the door."

"Yeah, so then?"

"Well, I guess I fell asleep 'cause the next thing I know it's around eleven in the morning. I check her room, no Chels. So, then I start callin' her friends. They tell me she never met them for the show. They didn't see her that night at all. So, I wait, still no Chels. But, she's stayed out before without callin' and…"

"God damn it! She's stayed out all night before? What's the matter with you?"

"What? It was like… she stayed over at a girl friend's and didn't call me."

"Why is this the first time I'm hearin' that *my* daughter stays out all night?"

"Like I say, hon, she stayed at a girl friend's."

"How do you know?"

"'Cause she told me."

"And this has got to do with Rick, how?"

"I'm tryin' to explain why I wasn't real worried, right off."

"Jesus!"

"Are ya gonna let me finish?"

"Stick to the fuckin' story, will ya?"

"So the next day, I go in'ta work at two. I figure maybe Rick can help me…ya know…advise me. Well, he ain't there. Called in sick, the other girls tell me. So, I do my shift and get home the same time that next morning."

"Did ya even consider callin' the house?"

"Of course I did. Every chance I got. Whad'ya take me for, Charlie?"

"Ya don't want to know."

"So, between my numbers, you know between the 'Firebird' *and* my 'Tribute to the Wild West'… they just can't seem to get enough of the Firebird…"

"God Damn It, Alma! I don't give a flyin' fuck about your dance numbers! Keep goin', will ya?"

"Okay! Don't get so excited! I'm just tryin' to tell ya… but you keep interruptin'. Anyway, I call the house off and on. No answer. But, I figure that she's prob'ly there and just isn't answering 'cause she's still pissed at me…ya know… 'bout makin' her change her skirt and all…"

"And you go home around three and then what?"

"Chelsea still ain't there. That's what I'm tellin' ya. Honest to God, Charlie, I really thought she came home and went out again that night, just to show me who's boss."

"You have got to be one of the stupidest broads I ever seen." Charlie grabbed her by the fleshy part of her arm. "Tell me, Alma, do you have any God damn sense at all?!"

"Oww! Cut it out, Charlie. I'm trying to tell you what happened. You're hurtin' me."

"Oh, you haven't seen hurt yet."

Brad tapped his pencil on the podium and stared hard at Charlie and Charlie let go of Alma.

"So wha'd ya do next?"

"So Saturday when I get up, I call her friends again. No one's seen her. So, I go into work, thinkin' that Rick will be there and he can give me some ideas or somethin'. He ain't there and no one's heard from him."

"SHIT!"

" I didn't know what to do, baby. I worked my shift thinkin' that she'll be home, for sure, when I get off. I figure she's just really mad at me and she's payin' me back."

"What about her school? Did you talk to them? Has she been to school at all?"

"Well see, I didn't want them to know she was cutting school again. So I…"

Charlie stared in disbelief. "Oh, this just keeps gettin' better and better. She's missed school so many times that you couldn't ask them this time? So wha'cha do?"

"I took a note to school saying she was sick."

"Christ, Alma!" Charlie almost wept with frustration.

"Well, she'd get suspended if they thought she was skipping again, Charlie."

"What a hair brained idea…"

"I kept lookin' everywhere I could think. Then I figure, I'm gonna see you in just a few days and you can help me figure out what to do."

"Shit! I gotta get outta here!"

"I knew you were gonna be so mad at me. That's why I didn't want to tell you, hon." Tears filled her eyes and ran down her face in black tracks from her mascara. "She's my daughter too and I didn't know what 'ta do, Charlie."

"Christ, Alma, don't cry. I can't stand it when you cry."

"I'm tryin' baby, I really am. She's missin' and you're mad at me and I don't know where else to look."

"Chelsea's only fifteen." Charlie thought he was going to lose his mind.

"Sixteen." Alma corrected him.

"Rick's what? Forty? Don'cha remember what he tried to pull last year? Where's yer brain?"

"Rick's thirty-five. And he claimed he didn't mean anythin' by that last summer. He said Chels over-reacted."

"Please, Alma, do yourself and me a favor and don't try to defend that son of a bitch. Now listen, ya gotta go to the cops, file a report that she's missin'."

"Is that what I should do, hon? I can't go 'til Monday."

"You go in and you tell them that Rick's missin' too, ya hear me, Alma? You tell em' you think he's kidnapped her."

"But he didn't! I don't want to get him in trouble."

"Alma! For fuck's sake!"

"But, what if Chelsea just run off with him and he didn't do nothin'?"

"Ya ever heard of crossin' a state line with a minor? Look! You do what I say! The cops are gonna treat a kidnappin' much more serious than just another run-away. You got that?"

"But…"

"Ya *got* that, Alma?"

"Sure, baby, okay."

"Christ, what am I gonna do, stuck in here? *I gotta get out!*"

"Well, I don't see how yer gonna do that, Charlie. Yer just gonna get into more trouble and get more time added to your sentence."

"Will you just shut up, please?" Charlie growled. "What kind'a mother are you, anyway?"

"I'm a good mother, for your information. I do the best I can with…"

Charlie jumped up and began to pace again. "Just shut up, will ya? Lemme think, for Chrissakes! I gotta find a way out!"

"Back in your chair, Baldwin." Brad started to rise from his chair. "Do it now, unless ya gotta go to the toilet or somethin'."

Charlie ignored Brad's instruction. He paced in wider circles.

"Charlie, please…" Alma said.

"Sit down, Baldwin! Now!"

Charlie waved Alma off and continued to pace. Suddenly he realized that he was behind 'the rich bitch'. *Look at her sitting there,* he seethed, *her spine 'finishing school' straight. Expensive clothes, designer hair-do. So much fuckin' money she could buy the world. She's too good to look at me. Just sits there watching that fuckin' door.*

Charlie leaned over, his hands on his bent knees. He felt faint with the frustration and fury that pounded in his head. When he stood up he held a short, deadly sharp shank in his hand. He stepped up behind Kitty and grabbed her.

"Get the fuck up, bitch!"

"Charlie!" Alma screamed.

He lifted Kitty out of the chair and held the knife to her throat. Kitty screamed. As he spoke, he quickly backed up, weaving between tables, to the far wall. Pandemonium broke out. Other inmates and their visitors scattered. Brad jumped to his feet and started around the podium.

Charlie reached the back wall and held Kitty in front of him. Joe grabbed Hattie by the arm, pulling her out of her chair and moved them both away from Charlie.

"Let me go!" Kitty screamed. "Oh, my God. Help! Someone do something!"

"Shut up! Shut up or I'll cut ya!" Charlie screamed in Kitty's ear.

"Help! Help me!" Kitty continued to scream. "Please, don't hurt me!"

Chapter 20

Alma ~ ten years ago

"Mommy, Mommy! Wake up! It's breaf'ist! Daddy made us somethin' really special!"

Six year old Chelsea bounced up on the bed and jumped on Alma buried under the comforter. She wore a pink and white jumper over a pink blouse. Pink bows were tied in her hair. She was shoeless wearing pink and white stripped socks. Leaning against the doorframe, Charlie stood in the doorway grinning.

"Tell Mommy what we made, Chels."

"Banana-dana pancakes! Your favorite, Mommy!"

Alma groaned from under the covers and one hand and arm came out and grabbed Chelsea. As the child squealed in delight the arm pulled her under the covers and she disappeared. Charlie could hear their muffled whispers.

"Shh…." Alma told Chelsea. "If we're real quiet maybe he will go away and we can have a nap."

"Mommy, I don't *need* a nap. Its morning…I've been sleeping *all* night."

"Oh. Well, it was worth a try. Peek out and see if he's gone."

Chelsea blond hair and big green eyes were all that could be seen as she peeked out at him. Charlie grinned at her and made a face. Chelsea giggled at him and darted back under the covers.

"He's still there, Mommy."

"Darn it! What does he want, do you know?"

Charlie sauntered over to the bed and sat down.

"He wants to feed you and your daughter banana pancakes." He began tickling Chelsea through the covers and she erupted in to more giggles.

"Daddy, stop!" Chelsea laughed. "Stop! I'm gonna wet Mommy's bed."

Alma pushed back the comforter and laughed up into Charlie's face. "Good morning! What time is it?"

"Chels, you're a big girl, tell Mommy how late it is."

Chelsea looked at the clock on the bedside table.

"The little hand is on the one and the big hand is on ....six, seven, eight.... the nine!"

"Good girl. You are so smart." Charlie praised her.

Alma groaned. "Do you two scallywags have any idea what time I got to bed this morning?"

"I'm not a scallywag, Mommy, I'm 'Daddy's little girl'."

"You tell her, Chels." Charlie laughed.

"Well, I can see that I'm outnumbered. No more sleep today for this hard workin' Mommy."

She nuzzled Chelsea's neck. *God, I will never tire of my daughter's powdery, sweet smell. How did I ever deserve this little miracle?*

Alma threw back the covers and sat on the edge of the bed. "Throw me my robe, will ya, hon?"

Charlie reached over and took her robe off the arm of a chair and handed it to her. Alma slipped into it and stood.

"*Now*, can we have banana-dana pancakes?" Chelsea asked. "Daddy says they're gonna get cold if we don't hurry, Mommy."

"Two minutes in the bathroom if you don't mind and then I'll be down."

As Alma walked across the room, Chelsea stood up

on the bed and began to bounce in earnest. Charlie rose
and walked a couple of feet from the bed. That was
Chelsea's cue and she bounced one more time and
jumped the short distance into Charlie's waiting arms.

"Cowabunga!" She screamed.

Alma turned at the bathroom door. "One of these
days, you two, you're gonna break my bed and then
what?"

"Tell her, Chels." Charlie grinned at his daughter.

"We sleep on the floor like bears!" Chelsea giggled.

Charlie turned to the bedroom door with Chelsea in
his arms.

"We'll see ya downstairs. Don't keep our banana-
dana pancakes waiting. We're not gonna save any for
you, are we Chels?"

Chelsea looked at her mother very seriously. "*I'll*
save you some, Mommy!"

* * * *

"Ugh! Your pancakes are *swimming* in maple syrup,
Chels." Alma remarked.

Charlie leaned over and inspected Chelsea's plate.

"Is that the back stroke or the dog paddle?" he asked.

"Mommy, pancakes can't swim. And I love the
syrup, especially the blueberry kind."

"Sorry, kid, we were all out." Charlie told her. "But
your second favorite is maple, right?"

"Second favorite, but my bestest favorite is
blueberry. We need to go to the store Daddy if you're
out of it." Chelsea chided him.

"Okay, pumpkin, maybe later today."Alma sipped
her strong, black coffee and let the conversation whirl
around her.

Charlie and Chelsea had their own little world and whether she was there in it or not was of little concern.

"What'd ya think, Chels, could you teach a pancake to swim?" He asked.

"Kermmie, the frog, can sing." Chelsea considered her plate of pancakes carefully. "I bet you could teach the pancake to swim, Daddy."

Alma rubbed her eyes and sighed.

"What's wrong, babe?" Charlie asked Alma.

"Tough shift. Couple of the girls was out sick so we had to double up on the dancin'. My legs feel like two blocks of wood."

"Well ya know what the solution to that is."

Alma glared at Charlie over Chelsea's head but kept her tone light.

"I'm not quitting my job, Charlie."

Charlie stared at her in silence. Then he turned to Chelsea.

"Hey, Princess, you done with your breakfast?"

"Yeah, Daddy, I'm full as a tock."

"'Tick, full as a tick' ya mean."

"Yeah, that's it. What's a tick, Daddy, and why is he always full?"

"I'll draw you a picture of one later. If you're finished why don't ya go in and watch your cartoons some more?"

Chelsea squirmed off her chair and ran towards the family room. "Okay!"

"Hold up there, partner. Come back. You forgot something." Charlie said.

Chelsea hurried back to her chair and stood for a nanosecond. She bounced from foot to foot.

"May I please be excused?"

"You may." Charlie smiled at her.

Chelsea rushed across the room.

"Tell Sponge-Bob I said 'hello'."

Chelsea stopped in mid-stride and turned back to her father.

"Daddy, Sponge-Bob can't hear me. He's in the television. Don't you know *anything*?" She said as she continued out of the room.

Charlie laughed. "God, what's she gonna be like when she's a teenager?"

"Don't ask. I don't have the strength to answer all her 'whys, when's, where's, at age six." Alma sighed.

"You need to spend more time with her."

Now that Charlie had gotten Chels out of the room he considered this conversation was long overdue.

"Please don't start on that again, hon."

"You come home in the middle of the night and sleep 'till the afternoon. You're here with her six hours tops and then you go to work."

"I ain't quitin'. We need the money. You're not makin' what you used to on the rigs."

"I promised you when you were carrying Chelsea, that I wouldn't leave and I'd quit the off shore work to be with you both. Nobody makes that kind'a money on the mainland."

"That's why I'm workin' dancin'. Nobody makes *that* kinda money doing some office job."

"It don't make any sense me takin' Chels to day care while her mother is here sleepin'."

"Well, excuse me, for needin' some rest when I get home."

"That's not what I mean. I just want Chels to have her mother around more."

"Why? She's totally happy with you, Mr. Mom."

"It's not the same." Charlie complained.

"Look, I like my job, Charlie. It's something I'm good at; better than good. Let's compromise. When she gets older like, I don't know, pre-teen? I'll be around more. Would that work for ya?"

"No."

"Well, I ain't quittin' Charlie. We can't afford it."

Suddenly Chelsea burst back into the room.

"Daddy, the picture on the TV died. Did you remember to pay the bill?"

Charlie got up from his chair and started towards his daughter.

"Let me come and see baby-girl."

Charlie turned to Alma, "This conversation ain't over, Alma."

"Surprise, surprise." Alma murmured.

Charlie swung Chelsea up into his arms. "Maybe Sponge-Bob broke it."

"Maybe you forgot to pay the bill, Daddy."

"Chelsea, where did you get this very serious streak? Certainly not from Mommy. What do you know about payin' bills and such?"

"I help you lick the envelopes, Daddy, when you pay for my TV."

"Oh, right, I forgot you're my 'letter-licker'" he said as they walked out of the room.

Charlie paused in the doorway and looked back at Alma.

"I'm thinkin' of comin' by the club tonight and seeing your new number." He told her in the way of a peace offering. "That okay with you?"

Alma's smile lit up the kitchen. "Sure baby, I'd like that."

"Does that mean I get a play date with Janie?" Chelsea piped up.

Charlie kissed the top of her head. "Sure, baby, let's go call her right now and see if she can come over to play tonight?"

"Cool beans, Daddy. I love Janie." She looked up coyly at her father. "Do I get to dial your cell and ask her myself?"

"You bet, sweetheart."

Chapter 21

Alma, Kitty, and Hattie

"Baldwin, let 'er go, you hear me?" Brad yelled.

"Charlie," Alma cried. "Oh'm God! Please!

"*Please* let me go!" Kitty struggled against the arm wrapped around her throat.

Charlie yelled over the mayhem. "Shut the fuck up! Ya hear me? Everybody, SHUT UP!"

"Charlie, my God, what are ya doin'?" Alma asked.

"I gotta get outta here! Shut up, all 'a yous!" The knife blade dug into Kitty's neck as Charlie shouted.

"Oh...no, please." Kitty moaned.

Charlie jerked Kitty up against him. "Be still or I'm gonna cut ya."

The other inmates and their families had crowded in the area of the exit doors. Some of the inmates murmured encouragement to Charlie while their women tried to shush them.

"Let her go, Baldwin." Brad said. "Don't make this any worse than it is."

"Oh, Charlie...please...don't do this." Alma told him. "I'm sorry. I promise I'll get Chels back!"

"Everybody, shut up!" Charlie screamed. "I gotta think... it's not supposed to be like this...*I gotta figure this out!*"

An unholy silence filled the room. Not making a sound, Kitty wept. The quiet was torn apart as a siren started up and a red light flashed above the door where the inmates entered and exited the visiting room.

The security locks on the steel doors could be heard snicking shut. A voice came over the speaker system.

"Attention, all inmates, return to your cells immediately! This is an emergency lock down."

No one in the room moved. All eyes were on Charlie and Kitty.

"Baldwin! Put the knife down and let Mrs. Lancaster go." There was a tiny tremble in Brad's voice. "You're gonna be in a world'a trouble if you don't. Come on now, you don't want to hurt her...do what I say and put the knife down."

"Fuck off! You don't give the orders here anymore ...this knife says *I* give the orders!"

"Okay, okay, you give the orders. But, Charlie, this is really a bad idea." Brad said.

"Shut up! Here's my first order! Get all these people outta here. Call up the control room and tell 'em."

"I can't do that, Baldwin."

"The hell you can't. You will or else." Charlie put pressure on the knife at Kitty's throat.

"Please." Kitty said to Brad. "He's going to kill me."

Brad backed up to the podium. "Take it easy. See? I'm getting to the intercom. Just wait, okay?" Brad pushed a button.

"Sir. I have a situation here..."

A voice boomed back, interrupting him. "What's going on in there, Kowalski?"

At his superior's tone, Brad grimaced. "I have a hostage situation, sir."

"WHAT? What's that you're saying?"

"Sir, an inmate, Baldwin, has taken a visitor. He is holding a knife to her throat. He wants the other inmates and visitors removed from the room."

"Stand by one...."

"Yes sir." Brad replied.

The intercom suddenly buzzed with static.

"Kowalski, we are unlocking the exit door chamber so that the civilians can exit. You tell the inmates to move to the wall where their door is and do it immediately."

"Yes sir." Brad turned to Charlie. "You hear that?"

"Yeah. Okay." Charlie raised his voice and said. "Listen up, you women and kids, as soon as those doors open I want you outta here."

Several of the inmates grumbled. "We ain't leavin'."

"If you're makin' a break, we're goin' with ya."

The sound system crackled to life.

"Attention. The inmates in the visiting room shall, in an orderly fashion, move to the far east wall and prepare to exit by your door. You will proceed to your cells immediately. Anyone not following these orders, exactly, will be written up and receive a minimum of fourteen days in restricted and visitation will be withheld for six months. Anyone who disobeys these orders will face charges and added time."

The inmates grumbled their displeasure. The large steel doors began to slide open. Inmates hurriedly kissed their family members goodbye. As their loved ones filed through, the inmates moved to the door that led back into the prison. Joe and Hattie were the last to move toward the exits. Hattie wept quietly and as they walked, Joe comforted her in quiet tones

"Hattie, you have to go. It's all gonna be fine. As soon as I see you out that door, I'll get back to my cell."

"Joe, I don't wanna leave you. That man is bad."

Just as they reached the doors Charlie's voice rang

out. "Not you, Washington!" Charlie yelled. "You and your wife get your asses back in a chair."

"Now, Baldwin, just a damn minute..." Brad objected.

"Shut up!" Charlie snarled at him.

Joe turned and stared at Charlie. "What the hell is goin' on, Baldwin?" he asked.

"Do like I said. You and the missus are stayin'." Charlie motioned with his knife to the chairs. "Sit."

Joe turned and looked at Brad. The guard shrugged.

Joe glared at Charlie as he guided Hattie into a chair and sat beside her. The loud slamming of the visitors' door echoed around the silent visiting room.

"Now tell control to get these bums outta here." Charlie indicated the other inmates who stood in a loose group, still grumbling.

Brad depressed the intercom button again.

"Sir, the inmates are ready to exit the visiting room."

"Roger that. Go ahead and unlock the door, Kowalski, we're ready for them on the other side."

Brad flipped the switch on his console that opened the door. With loud complaints and name calling aimed at Charlie, the inmates filed out.

Brad hit the intercom again. "Door secured, sir."

"Roger that. We'll get back to you."

Charlie looked over at Brad and then he smiled with an evil glint.

"Hand over the gun." Charlie said.

"How do you kno....?" Brad asked.

"I've noticed the same bulk under your pant leg for months now. I figured you weren't retaining water maybe it was swollen ankles 'cause of your flat feet." Charlie snickered at his own joke. "Hand over your piece, slow-like."

At the mention of a gun, Alma slipped to the floor and hid under the table.

"You know I can't give you my weapon, Baldwin."

"I know if ya don't you gonna see some blood. How much blood ya wanna see, *Kowalski*? I'll stick her! Shall we see if she bleeds blue… or red like the rest of us mortals?"

"Oh God no." Kitty pleaded. "Please don't hurt me."

"Okay okay, steady, Baldwin. Look, we can work this out. What's wrong? Why now?"

"Never mind. I don't need to tell you nothin'. Gimme the gun *now* or watch her bleed."

Brad carefully raised his pant leg and eased the snub nosed revolver out of its holster.

"This is going to cost me my job," he told Charlie.

"Boo hoo. Now sit down."

Brad didn't move. He stared at Charlie.

"Do it now, pig, or she gets cut. I ain't playin'."

Brad slowly placed the weapon on the table. "I'm layin' it down right here. This is not gonna end well for you, Baldwin…"

"Washington! Get his gun and come over here."

"Joe, no!" Rising, Hattie cried.

"Listen, Charlie, you're never gonna see daylight again unless you give this up now…" Brad said.

"Shut up. You heard me, Washington, get his gun and bring it to me. Do it now!"

Joe hesitated and then reached for the gun.

Brad lunged and picked the gun back up, aiming and swinging it between Joe and Charlie.

"Washington! You are not to approach me! Stay over there with your wife."

Charlie pressed the knife to Kitty's throat again and Kitty moaned.

Then he said to Joe. "Boy! Do what I say! You want me to cut her? I swear to God I will!"

"Please, please do it." Kitty begged Joe.

"Shut up, bitch!"

Joe stood perfectly still, looking from Charlie to Brad.

"Now Washington! Goddamn it! I swear, I'll slit her fuckin' throat!"

Joe made no move toward Brad. Slowly, Brad reversed his grip on the gun and held it out to Joe.

"Calm down, Baldwin! Take it easy... I'm giving the gun to Washington, see?"

"Joe, no! Don't!" Hattie cried.

"Shut up!" Charlie yelled at Hattie; then turned back to Joe. "Washington, tell your ol' lady to shut the fuck up and you do what I told ya."

"Hush now, Hattie, it's gonna be all right."

"Oh, no, Joe, please don't go near 'dat white man."

"Do it! Gimme his gun."

Joe took the gun from Brad and, holding it gingerly, started to walk over to Charlie.

"Get his two-way and check his pockets for any extra ammunition he might be carryin'."

Brad handed Joe his two way radio. "I don't carry any extra bullets."

"Bring 'em here, Washington." Charlie ordered.

"You!" He indicated Brad. "Sit down. You! Missus, sit next to 'im.

"Go on now, Hattie, do like he says. It's gonna be fine." Joe spoke to Hattie in a reassuring voice.

Joe patted Hattie's shoulder and then turned and walked over to Charlie.

"We gonna get outta here, Washington." Charlie said, taking the gun and radio.

Raising both hands into the air Joe began backing up. "Uh-uh, Baldwin, I ain't goin' nowheres. I just deliverin' the gun like ya told me. Now, I'm gonna walk back real slow over to my wife and sit down."

"You're nuts. We can get outta here, man."

"Uh-uh, not me." Joe said shaking his head and continued to back up.

Not making any sudden movements, Joe turned and walked to the chair next to Hattie. He sat down slowly and reached out to hold Hattie's hand.

"Okay, be stupid." Charlie sneered. "Ya gotta a chance to break outta here."

"Nope, not this way." Joe said.

Charlie broke the revolver open and checked the chamber to make sure it was loaded. Satisfied, he put the knife in his belt and held the gun on Kitty and the room.

"Okay, what's next Baldwin? What do you want?"

"I'll let you know in a Goddamn minute. Now, everybody just chill... I gotta think."

Charlie noticed some movement under one of the tables.

"Alma! What the fuck are you doin'?!"

Alma peered out from under the table.

"Nothin', Charlie. Honest."

"Get the hell out from under that table! What's wrong with you?"

"Sure thing, hon." Alma scrambled out. "Don't hurt me. I promise I'll get Chels back for you."

"Oh, for Chrissakes sit down and be quiet. I gotta think this out."

"Okay, hon. Just don't shoot nobody, Charlie."

"Alma, please! Stop talkin'."

"I hope you know what you're doin', baby. This is

gonna add so much time to your sentence, ya know?"

Charlie's smile was filled with an odd tenderness. "Alma! Please! Just shut up for one minute, will ya?"

Alma smiled back at him. "Sure, baby."

" Listen, Baldwin, why don't you let the women go, huh?"Brad asked. "Then we can work on getting this thing straightened out."

"Sure, sure that would put me right where ya want me. No, I like the odds jus' the way they are."

The shrill ringing of the telephone on the Brad's desk startled everyone. Brad stared at Charlie as it continued to ring.

"Ya gonna let me answer that?"

"No. Washington, get over there and answer. You say what I tell ya ta' say. One wrong word and the first bullet is for you. The second one goes into your ol' lady's head, ya got that? Now, go."

"Joe, no." Hattie held onto Joe's arm.

"It's gonna be all right, Hattie girl. Just doin' what the man tells me."

Joe rose and crossed to the podium. He looked at Charlie. Charlie nodded and Joe picked up the receiver.

"Hello. This is Joseph Washington, number 330407."

"Tell them where we're at in this deal. Tell 'em I got fancy-pants here. Tell 'em I got four more hostages besides."

"Baldwin wants me to tell you what the situation is here…He's got Mrs. Lancaster." Joe listened for a moment. "A shank in his shoe. He was gonna cut her. Now he's got Mr. Bradley's gun." Joe frowned while he listened again. "No, sir, I ain't no part of this.

He tol' me to answer the phone and tha's what I'm doin'. Ms. Gaynor here with my Hattie, er... Mrs. Washington, my wife. No, sir, he ain't said what he wants..."

Charlie interrupted. "Okay! That's enough!"

Joe didn't hang up and seemed to listen intently.

"Hey! I said stop talkin'." Charlie yelled. "Put the phone on that table there. I got somethin' to say. Then go sit back down."

"Hold on, sir. Baldwin wants to talk to you."

Joe placed the phone on the table then he crossed back to the chair next to Hattie and sat down. Charlie moved over to the telephone with Kitty held tightly to his side.

"Okay, Duchess, pick up the phone and hold it to my ear." Charlie told Kitty. Kitty fumbled the receiver and in doing so banged up against the gun being held to her head.

"No, Goddamn it! My other ear!" he told Kitty. Charlie yelled into the receiver. "Yo! ..." He listened for a second. "Cut the crap! I want outta here, that's what I want." Charlie listened for another minute and interrupted. "You ain't in no position to tell me you can't do that. Last time I looked I'm the one with five hostages ... No, you listen! I'm gonna call ya back in a little bit. Nobody is gonna get hurt if you do what I say, you got that?"

Charlie grabbed the receiver out of Kitty's hand and slammed it down.

"Okay, everybody just stay put. Washington, get up and find something to tie *Kowalski* up with."

"Listen, Baldwin, I don't want no part of this." Joe replied. "I'm gonna serve my time..."

"You ain't gonna serve shit if I put a bullet in ya.

Now find somethin' and tie that bastard up. Wait! I got a better idea. Get his cuffs and hook 'em to the leg of that table. That's...what'd ya call it?... poetical justice," Charlie laughed. "Using his own handcuffs. You! Pig! Get up. Come on, hurry it up."

Joe and Brad rose and moved to the table that Charlie had indicated.

Joe cuffed Brad's wrist to the table leg.

"Sorry, Mr. Brad, I don't got much choice."

"I know, Washington. It's okay."

"Ain't that touchin'. Always the model prisoner, huh Washington? Now, throw that key over here to me."

Joe tossed the key to Charlie. "Good. Go sit back down."

Joe crossed over and sat with Hattie again.

"Alma!"

"Yeah, sugar?"

"You got any idea where that son-a'bitch, Rick, might be? Him and Chels?"

"Well, ya know Rick likes to gamble. A casino somewheres?"

"Do ya think ya could narrow that down just a little, Alma?"

"Well, Jeez, baby, how should I know?"

"Yeah, I forgot who I was talkin' to..."

"Wait!" Alma held up her hand. "Chels told me once that Rick promised her a trip to Atlantic City. He said he hated the desert and Las Vegas. She wanted to go to Vegas but..."

"Jesus, Alma, give it a rest, will ya?! Why didn't ya tell me Rick was promising her stuff like that?"

"I donno know, hon. Chels and me was just talkin' one night. Ya know, like girls do..."

"Good Christ, Alma..." Charlie sighed. "You're not 'girl friends'; you're her mother."

Chapter 22

Hattie ~ sixteen years ago

Joe drove carefully down Longwood Drive on the south side of Chicago. Beside him Hattie sat looking out the window. She frequently turned around and gazed at the baby in the car seat in the back.

"I can't get over how pretty she is, Joe."

"I know. What I can't believe is that we made something so beautiful."

"She look just like her Daddy."

Joe patted Hattie's knee. "Uh-uh, she's the spit of you, darlin' girl."

Hattie turned back to look out the window. "Where ya takin' us, Joe? This ain't the way to our apartment."

"You'll see. It's a surprise for you and lit'l Ruby. My girls." Joe grinned.

"Well, let's not be too long, I wants to get this chil' home before she wakes up and wants another meal." Hattie laughed. "This chil' has one big whopper of an appetite. Where is it ya'll takin' us?"

"This here is the Beverly neighborhood. Nice, ain't it?"

"Yes, it's very nice, Joe. But can't we sightsee another day? What with the baby and me just now getting' outta the hospital, I really want to get home."

As Hattie spoke Joe pulled to the curb. The block was filled with modest but well kept homes. The green lawns were well cared for and there were flowerbeds full of pansies and daisies. The thwack of sprinklers could be heard through the open window of the car. Joe cut the engine and looked past Hattie at a little cottage that he had parked in front of. It was newly painted with a cheery light yellow color. The shutters sparkled with a new coat of forest green.

"What you doin', Joe? Do you know someone 'dat lives here?"

"Yeah, I guess you could say that." Joe opened his car door and stepped out. He sauntered around the front of the car, grinning through the windshield at Hattie. He stepped up to her door and opened it. He bowed from the waist and laughed.

"Ma'am. Could you please join me here on the sidewalk?"

"Joe, wha' mischief you up to?"

"Just step outside, I wanna show you somethin'."

Hattie stepped out and looked up and down the block. "Sure is pretty. Who lives here, Joey?"

"You do!" Joe crowed. "This is our new house; yours, baby Ruby's and mine."

Hattie stared at the cute little yellow cottage, her hand crept up to her mouth in shock.

"What ya goin' on 'bout, Joey? This ain't ours...is it?"

"Yes, Ma'am." Joe said as he opened the back door and unstrapped the car seat. He pulled the baby seat out of the car, being careful not to wake Ruby.

"While you was in the hospital, a few of the guys and me...we moved all our stuff from the apartment to here."

As Joe escorted Hattie up the front walk he continued talking.

"If'n ya don't like where we put the furniture, we'll move it around so it's like ya want."

"Oh, Joey-boy, this is so nice. How we gonna afford 'dis here place?"

"We can, don't you worry none. That apartment of mine was way too small for us with a baby and all. I never knew such a tiny mite like Ruby could own so many things." Joe laughed. "Come on in and look around."

He produced a key and handed it to Hattie. "After you, little-Mama."

Hattie fumbled with the key; certain someone would come by any minute and snatch it away. Tell her it was all a mistake. That they don't rent to nigras. She finally got the door open and stood looking into the living room.

"Well go on, girl, step in and see what ya think."

Hattie tiptoed in to the first room. The sun shining through the windows gave the hardwood floors a warm honey glow. Joe followed her in, carrying the baby, and closed the door.

"Is this really ours?" Hattie asked in a whisper.

"Well, I sure hope so since all our furniture and stuff is sitting right there."

Hattie walked to the center of the living room and turned slowly around. She touched her things as if to reassure herself that she wasn't dreaming.

Then Joe led her down a short hallway and into the bright kitchen. The walls were painted the palest blue and the cabinets were white. The appliances were pure white and the linoleum was black and white squares.

Joe wrapped his arms around her from behind as Hattie took it all in. "Do you like the color?"

"Oh, Joey, I love it. Did you paint this for me?"

"Yeah, after work I came straight over and did it. It was puke green before and I know how much you love blue."

Hattie hugged his arm. "Show me the bedroom, Joe."

Joe took her hand and they walked down another hallway. They stopped at the first bedroom.

"This here's the nursery, if you say so. I painted it too."

She looked around. "Pale pink for our baby-girl. Joey, I love it."

"I think the smell's almost gone. But if you want we can have Ruby in our room for a couple of nights."

Hattie laughed. "Oh, new-Daddy, I got some big news for ya. Ruby be in our room a lot longer than 'a coupl'a nights'. Long as I'm nursin' her she be right there by our bed. You don't wanna hav'ta get up every couple of hours and fetch her from the nursery, do ya?"

"Oh. I never thought about that. Well! Thas' okay 'cause it'll give me time to fix up her room the way we want. Now, come this way and let me show you our room."

"Joey, don' you fool wid' me. 'Dis cute little place got *two* separate bedrooms?"

"Yep. Come look." Joe said as he led Hattie to the next bedroom.

He opened the door as if opening the lid to a treasure chest. Their bedroom glowed in the afternoon sun. The walls were painted a soft deep rust. The woodwork was a shimmering cream. Their bed was between two windows and was freshly made up with new linens.

"Joey! We can't afford all this." Hattie exclaimed, her eyes shining with delight. "When? How did you get all this done? I was only in the hospital for two days."

"Do you like it?"

Hattie walked over to the bed and ran her hand over the new coverlet which had the exact same rust hue in the pattern as the color on the walls.

"Oh my, I love it." She sat down.

"Wanna try it out?" Joe teased.

Hattie looked at him sternly but with love lurking in her smile. "Now, Joe, you behave yourself. You know that there can be no lovin' for two weeks at least."

"That long?" Joe asked, crestfallen. "Really?"

Hattie laughed at his expression. "Yes, you know what that doctor said. No lovin' until I'm completely healed up."

Joe carefully set the baby carrier on the floor and sat next to Hattie. He wrapped his arms around her and tipped them both back on the bed. He nuzzled her neck.

"But cuddling is okay, right?"

Hattie kissed him. "Oh yes, Joey-boy, I loves ya more than life. You've made me so happy."

"Thank you for giving me a beautiful baby daughter, Hattie."

Suddenly the room filled with a hungry wail.

Hattie laughed. "A beautiful *loud* daughter."

Chapter 23

Sandy

Sandy Gerrard let herself into her apartment. She turned on a lamp and threw three days of mail and her keys onto the side table in the foyer. She turned the security locks and walked down the hallway.

She'd just finished a successful negotiation with a father who had run off with his son. Custody battles could be the messiest thing on earth and she hoped the Feds didn't come down too hard on the poor schmuck. At the end of the day, he was simply a desperate father worried about his child.

She walked into the stark living room and sat down on the charcoal leather sofa. She kicked off her regulation black pumps and swinging her feet up, she let out a moan of relief.

Federal negotiators were not allowed to wear her beloved, freshly f***** stilettos. And she had dozens of them in her closet. She did love her shoes. But for work gray or black suits and plain black pumps, with heels no higher than one inch, were the dress code. Even pastel blouses would be pushing it.

At forty-two years of age Sandy was a compact package. Five foot three and all muscle, thanks to her continuous training in Tae Kwon Do and kick boxing. Her shining black hair was cut in a neat short bob. Her Irish heritage had given her dark blue eyes.

Her living room decorated in black and white and soft grays always calmed her. Some would say the room was cold but she loved the clean lines of the furniture. The minimalist style of the room with only the huge, colorful impressionist painting over the gas fireplace. It was the only piece of singular boldness in the room. Sandy rose and padded into her kitchen of stainless steel and black granite.

I wonder if the romaine is still fresh enough for a salad, she pondered. *A glass of that lovely white wine I opened a week ago, a salad, a piece of the baguette and some cheese will be the perfect dinner after a shitty day.* She opened the frig door and got out the makings. *Yep, the lettuce was still good for at least one more salad.* She opened the bread drawer. The bread had not fared so well so she popped it in the microwave to soften it up.

Sandy took the bottle of wine over to the cabinet where she kept her Waterford wine glasses. Pouring out a half a glass she sipped the ice cold wine as she prepared her dinner. She then loaded everything onto a tray and took it into the living room. After setting the tray on the coffee table, she turned on the television and the fireplace with the remote control and sat down to eat and watch the news.

After a few bites she realized that nothing really had changed in the news; war, bloody murder, children lost, political scandal, a Hollywood starlet fake-dating her co-star to pump up the ratings. She muted the TV and sat back with her glass of wine and stared at the fire. The kidnapping case she'd just come off of had ended well. Nobody hurt and the child back in the arms of the mother. The mother seemed like a bit of a loser. Heavy makeup, ripped T-shirt and dirty jeans. Sandy was certain that she caught more than a whiff of alcohol on her breath as she cried big crocodile tears when reunited with her son. And the language she shouted at her ex would have had a sailor blushing. The father was carted off to jail and hopefully an understanding judge would hear the case. Poor jerk.

Sandy had just finished her light dinner when her door bell rang.

"Who the hell is that? At my door, unannounced at this time of night."

She rose and walked down the hall to the foyer. She looked through the peep hole in the door and sighed. Unlatching the security locks she opened the door.

"Come on in, Samuel."

She moved aside and a distinguished man in his mid-forties walked in. He was dressed casually in a golf shirt and grey sweat pants. He had a windbreaker slung over his shoulder. Sam was handsome but in a lived in sort of way. He was the type of man whose shirt tails never stayed tucked, whose shoes needed a polish ten minutes after their last shoe shine and whose hair always needed a trim. But his look contributed to his being a very successful and popular orthodontist.

"Your joy at seeing me is overwhelming." He told her with more sadness than sarcasm. "Great to see you too Sandy."

"What'd you want?"

"Gracious as always, I see. How about a drink for starters?"

Sandy looked at him for several minutes. She then turned and walked down the hallway.

"Why not? Your usual?"

Sam followed her. "Yes, please." *Maybe that's where we went wrong,* he thought, *me always following along behind her. Grateful for any small favor.*

In the living room Sandy went to the drinks cart and poured a scotch on the rocks, three cubes. Sam crossed the room and had taken one corner of the sofa, putting his feet on the coffee table.

Sandy walked over to him and handed him his drink. Almost as an afterthought and certainly not the first time she had said these exact same words to him, she told him, "Feet off the furniture."

Sam grinned and lowered his feet to the carpet.

"Join me." he invited, patting the seat next to him.

Sandy picked up her glass of wine and moved to the far end of the sofa and sat down. She sipped her wine and stared at him.

Sam looked around the room. "I see you still live in a monk's cell, Sands."

"Is that why you came? To critique my decorating style, *again*?"

"No, just making conversation."

"Well, if you don't mind I'm really tired. I just got in off a kidnapping case and I'm beat. Why are you here?"

"Did it end well?"

"What?"

"Your case, did it end well?"

"Oh. Yes. It was a custodial 'napping so the child was safe. I always feel a bit sorry for the parent who takes the kid. They get slammed by the justice system. I know it's the right thing but I don't have to like it."

Sam sighed. *How can she be so empathetic to these missing children and still not want any of her own.* He wondered. *Maybe if she had consented to having a kid or two it would've worked out.*

"Sam!" Sandy had said his name several times. *But as usual he's off in his never-never-land. What a dreamer*

"What? Oh, sorry I was thinking about kids."

"Sam, what is it that you want? I gotta get some rest. I've got a full day of paperwork tomorrow."

He looked over at her, his eyes full of grief.

The guy is so soft hearted and sweet. Why couldn't I love him more? Why couldn't I give him the kids he so desperately wanted? Why couldn't I have been little Miss Homemaker? Sam certainly deserves all of that and more.

"The divorce papers are ready and will be delivered to you tomorrow. I just wanted to see you in person to tell you," he told her.

"Okay."

"Sands, won't you please reconsider? I still love...."

Sandy set her glass down and moved over to him. She took his hand.

"Sam, don't. We've been over this a thousand times. You know I will always love you but I can't give you what you want; what you deserve."

Sam hung his head and watched his own fingers making lazy circles on the back of Sandy's hand.

"I loved you so much. Still do. This divorce is killing me."

Sandy's cell phone began its distinctive chirp signaling that it was the office. Sandy groaned and picked it up off the table. The caller ID confirmed that someone at the office needed her.

"Sorry, it's the office." She told Sam before she answered it.

"Yeah, I figured."

"Gerrard, here."

"Got a hot one for ya. Report to the state prison immediately. An inmate grabbed some rich old broad and they're holed up in the visiting room. The team coordinator will call you on the road and brief you. Pack a toothbrush; it's gonna be a long sum-a-bitch."

"Roger that. I'll be in my car in fifteen minutes." Sandy ended the call and turned to Sam. "I'm sorry, I have to go."

"But you're wiped out. Can't they call someone else?"

She began to squeeze her tired feet back into her shoes. "We've got a hostage situation at Statesville."

"Oh."

"I'm so sorry to cut you off like this Sam. But there's nothing more to be said. You and I both know that a divorce is right for us. I'll never be different than who I am. In a little while you'll meet a wonderful woman who can give you all the things I can't. I love you and you know we will always be friends."

Sandy was up and moving; she was in negotiator mode in a blink of an eye. She loaded the tray with her dishes and both glasses and moved to the kitchen.

"I'll sign the papers as soon as I get back. Will you sign yours, Sam?"

"Yes. I didn't want to until I had a chance to talk to you one last time."

As Sandy loaded the dishwasher she wondered to herself, *what's he waiting for now? Can't he see that I have to throw some fresh things in my bag and get on the road? Maybe if I ease towards the door, he'll take the hint.*

Sandy left the kitchen and walked down the hall. Sam really had no other choice but to follow her. He stood up, took one last look around the cold, remote room and walked towards the front door.

Sandy was standing there with her hand on the door knob.

"We'll talk after I get back and have signed the papers, okay?" she said.

"Yeah, that's fine." Sam leaned in to kiss her and Sandy quickly turned so he kissed her cheek. "Drive safe, will you?"

"I always do Sam. Again, sorry about the 'bum's rush' but crime never sleeps." Her laugh came out flat and Sam didn't even smile.

Sandy opened the door and as Sam walked through it she patted him on the back.

"Talk to you when I get back, okay?"

"Good night, Sands." Sam said as he walked toward the elevator. Sandy had closed her door before he had gone six feet. He stood alone in the hallway, waiting for the elevator, tears trickling down his face.

Chapter 24

Sandy, Kitty, Alma and Hattie

Sandy Gerrard stood just outside the security doors that led to the visiting room. Inside the telephone began to ring. Charlie looked over at his hostages.

"Washington, answer that!" he ordered.

Joe stepped over to the phone. "Yeah?... Okay, hold on." He turned to Charlie. "It's a FBI negotiator, name's Gerrard."

"Tell him I ain't negotiatin' nothin'!" Charlie snarled.

Joe spoke into the phone. "Baldwin says... yeah, ya heard? Okay, hang on a sec... Gerrard wants to know, will you just talk a minute?" Joe told Charlie as he held the receiver out to him.

"Sure, why not? I'm not doin' nothin' else." Charlie laughed. "Okay, Duchess, hold the phone up to my ear. Yo! Mr. Ne-go-ti-a-tor Man, wha'd ya say?"

Charlie's eyebrows went up when he heard a calm, but definitely female voice on the other end of the telephone.

"Mr. Baldwin, my name is Gerrard. Sandy Gerrard. See me? I'm just outside the doors here."

"Yeah, I see ya. A broad?! They sent a broad?"

"Is that a problem?" Sandy asked.

"I don' know. Can ya cook?" Charlie laughed at his joke. Sandy chuckled.

"You let those folks go, and I'll cook you up a big

ole' steak."

"Ha. Ha. Very funny. I don't think so." Charlie wiped the laugh off his face. "You can see me too, right?"

Charlie indicated Kitty with his gun hand, then placed the end of the barrel to Kitty's head.

"See what I got here?"

"Yes, I see. No need for anyone to get hurt, Baldwin."

"Well, that's sort'a up to you, now, isn't it?"

"Look, you need to work this out with me."

"Says who?" Charlie asked.

"That's the only way you can get what you want. I'm here to help you."

Charlie snorted out a laugh. "Yeah, sure." He considered what she had said for a moment. "Okay, let's say I'm willing to talk to you. You the 'go-to' girl? 'Cause I ain't talkin' unless it's to somebody can get me outta here."

"I'm the one." She took a minute. "How's everyone doin'?"

"Oh, we're peachy keen, Gerrard. Maybe a little hungry since we missed lunch."

"What can I send into you, you know, to make you and the others more comfortable?" she asked.

"How 'bout some beer? A six pack would go down nice. No, make that a twelve pack, it's gonna be a long night. A cold brew would taste pretty good. Some pizza too and not that prison crap they pass off as pizza!"

Sandy laughed. "I know. Pretty awful, isn't it? How about some water and I'll see what can be done about some real pizza?"

"No beer, huh? Didn't think so. Oh! And I wanna a cell phone."

Charlie took the receiver from Kitty and waggled it in the air. "This piece 'a shit ain't worth nothin'. I need to move around."

Charlie turned to Kitty and pointed to the floor. "Sit down, there."

Kitty sat down against the wall and curled her legs under her. She laid her head back and closed her eyes. Finally Charlie's attention was on someone else so she relaxed a little.

"Can do! I'll bring you the cell phone and some water when I bring in the food." Sandy reassured him.

"Wrong, Gerrard. You ain't comin' in here. You put it in the lock down and my ol' lady will get it. Oh, and Gerrard?"

"Yeah?"

"Everything comes through the lock down. If I see that personnel door open, for any reason, whoever it is gets the first bullet. Understood?"

"Understood. Give me half an hour, okay?"

"Just hurry it up. I'm real hungry now that I think about it. This hostage stuff stirs up a man's appetite, don't it?"

"Listen, while we're waiting on the pizza, why not tell me what's going on? Give me some details."

"Why?"

"'Cause I'm here to help you if I can. We all want this to end safely."

"No. How we want this to end is for me to get outta here. I got five hostages. That says you're gonna let me out so I can find my little girl."

"Your daughter?"

"Yeah."

Sandy hid her smile. *So now we know why all of this hit the fan,* she thought to herself. *We gotta find the kid ASAP.* She turned away from the window and spoke into her lapel.

"You getting this?"

"Roger that." A male voice came back.

"Let me get some details and then you guys jump on finding his kid, before this gets any uglier."

"Roger."

Sandy turned back to the window. "Just checking on the pizza." She told Charlie. "You got any other kids? I've got two myself."

"Nope, just the one and she's missin'."

"How, missing?"

"As in gone, disappeared, vanished, poof! What's wrong with you, ya stupid?"

Sandy ignored Charlie's insult. *A good, no, a great negotiator ignored the hostage takers' insults and fury. Keep them on track and don't let it escalate.*

"Did she run away?"

"Naw... um..." Charlie fired a glare at Alma. "We don't know for sure."

"How old is she?"

"Fifteen. She's just a kid."

"Charlie...." Alma started to correct him.

"Gonna turn sixteen in a couple of months." He sighed.

"What do you think happened?" Sandy gently prodded. "Does your wife have any thoughts?"

Charlie's laugh was derisive. "I don't think... I know what happened! She's disappeared for over a week now. A guy my wife works for... Rick... she's with him and he's got a hard on for her. And I don't mean he's mad at her. He's had his eye on my daughter since she was thirteen. Jesus! I gotta get outta here! I gotta find her!"

"What's Rick's last name?"

"Santana. Why?"

"Give me some details, maybe I can help. Where does your wife work?"

"A strip joint out on highway 30. The Paradise Lounge. Santana owns it."

"What's your daughter's name?"

"Chelsea, Chelsea Marie."

"Pretty name, Chelsea a family name?"

"After my mother, okay? What's with all the chit-chat?"

"Is Chelsea close to her grandmother? Would she maybe call her instead of her mother?"

"My mother died eight years ago."

"Oh, I'm sorry."

"Yeah well cancer will do that to ya."

"How old is this Santana guy?" Sandy asked.

"Thirty-five, forty. You got kids, Gerrard. Ya got any idea how this feels? Me locked up in here and my daughter's with some ol' pervert? My dimwit wife tells me just now, that Rick promised Chelsea a trip to Atlantic City."

"I do know how you must feel Charlie...can I call you Charlie?" She always tried to get on first name basis as quickly as possible.

"You can call me Charlie, Baldwin or a '*horse's ass*' for all I care. I got every reason in the world not to trust you, *Sandy*. A fucking cop!"

Sandy ignored his slurs. "I got two girls. Nine and eleven. I know how frantic you must feel. I would be going out of my mind right about now."

"But we can help you find her. Whad'ya say? Put the gun down, walk away from this right now.

Let the others go and I promise you, we will do every-thing we can to find your daughter."

"No way."

"Look, Charlie, if you give this thing up, right now, you're looking at a few good days being taken away. Some lock down time. A couple of weeks in the hole at the most…"

"Like I give a shit…"

Sandy went on as if he hadn't spoken. "You let this go any further; you're jeopardizing your future with your daughter. Come on, be smart and give it up now."

"Nice try, Gerrard. No deal. The way I see it, I hold all the cards. I get outta here, I'm the one finds my kid, and I find that bastard, Rick, end of story. So where's the food ya promised?"

"It just walked in the door, Charlie… you ought 'a be able to smell the pizza from in there. Let me bring it in, we'll have a slice together and talk… how 'bout it?"

"Uh-uh… you just put the stuff in the lock down and back out. You got the phone?"

"Yep. All right here." The first door slid open and Sandy walked into the chamber. "I'm coming into the lock down now. Why not let me come on in and we'll talk about getting your daughter back."

Sandy stood, pizza boxes in one hand, a six pack of water dangling from her fingers. Charlie yelled into the receiver.

"I said no! You stay where you are. Just set everything down and back out."

Sandy laid the supplies down on the floor. "Whatever you say, Charlie." She removed the cell phone from her pocket and showed it to Charlie.

" Here's the phone. You can call me anytime. Just hit number one on the speed dial. And there's some real, Chicago style pizza. Hope ya like sausage and green peppers. "

"The phone's probably bugged." He grumbled to himself. "Go on, get out." He waved the gun at the doors. "As soon as you're out, open the inside door. Alma! Go get that stuff."

"Okay, hon."

Alma rose from her chair and crossed to the inner door as it slid silently open. She gathered up the food and phone. She walked across to her table and looked at Charlie.

"Put the food and water on the table, Alma. Bring me the cell phone and one of them waters."

"What about Mrs. Lancaster, hon?" Alma asked.

"What about her?"

"Maybe she'd like some water too, Charlie."

"Yeah, sure. What the hell."

Alma pulled two bottles from the pack and picking up the phone scurried over to Charlie. He took the water and cell phone. Alma reached down to Kitty, who was still sat on the floor, and handed her a bottle.

"Thank you." Kitty looked up at Alma, her eyes full of desperate pleading.

"Welcome." Alma's eyes locked with Kitty.

"Please. Make him let me go…make him stop." Kitty pleaded.

"Don't worry, Mrs. Lancaster, Charlie won't hurt ya…he talks real tough but he won't do nothin' bad to ya."

"I have a daughter too, Alma. She's pregnant. She'll be worried. Please help me." Kitty whispered.

"Jeez, that's rough…" Alma sighed.

"For Chrissakes, Alma, shut up and go sit down." Charlie barked at her.

"Okay, baby, don't get mad."

Kitty slumped in defeat. Why would no one help her?

Charlie could hear the faint voice of Sandy coming from the forgotten phone in his hand. He raised it to his ear.

"Charlie, you can hang up now and call me on the cell phone. Let's talk. See how we can work this out."

"Later." Charlie sneered. "Don't call me...I'll call you."

Chapter 25

Kitty ~ Seven months earlier

"What a beautiful morning!" exclaimed Kitty as she stood at the foot of the huge dining table.

"Here we are, all together around the table. I'm so happy you could get away for a Sunday, Danny."

Kitty beamed at her children, Elizabeth and Daniel. Next to Elizabeth sat her husband, Hunter.

The formal dining room was filled with sunshine and the scent of pine from the Christmas tree, rising twenty feet, in the corner. Muted pink and gold damask wallpaper covered the walls. The pink was repeated in the chair fabric and drapes. The Kashan Persian carpet of dark greens and gold covered the polished oak floor. White roses mixed in with bright red Poinsettias crowned the antique table.

"Isn't it lovely, Edward?" she asked her husband seated at the head of the long table. Edward's head was down as he pushed his food around his plate. He appeared to be a million miles away and didn't seem to hear his wife. "Edward?"

Edward's head snapped up. "Excuse me, my dear, what was that you were saying?"

"I said, isn't it wonderful having all of our children here with us?" replied Kitty.

"Oh! Yes, yes, wonderful"! Edward returned to studying his food and Kitty frowned, wondering what was troubling her husband.

Edward was usually as thrilled as she was when all their kids were home at the same time. The oldest child, Elizabeth, was a beautiful young woman with shining, chestnut brown hair and hazel eyes that she had inherited from her father. She was perfectly groomed in a silk shirt-waist dress in a rich burgundy color. Her Jimmy Choo shoes were the exact color of her dress.

Their son, Daniel, fresh out of college, was as handsome as his sister was pretty. Blond and blue eyed he was their 'golden boy'. An athlete with a 4.0 grade average, he had been popular with teachers and friends at prep school. He was equally popular with his new employers and was on the fast track in a prestigious law firm in New York who had hired him right out of law school.

Elizabeth and Daniel were especially close now that they were adults but a little sibling teasing was never far from the surface.

Grinning, Elizabeth addressed her brother. "How's the new associate ambulance chaser, brat?"

"A glorified research gofer, you mean", replied Daniel sighing. "How long is it going to be before they let me do more, Dad?"

Edward didn't respond and everyone turned to stare at him. Finally, raising his head, he looked around the table.

"Excuse me?"

"Edward, for heaven's sake, what's the matter with you, darling? You haven't heard a word anyone has said to you!" Kitty exclaimed.

Edward ran his fingers through his thinning hair and grinned, rather sickly, at his wife. "Old age, I'm afraid. Sorry all, I've quite a bit on my mind at the moment. I apologize, Danny, what was it you asked?"

"No worries, Dad. I was just wondering when they would give me a couple of briefs to write or something besides all this research. It seems like right now I'm just an errand boy living in the law library."

"Ah." *I know all about paying one's dues.* He smiled at his son. *I can remember those days when I wanted to light the world on fire with my brilliance. The apple didn't fall very far from this tree.*

"Anxious to get your feet wet, my boy? I remember those days. Just be patient, do whatever they asked of you and above all be discreet! They're testing you at the moment. It will come; just have a little patience."

"Your Dad's right, Danny." Hunter chimed in. "It'll probably be a year before you feel like you're doing anything meaningful and what you went to school for. That first year with my firm had to be the most frustrating of my life."

Their maid, Mary, walked in from the kitchen with a silver coffee server held in both hands.

"Ah, Mary, thank you. I believe we're all ready for some fresh coffee," Kitty said.

"Any chance there's a bottle of champagne chilling in the kitchen, Mary?" asked Hunter as he declined more coffee.

He and Elizabeth had been married a little less than two years and were a perfect match. Tall and slim, Hunter was Boston aristocracy from the tip of his Italian loafers to his four hundred dollar haircut. He had graduated from Harvard Law and was now an associate at a respected Chicago law firm.

"I'm in the mood for a mimosa." He continued, winking at Elizabeth.

"I'll ask Cook, Master Hunter." Mary said as she finished serving the coffee and left the room.

"Are we celebrating, dear?" Kitty asked. "Did you receive your promotion?"

"Why don't you tell them, Liz?" Hunter said hugging his wife.

Elizabeth grinned at her mother and turned to her father, "Well, Grandpa…."

Kitty screamed and jumped to her feet. She rushed around the table and Elizabeth rose to meet her. Kitty embraced her and said, "Lizzy! You're expecting? When, how? Oh, Lizzy, how wonderful!"

Hunter rose laughing, "Here Grandma, sit next to your daughter."

Kitty hugged her son-in-law. "Hunter, you've made me so happy!"

Edward rose and crossed to him. "Congratulations, son!" he said as he shook Hunter's hand.

As he kissed the top of his daughter's head he told her, "Going to make your ole' Dad a grandpa, huh, Lizzy?" He walked towards the kitchen door. "I'll get the champagne from the kitchen."

Elizabeth glanced over to her brother. "Nothing to say, Uncle Danny?" she asked him.

"Jeez, sis, I'm too young to be an uncle."

They all laughed at Daniel's reaction.

"How far along are you, darling?" Kitty asked.

"Ten weeks. We wanted to wait until we were well into the first trimester before we told anyone. I was feeling a little superstitious. I hope you understand, Mom." Elizabeth told her mother.

"Of course, my dear. How's your health? What does the doctor say? Are you having morning sickness? Are you retaining water? You must get lots of rest. Maybe you should spend this first trimester in bed. Just to be on the safe side."

Elizabeth took her mother's hands in hers and smiled gently. "Mom, nothing's going to happen. Miscarriages don't necessarily run in families."

"I know, my darling, but what if something should happen?"

"Mom, you had the very bad luck of losing three fetuses. Things were different back then. They didn't know about all the things that could affect a baby. I'm going to be fine, I promise."

"I know, my darling girl. My head says you're a healthy young woman. But my heart is frightened. The pain of losing those babies....I'll never forget them." Kitty's eyes glistened with unshed tears.

Edward had returned, a bottle of wine cradled in his arms. "Slow down, Kit. She's going to be just fine." He walked over to the side board to open the champagne.

"Danny, hand me that pitcher of orange juice, will you son?"

Kitty laid her head on her daughter's shoulder. "Please, Lizzy, be extra careful....for me?"

"I promise, Mama. Just orange juice for me, Dad," Elizabeth said. She turned back to her mother, "The doctor says everything is normal and if I was any healthier I wouldn't need him at all. A little nausea in the mornings but a bite of toast and a cup of tea and I feel fine."

"I'm the one with morning sickness," Hunter laughed. "Ever since I found out, I've got butterflies like you would not believe!"

Edward laughed. "Get used to it, son. Once the baby's here and you're sleep deprived, the butterflies are the least of your worries."

"Oh, Edward, it wasn't that bad!" Kitty laughed. "He's just trying to scare you, Hunt. You'll have to begin interviewing for a Nanny soon, Lizzy, it takes quite awhile to find just the right person."

"Mom! I'm barely 10 weeks. We have months to find a Nanny."

"My darling, it took me six months to find Helgie. Thank God for her!"

"Helgie," Elizabeth sighed. "How I loved her. How patient she was with you, Danny, throughout your frog, bug and snake phase."

She paused, thinking. "Mom! Do you think she would consider coming out of retirement for me?"

"Well, that's certainly a thought, dear," Kitty mused. "She told me when we last spoke that she loved all the traveling she's been doing but really missed her 'babies'. Let me give her a call tomorrow."

"Oh, Mommy, would you? I would feel so much more confident if she was with me when the baby comes," Elizabeth replied.

"Hey, what about me?" Hunter joked.

Edward passed around the champagne glasses.

As he set one down at Elizabeth's place he said, "Orange juice for you, Mommy." He kissed Elizabeth's cheek. "A toast! To the first grand-baby, Edward Daniel Lancaster, the fourth." Edward crowed.

"What if she's a girl, Dad?" Elizabeth laughed.

"She wouldn't dare!" He chortled.

"We did put in an order for a boy, sir, but we really don't care what we get as long as all toes and fingers are present." Hunter said.

"Of course, my boy. But a grandfather can always hope. Raise your glasses high everyone. To the first Lancaster grandchild, may he or *she* arrive with all fingers and toes present."

"Here, here!" Daniel replied.

Hunter and Edward clinked glasses. Kitty took a sip and set her glass down. She reached for her handkerchief, wiping away tears.

"Mom, what's wrong?" Elizabeth cried.

Dabbing at her eyes Kitty said, "My little girl expecting her first baby. The years have just flown by...and now here I am, going to be a grandmother. I'm so happy," she said as she hugged Elizabeth close.

"Why do women always cry when it's good news?" Daniel asked.

"Ours is not to reason why, son," Edward laughed.

The maid entered the dining room from the foyer. She waited silently until Kitty noticed her. "Yes, Mary, what is it?"

"Excuse me, Mrs. Lancaster, ma'am, there's gentlemen at the door asking for Mr. Lancaster."

Edward paled and his hand trembled as he set down his wine glass. "I'll go, my dear. Don't disturb yourself."

"But, Edward, it's Sunday. Who could it be?" Kitty said.

"Just stay here with the children, I'll be right back." Edward said. He rose and left the room.

Kitty turned to her children, "Who on earth arrives on a Sunday morning without calling first?"

Danny laughed. "Probably Jehovah Witnesses. Dad will make short work of them."

Kitty turned toward the dining room door when she heard raised masculine voices. She rose from her chair and began to walk towards the foyer.

"Wait, Mom," Daniel said. "Let me go and see what's going on."

"Would you, darling?"

Daniel walked out of the room and Kitty sat down

again beside her daughter. "Now, have you thought about names…?"

Suddenly, voices were raised and they heard Daniel say, 'Wait just a damn minute! You can't waltz in here…"

Upon hearing her son's strident tone, Kitty jumped up and ran toward the door, followed closely by Elizabeth and Hunter. All three rushed into the foyer but were brought up short when they found three men in suits and a uniformed police officer standing there.

One of the men was holding Daniel's arm to restrain him, while the police officer proceeded to hand cuffed Edward.

"You have the right to remain silent. Anything you say can…" the police officer began reading Edward his rights.

"My God, Edward! What is going on?" Kitty rushed to Edward's side.

"Daddy, who are these men?" Elizabeth cried.

The officer continued, "…be used against you in a court of law. You have the right to speak to an attorney,"…

"Dad, what the hell….? Who are these guys?" Daniel struggled to get away from the man holding him.

The man who seemed to be in charge of this fiasco glared at Daniel. "Settle down son, don't make any trouble."

He turned to Kitty. "Mrs. Lancaster?"

Kitty nodded. "Yes, what's this about? You've obviously made a serious mistake. "

"I'm Special Agent Robert Smythe. Sorry, Ma'am but your husband has to go with us. I have a warrant for his arrest."

Hunter stepped up. "I'm Mr. Lancaster's attorney."

"Hunter..." Edward began.

"Please, Edward, let me handle this. Do not speak to any of these gentlemen." Hunter advised. "There has got to be some kind of mistake, Special Agent Smythe. Let me see the warrant, please."

The agent pulled several pages out of his breast pocket and handed them to Hunter.

"There you are. He's being arrested for alleged insider trading and money laundering."

"...If you cannot afford an attorney,"...the police officer continued as if there was no one in the room but he and his suspect. "....one will be appointed for you. Do you understand these rights as they have been read to you?"

"Yes," Edward murmured, docile and unresisting.

Kitty moved in front of Edward. "Remove those *hand cuffs* immediately! Who do you think you are?"

"FBI, ma'am."

She moved closer to her husband. "Edward, I don't understand, what's going on?"

"I'm sorry, Kitten, I tried to tell you," whispered Edward.

"Tell me what?" She gazed into his eyes and saw the truth.

"You knew? You knew they were coming?" Kitty gasped.

"Yes, I told them... that is Richard told them, I would surrender myself today. But I thought they would have the decency to come this afternoon. I'm so sorry."

"'Surrender'......but, Edward, what's this about? I don't understand," Kitty cried, grabbing his arm.

"Excuse me, Ma'am, but he has to go now. Mr. Lancaster will be arraigned tomorrow at Cook County

Jail." The FBI agent gently began to pry Kitty's hand off Edward's arm. "You have to let go now, Ma'am."

"Hunter! Do something!" Elizabeth cried.

"Edward...." Kitty gasped.

"Daddy..." Elizabeth began to weep.

Edward turned to Hunter, "Hunt, take Lizzy into the next room. Will you call Richard and tell him what's happened? Ask him to meet me downtown."

"Yes, sir, I'll call immediately. Edward, you shouldn't speak to these gentlemen until Richard is with you."

Edward smiled at his son-in-law. "I know, Hunt."

"Lizzy darling, come with me," Hunter put his arm around a sobbing Elizabeth. She broke free and threw her arms around her father's neck.

"Daddy...please, why are these men arresting you? Don't let them take you."

"Lizzy go with Hunt now. I don't want you to see me like this. It's going to be all right... everything will work itself out, you'll see."

Hunter put his arms around Elizabeth once again and led her from the room.

"I demand that you release my husband at once. You've made a terrible mistake. I will speak to your superiors about this....do you know who you are dealing with?" Kitty sputtered.

"Ma'am, it's all there, in the warrant. Please let go of your husband now."

He turned to the policeman. Officer, take Mr. Lancaster out to the car."

The officer took Edward by the arm and walked him out the front door. Kitty stood dumbfounded and stared after Edward's retreating back.

"We also have a search warrant for all electronic equipment. We'll try to be as quick as we can. If you'll just show us your husband's office and any other location with computer equipment."

"I most certainly will not! You will not go pawing through my husband's private papers." She turned to her son, "Danny, stop them; they can't do this!"

"Mom, calm down; we'll go with Richard tomorrow and this will all be straightened out. I'm certain there's been a mistake of some kind."

Danny rushed to the front door and called out to his father as he was being put into the back of the squad car, "Dad, don't worry, we'll see you tomorrow."

Danny walked back into the house and crossed to his mother's side. "Come on, Mom, let's go see what Hunter found out from Richard."

"But, Danny, your father," Kitty pleaded. "They put hand cuffs on your father!"

"I know, Mom. We'll take care of it tomorrow. Right now you have to see to Liz," replied Daniel. "And I'll show these *gentlemen* where Dad's computer is." Daniel turned to the agents. "If you'll wait here a moment?"

"Certainly. But don't be too long," one of the agents replied.

"Come on Mom. We need to be certain that Lizzy is okay." Daniel urged Kitty.

"Yes, Lizzy," Kitty said as Daniel began to lead her back into the dining room. "You'll go with me tomorrow, won't you Danny?"

"Of course. Try not to worry. Everything will straighten itself out, you'll see."

They walked into the dining room and Elizabeth ran to her mother.

Sobbing she threw herself into Kitty's arms.

"Mommy!"

"Lizzy, please don't cry so hard. You have to think of the baby," Kitty urged.

Hunter was just hanging up the telephone. With a glimmer of hope in his eyes, Daniel looked at Hunter over the heads of the two women. Hunter shook his head at Daniel's unspoken question. Daniel crossed to Hunter. "What did you find out?"

"Later." Hunter sighed. "It's not good."

Chapter 26

Alma, Hattie and Kitty

Early the next morning Charlie sat against the wall, an empty pizza box and water bottles nearby. For the night, Charlie had tied a piece of rope from his ankle to Kitty's.

Kitty was curled up in a tight ball asleep. Periodically, she would flinch in her sleep and sigh. Gone was the perfectly groomed socialite. In her place was a haggard older woman whose clothes were smudged with dirt and wrinkled. Most of her makeup had worn off leaving deep lines between her eyes and around her mouth.

Charlie's head lolled back against the wall, eyes closed but he was awake and alert to anyone's movements.

Alma sat at a table, her head resting on her folded arms. Her face was turned away from Charlie and the room as if to block out what was happening.

Hattie and Joe, holding hands, sat close together on the floor across from Charlie. Hattie's head rested on Joe's shoulder.

Brad, handcuffed to a table leg, had spent a cramped night and squirmed around trying to find a more comfortable position.

Hattie raised her head and peered around the room. She stared at Charlie and thought he might have finally fallen asleep.

"Psst! Miss Alma!" Hattie whispered.

"Yeah? Wha'd ya want?" Alma raised her head and looked at her.

"Please, can't ya do sumpin'?"

"Me? What can I do?"

"He's your husband, girl! Talk some sense in'ta him, make him let us go...he's gonna get into a world'a hurt here if he don't stop this nonsense."

"I can't talk him into nothin'. Not when it's about his daughter."

"But, Miss Alma, I got kids waitin' on me." Hattie whispered urgently. "Four of 'em. Joe's gettin' out soon. Please, won'cha try?"

"I'm sorry, Mrs. Washington. There's nothin' I can do. You don' know him. He loves our daughter more than anything in this world."

"Well then, I'm sorry too...sorry to tell you that you is a mess of a mother and a woman, lettin' this happen in the first place."

"I'm doin' the best I know how. What'ya know about it anyway? Besides, he ain't gonna hurt nobody, Mrs. Washington." Alma whispered.

"I can hear you..." Charlie spoke without opening his eyes.

Charlie opened his eyes after a moment and glared at Hattie. "Thought I was asleep, didn'cha. Washington, shut your woman up! Alma..."

"I wasn't doin' nothin', Charlie, honest. She started it."

"Hey, Baldwin." Brad called out. "I gotta take a leak real bad. And I'm sure the ladies would like to use the rest room too. It's been a long night."

The women voiced their need.

"God, yes, Charlie we all need a bathroom break." Alma said.

"Well, let me think on that." Charlie said. "It's gotta be on a buddy system." He laughed.

They all sat and stared at Charlie. Now that someone had mentioned it, they couldn't wait to relieve themselves; maybe be able to splash some water on their face, finger brush their teeth.

Their voices woke Kitty and she jumped up and scrambled away from Charlie as far as the four foot length of rope would go. Charlie, nonchalantly, reeled her back in and motioned for her to sit next to him.

"Good morning, Duchess." He grinned at her. "We're just figuring out bathroom breaks. Okay. Alma, you take Washington's wife and the duchess here to the bathroom."

Charlie stared hard at Hattie. "Missus Washington, no funny business in there. Remember I got your husband right here. You don't say a word to my wife, you got it? You got five minutes."

As he spoke he was untying the rope around Kitty's ankle. Standing up, Charlie yanked Kitty up by the arm.

"Duchess, you keep your mouth shut while you're in there. No talking."

He pushed Kitty towards to restrooms. "Alma, take them in there. If either one of them says a word to you or the duchess here tries to buy you off, I want you to tell me. Got it?"

"Sure, baby. I know."

"Washington, get on over here and sit in front of me 'till your wife gets back."

Alma and Hattie joined Kitty and the three women walked across to the rest rooms by the soda machines.

"Missus!" Charlie called to Hattie. All three women turned back at the sound of his voice.

"See this here gun? You wouldn't want to do

nothing that might cause your children to be fatherless. You get my meaning?"

"Yes, sir." Hattie mumbled.

"Alma, leave the door open while you're in there."

"Sure thing, sugar."

As the women filed into the rest room, Alma propped the door open with a trash can.

"Won't ya let my wife go, Baldwin?" Joe asked. "She ain't done nothin' to you. And besides, she's sick."

"Not a chance, I got just the right number of hostages to keep control of that bitch-cop out there."

The men sat silently. The sound of toilets flushing and water running could be heard. A few minutes later the women filed out and crossed to the tables in front of Charlie.

"Okay, did everyone behave themselves? Duchess, come on over here and sit down." Charlie told Kitty.

She didn't move but stood and stared defiantly at him.

Charlie barked out a laugh. "Funny things, bullets, they can fly across the room and get'cha."

Kitty's body slumped in defeat and head down, Kitty slowly walked over and slid down the wall beside Charlie.

"Now Missus trade places with your husband." Hattie reluctantly walked over to Charlie. "Sit. Washington here's the key to the handcuffs."

Charlie tossed the key to Joe. "Uncuff him," he indicated Brad, "and cuff yourself together."

Joe walked over to Brad and did what Charlie told him. "Jus' remember, Washington, I got your wife here. Any funny business and she takes a bullet.You and the pig got three minutes in there.

Take a piss and wash up if you want and get back out here. No talking. Leave the door open. Got it?"

"Yes. Just take it easy, Baldwin. I ain't gonna do nothin'." Joe replied.

"That's for damn certain if ya got any brains."

Cuffed together, Brad and Joe crossed to the restroom and went in. Inside the rest room Brad dragged Joe with him as he turned on the water at the sink. Under the noise of the water Brad whispered to Joe.

"Washington, ya gotta help me put a stop to this."

They crossed over to the urinals and each clumsily unzipped their pants.

"Uh-Uh, not me, Mr. Brad. I'm stayin' outta this mess." Joe zipped up and waited for Brad to finish relieving himself.

They walked over to the sinks and Joe waited while Brad washed his hands and face. The cuffs rattled nosily against the metal sink. Then Brad leaned over to give Joe enough room to wash up. Brad kept his voice very low over the flushing of the urinals.

"This is gonna get worse before it gets better, Washington. None of us are safe with this wack-o, including you and your wife. Help me so we can all get outta here in one piece."

"Sorry, Mr. Brad, I'm keepin' quiet and doin' what the man says."

"At least fake it when you recuff me. Leave me loose so I can *do* something."

Charlie yelled from the other room. "Hey! Time's up. Get your asses back in here, *now*!"

Turning off the water, Brad and Joe grabbed some paper towels and dried their face and hands. Brad and Joe walked out of the rest room and crossed back to where Brad had been cuffed to the leg of a table.

"Great! You two read my mind. Uncuff yourself, Washington and secure Kowalski there. Now, les' see. Who are the lucky ones to accompany me while I take a much needed piss?" Charlie laughed. "All that runnin' water is making me need to go real bad. Toss me the key when you're done Washington."

Joe did as he was directed. As he locked the cuff to the table leg he gave Brad an apologetic look and shook his head. He then threw the keys, none too gently, to Charlie who caught them with ease. He chuckled.

"Nice fast ball for a negro, boy."

Joe ignored him and walked over to Hattie.

"Okay then, my turn." He smirked at Hattie and Kitty. "Sorry, ladies but you are going to have to go with me while I pee."

"Wait just a minute, Baldwin. You ain't takin' my wife nowhere." Joe told him.

"No other way I can see to keep control of all of you. Just be a good *boy* and we'll be back in a minute. I'm sure I don't got nothing she ain't seen before. Alma, you keep your eye on Washington. If he so much as blinks, you call me."

"Okay, Charlie." Alma said.

"Okay, ladies if you will just walk ahead of me." Charlie directed, waving the gun toward the rest room.

Kitty and Hattie walked back across the room. Hattie reached over and quietly took Kitty's hand. As they disappeared into the ladies room, Charlie could be heard telling the ladies, "You can face the wall if you don't wanna look." He laughed.

The two women faced the wall holding hands.

"It's gonna be al'right, Miss Kitty. Just be brave for a little longer." Hattie whispered.

"Shut up, no talkin'."

Charlie finished at the urinal and crossed to the sink. He doused his head and face in cold water and rinsed his mouth out.

"Like 7-up, 'the pause that refreshes'. He laughed.

Wiping his face and hair with paper towels he motioned to the women to precede him out the door.

A few moments later Charlie, finger combing his hair, followed Hattie and Kitty back out into the visiting area.

"Goddamn! That felt good. Everybody behave themselves, Alma?"

"Yes, Charlie. Nobody moved a muscle."

"Good girl."

Chapter 27

Kitty ~ eight years ago

Kitty lay in the hospital bed, her face turned to the wall. The tears silently ran down her cheeks and quickly soaked the pillowcase.

Edward tapped on the door and walked in. Stepping quietly, he crossed to the bed and stood looking down at Kitty.

"Kitty, darling," Edward whispered. "Are you awake?"

Kitty tried to pretend to be asleep....*Why can't he leave me alone? All of them, just go away and leave me to die*... but the tears streaming down her face gave her away. Edward rubbed her shoulder tentatively.

"Kitten, turn over and talk to me, please?"

Wearily, she turned over and faced him. She hugged the sheet to her chest with both hands so she wouldn't be forced to touch him.

"I don't want to talk. There's nothing to say."

"But, sweetheart, you've been laying here for a week. Won't you let me take you home?"

"No! I couldn't bear to see the nursery." She began to cry harder. "Oh, Eddie, I wanted this baby so much. I knew I was a little old to be pregnant but the doctor said I was in perfect health."

She stared past his shoulder at nothing. "Did they tell you? It was a boy."

Edward reached up and dashed the tears from his eyes. "Yes, Kit, they told me."

"And I lost him. I killed our son." Kitty cried.

"No! Darling, what are you talking about...? that's crazy. You had a miscarriage. No one knows why these things happen. It's not your fault."

"Yes, it is completely my fault. My body betrayed us, killed our beautiful baby boy. Six months I carried him with no sign of any trouble. I was so happy."

"I know, darling, I was too. But I guess it wasn't meant to be."

"How can you say that? There was nothing wrong, I tell you. Then he just got really quiet. He didn't move, didn't move at all. How can that be?"

"The doctors said it was an intrauterine death."

At the word, 'death' Kitty flinched and fresh tears flowed down her face and unchecked, dripped off her chin.

"No one knows why." Edward continued. "It just happens."

"It's not fair. We can give a child everything."

"Kitty, we've been blessed with a fine son and daughter. Try to focus on them."

"I don't want to. I wanted this *new* baby. After all the other miscarriages I was so certain that this child would go full term....be in my arms in just a few months."

"I know, I know."

Silence stalked the room. Edward didn't know what else he could say to her. He had no words to tell her how sorry he was.

"Kitten, Dr. Schlossmeyer is coming by to see you tomorrow."

Kitty barked out a near hysterical laugh. "You think I'm crazy? That I need a shrink? Why? For mourning my baby? That's rich, Edward.

Why aren't *you* grieving?"

"Oh, Kitty I *am*."

She ranted on as if he hadn't spoken. "Didn't you want this baby? That's it, isn't it?" She screamed, "You're secretly glad it's gone. *I knew it!*"

Edward reached for the call button and silently pressed it.

"What are you doing?" Kitty cried. She grabbed the cord and tried to wrestled it away from Edward.

"Just getting a nurse. I think you need some rest, darling."

Kitty suddenly struck out at Edward, hitting him in the chest with her fist. Edward did nothing to defend himself.

"Goddamn you! You didn't want this child. You wished him dead!" Kitty hit him again and again.

"I won't be drugged. I want to feel this pain. I want to grieve for my baby...." Kitty sobbed.

The nurse came through the door with a small tray on which lay a syringe. Kitty crouched on the bed trying to make herself as small as possible.

"Get away from me!" she screamed.

"Mrs. Lancaster!" The nurse said. "You mustn't get yourself this worked up. You'll start to bleed again."

Kitty screamed. "Get out of here! I don't care! I wish I would bleed...to death."

As she sobbed the nurse stepped to the IV tube and uncapped the syringe. She plunged the needle into the receptacle. As the sedative hit her blood stream Kitty's shouts and cries subsided to a moan.

"I don't care....I don't want to live without my baby...leave me alone."

Edward had stepped out of the nurse's way and stood

helplessly by the door, his face a mask of grief and loneliness.

"You should go for now, Mr. Lancaster." The nurse told Edward. "She'll sleep for several hours."

"Yes, I'll return a little later."

He followed the nurse out the door and it softly clicked shut.

"I'm sorry, Edward." Kitty mumbled. "I killed our baby, our sweet little boy. I'm so very sorry."

Chapter 28

Sandy, Kitty, Hattie and Alma

Sandy Gerrard stood near the control room outside the visiting room. Her cell phone rang and she scrambled to get it out of her pocket.

"Gerrard here." She listened for a moment. "Hey George." FBI Special Agent George Bryant was calling Sandy with an update.

"What does Atlantic City say? Is there any word on the kid?"

"Nothing yet I'm sorry to say. ACPD could be moving faster on this." George replied.

"Do they know how urgent it is?"

"Yeah, they know."

"Well, tell the detectives down there, we can only wait so long then we'll have to get you guys officially involved. That ought 'a light a fire under their butts."

"They're whining about budget cuts and personnel. And they're still callin' it a missing persons case."

"Christ on a crutch, it is no longer a missing kid. The minute this inmate took hold of a hostage and a gun, it became much bigger than a teen runnin' away with some guy."

"I know, I know…" George said.

"And tell them I don't give a rat's behind about their budget cuts or how thin they're spread."

"I did, boss. They said they're workin' it as hard as they can."

"Yeah well, tell 'em to work harder! If we can find her and this Santana character, maybe I can talk

Baldwin into giving up and letting the hostages go…
and for Chrissakes, if you do get lucky and find
Chelsea, bring her here immediately! *I need her here
pronto!* If Baldwin sees his daughter's safe he may
stand down."

"Roger that."

"Okay, let me know if there's any more news."

"You'll be the first call."

Sandy hit the disconnect button and immediately
dialed another number.

"Commissioner Randolph, please… yes, I'll hold…
tell him it's Special Agent Gerrard."

"Commissioner Randolph speaking."

"Sandy Gerrard, Sir."

"What have ya got for me, Gerrard?" a deep voice
asked.

"What we have ascertained, sir, is that the girl's
mother works for this Rick Santana who's had the hots
for the daughter for some time. Now, both the girl and
Santana are missing. To complicate matters, the mother
didn't report the girl missing for over a week. We may
have a lead in Atlantic City. The ACPD is working that
now."

"And?"

"Nothing so far, sir. I just got off the phone with
Special Agent Bryant. ACPD is treating this like a
missing persons."

"Let me make a phone call to the police
commissioner down there. See if we can get them to
change the status to kidnapping."

"That would be very helpful, sir." Sandy replied.

"What about the girl's father? What's he in for?
Does he seem like he might take a deal that *does not*
include his escaping?" Sarcasm dripped from his voice.

"Well, sir, he's a pretty hard case. He's in for murder; took a plea down to voluntary manslaughter. Killed some guy with his bare hands. Eight to fifteen. So far I'm not making much progress on getting him to stand down."

"You told him we are pulling out all the stops to find his daughter?"

"Yes, I made that very clear, sir. But, he's adamant! He wants out so he can find his daughter himself."

"Well, that isn't going to happen."

"Yes, sir, I realize that we can't just open the door and let him go. But, I am going to need more time with him."

"Listen, Gerrard, the press is going to get this very, very soon. Then the real pressure will be on."

"Understood, sir. I know there's a lot of pressure. We're feeling it too. I've got five hostages and a very unstable situation. If we can just take it slow I think I might be able to talk him down."

"Do you need any extra help, Gerrard? Maybe a male negotiator would be better in these circumstances."

"No, Sir, I don't think so. It seems to amuse him that I'm a woman. I think I can work that to our benefit."

"Roger. Call me with updates as things progress. You have forty-eight hours then I'm calling in SWAT."

"Sir…"

Sandy held a dead phone. "Damn it!"

* * * *

Inside the visiting room Charlie took the cell phone from his pocket and hit the speed dial key.

"Gerrard here." Sandy spoke harshly into the phone.

"Guess who, Sandy?"

"Hey, Charlie, good news! We've got your daughter's picture out nationwide on the Amber Alert system and we've got the Atlantic City police department checking the casinos. Also an APB's out on Rick Santana. That's a pretty raunchy club he owns."

"Yeah... tell me about it. Big shot Rick hires only the best 'exotic dancers'." Charlie looked over at Alma as he said this. "Whatever he finds under any ole' rock."

Alma stuck her tongue out at Charlie.

"Ya find out anything?" he asked.

"It takes time, Charlie. I'm sure we can find Chelsea if you'll be patient."

"Well, time's the one thing I ain't got, Gerrard. And time's runnin' out for you too."

"Listen, Charlie, let me come in there and talk."

"Why?"

"I think we can accomplish more if we're face to face. We need to work this out so nobody gets hurt and everybody wins."

"Well... shit, why not? I'm feelin' generous this morning. Come on in and join the party. But ya better not try anything, see? We wouldn't want any accidents to happen, would we?"

"No definitely not, Charlie. At least not because of something I do. I'll be coming in unarmed. How about trading me for one of the women?"

"Ha! You're a laugh a minute, Gerrard, you really are. Why should I?"

"Show of good faith."

"I don't gotta show you nothin'. No way. No trades."

"I'm coming in. No tricks. Okay?"

Charlie grabbed Kitty's wrist and pulled her up and in front of him. He continued to talk to Sandy on his phone.

"You just take it nice and easy, Sandy. When you get into the lock down, make sure that outside door is closed before they open this door, ya got it? When you get in, stay right by the door."

"Whatever you say, Charlie."

The outside door slid open and Sandy stepped into the chamber. The door slammed shut and instantly the inner door began to slide open. Sandy stepped slowly into the visiting room and the second door noiselessly closed behind her. Almost simultaneously Charlie and Sandy disconnected their cell phones.

"Alright, Gerrard, turn around real slow. Lift your coat so I can see if ya gotta a gun." Charlie told her.

Sandy lifted the hem of her jacket with both hands and turned slowly. "No weapon, Charlie."

"Now your pant legs."

Sandy had anticipated this. Her back up weapon was holstered in a state-of-the-arts calf holster with a S&W Airlite revolver. She reached down and raised the cuffs of her trousers to expose her ankles.

"Okay." Pointing to a table several yards away from him he said, "Sit down over there."

Sandy walked between the tables and sat where Charlie had indicated. "Mrs. Lancaster, are you all right?"

"Please! Help me. Make him let me go."

"Shut up! Did I say you could talk?"

"It's going to be all right, Mrs. Lancaster. Charlie, you can let Mrs. Lancaster sit down again. I came unarmed, as you can see. I just want to talk, work this out."

"What?… now you givin' me orders?"

"No, not at all. It looks like Mrs. Lancaster is ready to drop and since you hold all the cards, why not let her sit down?"

"Jesus, okay! Another bossy woman in my life." Charlie poked Kitty with his elbow. "Sit!"

Kitty flashed a grateful look at Sandy and sank to the floor once again.

"How's everybody doing? Mrs. Washington?"

"Please, ma'am… can't ya do sumthin'? My kids is home waitin' on me. They'll be so scared if'n I don' come home."

"Just hold on, Mrs. Washington. This is going to be over soon. Ms. Gaynor, how are you holding up?"

"I'm fine, Ms. Gerrard. Charlie don't mean no harm to anybody. He's worried about our little girl. I tried to tell him how much trouble he's gonna be in."

Charlie sighed wearily. "Alma! For fuck's sake shut up."

"Sorry, hon."

"Officer, you all right?" Sandy continued to poll the hostages.

"Yes, sir. Sorry 'bout this, sir. I had an unauthorized back up weapon and the prisoner got it. I'm sorry, but he was going to cut Mrs. Lancaster."

"We'll worry about that later, Officer. You did the right thing given the circumstances." She turned to Joe. "Mr. Washington? Do I have that right?"

"Yes, Ma'am." Joe replied. "And I don' want no part of this mess."

Nodding, Sandy turned back to Charlie.

"You through checking your little group of kiddies, Sandy? God, you sound like my first grade teacher." Charlie laughed.

"Charlie, what are we going to do?" Sandy asked shaking her head.

"I don't know that you can do much... but me, I'm gettin' outta here. Ya say ya can help me. So, start talkin'."

"We all want this situation to end well. Get your daughter home. These nice ladies get to go home. You serve the rest of your time out peacefully."

"Sounds like a fairy tale I used to tell Chels when she was little."

"Put the gun away."

"Like hell I will!"

"I'm no threat. I'm here solely to help. I can't talk to you down the barrel of a gun. Come on, put it away."

Charlie stared at Sandy for a few moments. He lowered the gun to his lap and then, sighing, tucked it into his belt.

"Okay, so the gun's put away. Don't nobody give me a reason to get it out 'cause if I hav'ta, the Duchess here she gets it first."

"No one's going to give you any reason to use the gun, Charlie. I want to talk to you about your daughter and how we can help find her."

"Start talkin'."

"What did you and your daughter like to do together? You know, before you were sent here."

"Oh, *come on*, Sandy." Charlie scoffed. "What is this, Negotiating, 101? Get cozy with the felon?"

"Not at all. It helps all the people who are looking for Chelsea to get a feel for the type of kid she is. Will she run when we approach her? Has she been in much trouble as a teen?"

Charlie shot a look at Alma. "Not that I know of. A few times she skipped school.

Stayed out all night at a girl friend's house. That one I didn't know about until now. Her mother seemed to think that was okay and didn't bother tellin' me."

"She get good grades?"

"Yeah, she's always been really smart." Charlie bragged.

"She's a good kid, Ms. Gerrard." Alma said.

"What about Chelsea's younger years? I'd like to hear how she spent time with you before your trouble. Did Chelsea like the zoo? My two are crazy about the place. Every weekend it's, "Mommy, can we go see the animals?"

Sandy had hit a nerve. Charlie's face softened thinking of his baby daughter and his freedom to be with her.

"Yeah, Chelsea too. When she was little we'd go to the zoo all the time. She loved the snakes. Never could understand that, a little girl lovin' snakes."

Sandy laughed. "Mine too…only it's spiders with Susie."

The tension began to drain from the room.

"How about you, Sandy, what else ya do with your kids?" Charlie asked. "That is when you ain't talkin' down bad guys like me?"

"Oh, you know the usual parent stuff. Soccer Mom, play board games, read bedtime stories. I must have read Harry Potter a dozen times." She laughed. "Help with homework, watch old movies…"

"Oh yeah? Old movies?"

"Yeah, we love them."

Charlie was a big fan of old black and white movies and he had collected quite a few when he was a free man and working off shore.

Let's test this broad; see if she knows jack-shit about some of the classics, Charlie thought.

"What's your favorite? And don't make me puke by sayin' 'It's a Wonderful Life.'"

Sandy laughed. "No. That's a little too saccharine for my taste. Actually, it's an old one from the forties with Charles Boyer as the bad guy. Ever heard of 'Gas Light'?"

Charlie was surprised. She pulled one out that he had never heard of. "Naw, don't know that one."

"Charles Boyer is a real bad ass." Sandy told him. "He wants to get rid of his wife by driving her crazy."

"Yeah, I can relate." Charlie glanced over at Alma. "Only she's drivin' *me* crazy."

Ignoring Charlie's dig at Alma, Sandy went on with the thumbnail sketch of the story.

"Ingrid Bergman plays the wife. Boyer's a great villain. And Angela Lansbury is the young housemaid. You know her from 'Murder She Wrote'? What a cast! I'm certain you'd like it."

"Oh yeah, that Lansbury broad was a looker when she was young." Charlie reached down and taps Kitty on the top of her head in mock affection.

"What's your favorite flick, Duchess? I bet its 'Breakfast at Tiffany's'." Charlie laughs again. "Starring that tall, skinny broad, what's her name?

Kitty doesn't speak. Charlie leaned down, menacingly. "I asked you a question, Duchess."

"I don't know...Kitty whispered and grasped at the first title that came to mind. "'African Queen'?"

"It figures! The broads all love Bogart, don't they Duchess?" Charlie straightened up. "What was that skinny broad's name in 'Breakfast'? You remember her name, Gerrard?"

"Audrey Hepburn, Charlie."

"Naw, that ain't right. Hepburn was Spencer Tracy's lady. She played in 'African Queen' with Bogie."

"Yes, but that was *Kathryn* Hepburn. We're talking about Audrey Hepburn."

"No kidding. That's weird... two movie stars with the same last name. They related?"

"Not that I know of. Audrey Hepburn is from Belgium originally and Kathryn is from Connecticut."

"I'll be damned." Charlie said, truly impressed with Gerrard's knowledge of some of the old great actors.

This is going well, Sandy thought. There was a particular phenomenon between hostage takers and the negotiator that if a common ground of any sort could be found between the two, there was ultimately a better outcome at the end.

"What's your favorite movie, Charlie?"

"Oh, that's easy. Hands down! 'Shane'. Now, there was a guy you could respect!"

"That's a good one. Alan Ladd, right?"

"Yeah, Ladd. Bogart, Ladd, Randolph Scott, Jimmy Cagney. They don't make actors like them no more."

"Too bad, Shane dying in the end, huh?"

"Hey! He didn't fucking die!"

"Sure he did. He's all slumped over in the saddle as he rides away."

"You don't know shit! He's just wounded, see?"

"Well, yeah, he could be wounded. I never thought of it like that." Sandy agreed.

"Damn straight! 'Cause he's gotta come back for the boy."

"Who played the little kid?"

"How the hell should I know?"

Charlie was suddenly fed up with all this talk.

"Wha'd I look like, those Sickles and Hebert faggots? Hey, enough of the chatter. When am I getting' outta here, Gerrard?"

"We're workin' on it, Charlie…we're also trying our darnest to find Chelsea."

"Well, you can dance me around the room just so long but we still come back to the same place when the music stops… I WANT OUT!"

"I know you do. That's what I want to talk to you about. Here's the plan. Give us forty-eight hours to find Chelsea. You're just one guy, I've got dozens of guys on the lookout. We'll…"

"To hell with that! I'm just one guy but I know all the holes Rick can crawl into. Places your guys never dreamed about."

"But…"

"Forget it! Here's the way this is gonna play out, Gerrard. I want a car, full size, gassed up. And police issue vests. I want one hundred large in unmarked bills…

"One hundred thousand? That changes things, Charlie. Ups the ante on the time you'll face when you're caught."

"*If* I'm caught…Oh yeah, and don't try to dye bomb the cash 'cause that bag is gonna get the hell beat outta it before I leave here."

"Okay, say I can guarantee all that for you, right now. What are you going to give me?"

"I ain't givin' you shit!"

"If I guarantee the car, the cash, I want two hostages released now."

"Fuck you, Gerrard. Ya get nothin' now. When I see the car and the cash, maybe I'll think about giving you Kowalski over there and Washington."

"Before you walk, I get Mrs. Washington and Ms. Gaynor." Sandy insisted.

"Uh-uh…no deal. They go with me."

Joe's head snapped up upon hearing Charlie's plan.

"That's not a good idea, Charlie. That adds kidnapping to the other charges. How about this? Leave everybody and take me with you."

"Nope. The women they go with me."

Hattie frantically whispered to Joe. Joe put his arm around her and shook his head.

"Joe, don't let him take me." Hattie pleaded. "My kids…" Hattie turned to Charlie and raised her voice. "Please Mister, don't take me. I got four kids alone at home."

"Shut up! Washington! Shut her up."

"Hattie, hush girl." Joe said. "Do like the man says now and be quiet."

"But, Joe, what's to become…"

Joe gently put his fingers to Hattie's lips, silencing her.

"It's gonna be all right." Joe whispered. "I won't let you go."

Tears tracked a dusty trail down Hattie's cheeks but she remained silent as she looked at Joe.

"Charlie, let's see if we can find another solution. You don't want to be in here for the rest of your life. Kidnapping these ladies will add twenty years at least to your sentence. Don't you want to eventually go out into the real world and be with your daughter?"

"Wha'cha mean? This *here* is the real world. Why else do ya think these stiffs keep comin' back?"

"Charlie…." Sandy said.

"Enough!   I'm through talkin, Gerrard. I get away clean. You and your guys back off for forty-eight hours and I let the Duchess here go. And Washington's ol' lady too."

"What about your wife, Charlie? Why get her mixed up in this?"

"She's already in it up to her pretty little neck!" Frustration poured off Charlie in waves. "Did ya know, Gerrard, that Chels was gone for a week before she said a fuckin' word to me? God! Alma, how stupid can you be?"

"I didn't know what to do, Charlie, honest."

"Listen, Charlie... reconsider, let's give the Feds time to find Chelsea." Sandy asked.

"*I said,* NO! Now get your ass in gear and get me that car and the cash. Go on now, get outta here. And be quick about it! I ain't waitin' around!"

Sandy rose and walked towards the door.

"Hey! Gerrard!"

Sandy turned around. "Yes?"

"Send Lancaster down here."

Kitty looked up in shock and with a glimmer of hope.

"I wanna talk to 'im while you're gettin' me the wheels and the moola."

"Excuse me?"

"Ya heard me. Get Lancaster down here now."

"Everything's locked down. What do you want with Mr. Lancaster?"

"We got some unfinished business. Get him down here; I ain't gonna tell ya again."

Charlie pulled the gun from his waistband and put the barrel to Kitty's head.

"Please, Ms. Gerrard," Kitty pleaded. "Let my husband come in. He must be frantic!"

"Hey, Duchess…did I give you a vote? Huh?"

Kitty flinched and didn't speak. "Answer me, Duchess. Did I give you a vote or not?"

"No." Kitty whispered.

"That's what I thought."

Sandy frowned. "Look, Charlie, I've been fair with you so far…but, I can't hand you another hostage."

"Shit, I don't want that little weasel as a hostage, Gerrard."

"What, then?"

"I just want to talk to him." Charlie patted Kitty's head. "Show him what I got here. He's been a pain in my ass since he got here. Thinks he's better than everybody but he wears con-denim just like the rest of us."

"What's the point, Baldwin?" Joe asked. "Leave him alone."

"Oh, ho…now everybody's got an opinion."

"Mr. Washington, please stay out of this." Sandy said.

"Yeah, shut up, Washington. This is between me and Lancaster now. Get movin', Gerrard."

"I need your word, Charlie. You just want to talk to him. Is that right?"

"I give you my word of *honor,* Sandy. I won't keep Lancaster more'n ten minutes, then you can have him back."

"And I need to be here the whole time."

"Sure, sure. Get busy!" Charlie waved Sandy on with his gun.

"It's going to take a few hours to arrange everything you've demanded, Charlie." Sandy moved to the opening doors to exit the visiting room.

"And Gerrard? Send in some more food and water...
please? I'm gettin' hungry again."

As Sandy walked through the second door, she could
still hear Charlie's laughter.

Chapter 29

Sandy ~ much later that night

Sandy walked into her apartment around two in the morning. *A shower, a couple hours of sleep, a change of clothes then back to the prison.* She'd been away three days and had run out of clean clothes. Her apartment smelled closed up and neglected. Sandy walked to the kitchen and opened the window over the sink a crack.

Sandy had talked, at length, to the prisoner about his daughter. She had seen his devotion. He wasn't a hardened, brutal killer while he spoke of her. He was simply a father desperate to find her, to keep her safe. She wondered if she had missed out by not having children. Instead, she had fabricated two imaginary daughters to try to get next to Charlie. This was what negotiators did, invented a life close to the bad guy's; got a dialogue going separate from the dire situation they all found themselves in.

She could have chosen to stay with Sam, have the kids he wanted so desperately. The house, the white picket fence, the dog, *and* her career. But she knew her career would always be front and center. She would always, if a choice needed to be made, have chosen it first. That would have been unfair to the kids and husband she didn't have. No, this was better. Her life was exactly what she wanted.

But, she wondered what it would feel like to risk it all to protect a child. Right or wrong, that's what this inmate was doing. In mortal fear for his daughter, he had been pushed to the edge.

This rough, foul mouthed bully would risk a life time in prison and even death to get out, to get free long enough to find his daughter and kill the man who had taken her.

And Sandy's job was to not let that happen. It was further complicated by the inmate's wife being among the other hostages. What a mess!

Sandy walked into her living room, flipped her shoes off and stripped out of her jacket. She crossed to the drinks cart and poured a whiskey, neat. Carrying her glass, she sank back into the soft leather of her expensive sofa.

Funny how we got off on old movies, she mused. *Sometimes I forget that these felons had a life before crime. Charlie insisted that Shane was just wounded, slumped over the saddle horn like that, and would be back. Wonder what that was all about. Could an incurable romantic be hidden inside that crude exterior? And I stumped him with 'Gas Light'.* That made her smile.

She sipped her drink and thought of the pain that lurked behind the rage in Charlie's eyes. *Every second must be a living hell for him, thinking of good ol' Rick Santana with his daughter.* She could certainly understand his desperation. *It seemed that Santana had been after the girl for a couple of years now. And the mother, Elma?....no that's not right...Alma, that's it! She was complicit in that Santana was her boss at the club. Letting the slime bag get anywhere near the girl.*

How 'f'd' was that? Sandy wondered. *Ah well it was hard to figure some people.*

She sighed and closed her eyes. A couple of hours of down time and she'd be good to go.

Chapter 30

Sandy and Kitty

Early the next morning Sandy Gerrard was standing near the control room with inmate, Edward Lancaster. Sandy needed to set down some rules and coach the prisoner.

"....so no matter how he provokes you, you've got to keep your head, Mr. Lancaster. Our whole goal here is to get everyone out safely, especially Mrs. Lancaster."

"My wife, she's all right... she's unharmed?" Edward replied.

"Yes, she's doing fine. A little tired, but they all are. Did you hear what I was saying? About keeping your composure?"

"Yes, yes. Please, when can I see her?"

"Right now. I want you to stay close to me. Be certain to stay out of reach of Baldwin. You ready?"

"Yes, I just want to see my wife, make certain she's all right."

Okay, then, here we go."

Sandy speed dialed Charlie's phone. "Hey, Charlie, as you requested I've to Mr. Lancaster here with me. We'd like to come in."

Charlie grinned at them through the glass. The distortion in the double glass made it look more like a horror movie grimace.

"Sure thing, doll. I've been lookin' forward to this."

Sandy led Edward through the doors and into the visiting room.

As Edward entered Charlie said. "Well, well, well, look at who the cat dragged in, Duchess. How's it hangin', *Eddie?*"

Kitty tried to jump up when she saw her husband. Just as quickly, Charlie roughly pushed her back down to the floor.

"Edward! My God, help me. Stop this maniac. Make him let me go! Please!"

"Kitty darling, it's going to be all right. Just stay calm, and do what this man tells you. We'll work it out Kitten, I promise."

"Ohh...ain't that sweet? 'Kitten'...that what he calls you, Duchess? Maybe in the sack?"

"Okay, Charlie, let's keep it constructive." Sandy said. "Mr. Lancaster's here. What now?"

"Shut up, Gerrard. Sit over there where I can see ya while I talk to Mr. Big Shot here." Charlie turned back to Edward.

"That's you, ain't it Eddie? Mr. Big Shot?

Edward followed Sandy to the table.

"Uh-uh...Lancaster, you sit right here in front'a me. We got some serious negotiatin' to do."

Edward turned and sat at a table in front of Charlie. He smiled reassuringly at Kitty.

" Eddie, please, help me...do something."

"Shut up, *Kitten!* See what I got here, Lancaster?" Charlie patted her head. "Where's your protection now, huh? Where's Washington now? He ain't so big and mean now, is he?"

"What is it you want, Baldwin? You want me instead of my wife? Fair enough! Let's trade."

"Edward, no!" cried Kitty.

"That's not going to happen. Charlie." Sandy interjected.

"We had an agreement that if I brought Mr. Lancaster down it was just for talk. If you think you're going to bargain with who stays and who goes, I'm taking him right out of here."

"All ya! Shut up!" Charlie yelled. "What the fuck? Like any of you's got any say here. Who's got the gun, huh? Dumb shits!" He turned his attention back to Edward. "I don't want you, Lancaster."

"Okay, so you don't want me...then, it must be money, right?"

"Bingo! You're not as dumb as you look, Lancaster. When I leave, I'm takin' the Duchess here with me. I'd be willing to drop her off somewheres, all safe and warm, if you make it worth my while."

"Baldwin, I cannot sit here and watch while you extort money right in front of me. I'm taking Mr. Lancaster out of here, now!"

"How much, Baldwin?" Edward asked ignoring Sandy.

"Oh...I don't know...what's she worth to ya?" Charlie scoffed.

"The world...she's worth the world to me. How much?"

"Let's see...how much ya weigh, Duchess? One forty? One fifty?"

"One hundred twenty-three." Kitty said. "Edward...don't give..."

"I told ya to shut up! Okay, we'll call it one thirty. Women always lie about their weight, don't they guys? So, let's sell the Duchess by the pound, how 'bout that, Lancaster?"

"Whatever you say, Baldwin."

"Mr. Lancaster, I must insist...." Sandy tried to interject.

"Now that's the spirit!" Charlie said as if Sandy hadn't spoken. "Let's see…one hundred thirty times five thousand bucks a pound, what does that come up to?"

"Six hundred fifty thousand." Edward said.

Charlie whistled through his teeth. "That's some serious money." He patted Kitty on the head. "That sounds about right, don't it Duchess? You worth six hundred, fifty large?"

"Edward, what are you doing?" Kitty whispered.

"I need some paper…something I can write on." Edward said.

"Gerrard, find something this fine gentleman can write on." Charlie instructed.

Sandy reached into her jacket for a pen and a scrap of paper and handed them to Edward.

"You don't have to do this, Mr. Lancaster."

"Thank you, Ms. Gerrard, but I think I do." He began writing.

"Here's the phone number for my attorney, Baldwin. Call him and instruct him how to get the money to you. He'll be expecting your call and will already have the money available. Please don't harm my wife. I give you my word that the money will be there if you just let my wife go."

"Now, see, Sandy…that's ne-goti-at-in'! See how smooth that went? Why can't you be that way with me?" Charlie chuckled. "Nice doin' business with ya, Lancaster."

"Will you give me your word that you won't hurt her? Gentleman to gentleman?"

Charlie burst out laughing, slapping his knee. "Oh..…Goddamn…Lancaster! You slay me…you really do…'gentleman to gentleman'? Okay, what the hell? I'll even shake on it."

Charlie leaned forward, and extended his hand to Edward. "Ya wanna shake, Lancaster?"

"Mr. Lancaster...." Before Sandy could react, Edward stood and leaned across the table to take Charlie's offered hand. Charlie took Edward's hand and suddenly pulled him up close to his face. Edward tried to break free. Sandy jumped to her feet and stood frozen.

"It's a deal, Lancaster. But, listen up close." Charlie jerked Edward closer. "If you screw me, I'll kill your little kitten here. And before I do, I'll make her sorry she was ever born. Ya got that?"

Edward tried not to flinch. "Yeah, I got it. You just call my attorney; you'll get your money."

Charlie let Edward go and shoved him back.

"Okay, then, get the hell outta here. Gerrard, get 'im outta here and get things movin'."

"Edward..." Kitty cried.

"Just stay calm, Kit. Do everything he says...it'll all be over soon, I promise."

"Eddie...I love you..."

Edward smiled at Kitty. "I know...I love you too, Kitten. I'll see you soon. Don't worry."

"'I love you too, Kitten'" Charlie mimicked Edward. "Ain't that sweet? Go on you two, get!"

Sandy stood and walked to Edward. She took him by the elbow and they turned and crossed to the door. Edward kept his eyes locked on Kitty as long as possible as they left.

As the door closed Edward said, "I'll see you soon, Kit."

* * * *

The inmates complained loudly about the lockdown and cold food served to their cells. No one was allowed in the chow hall. Sandy Gerrard stood gazing through the glass as meals were served to each cell through the narrow slot in the cell's door.

A few minutes ago six trays had been placed in the lock down chamber for the people in the visiting room. There was an air of expectation in the control room. She held her cell phone to her ear and waited impatiently for her call to be connected.

"Yes, it's Sandy Gerrard. What's the latest?"

"Sorry, its bad news, I'm afraid," Agent George Bryant replied. "Santana was gone by the time we got there. But at least now we know they're in AC."

"Damn it! Didn't ACPD have the casino covered? Christ! What about the girl?"

"No sign of her yet."

" Okay. Once you've found her how soon can you get her here?" Sandy asked.

"About that...we've hit a snag here. My supervisor wants to hold her here as a material witness? Until they take Santana into custody."

"Goddamn it!" Sandy exploded. "Don't they know I needed her here like yesterday?"

"I know, I tried to explain the urgency of your situation. They said they'd consider it."

"Listen, George I don't care what you have to promise your boss, find that girl and get her on the first flight here! Understood?"

"Roger that."

"Please keep me posted."

Sandy hung up and her phone immediately began ringing. "Damn it! Yeah! Gerrard here."

"Guess who, Sandy?" Charlie's voice barked out.

"Why're ya so cranky?"

"Hey, Charlie. Sorry about that. I thought you were someone else."

"What the fuck's goin' on, Gerrard. It's been five hours. When am I gonna get outta here? Where's the fuckin' car?

"Cool it, Charlie... these things take a little time."

"As long as yer takin', you could'a *built* the damn thing. I asked you a question, Gerrard. If I have to ask again, maybe one of my hostages has an accident."

"Just like we talked about, the car's on the way. Stay calm and nobody gets hurt, okay?"

"What about the money?"

"It's the money that's holding things up. But listen, what if I told you we have a couple of good solid leads on Rick Santana? He's been spotted in Atlantic City, just like your wife said."

"First of all, why should I believe you? Why should I believe a fuckin' cop?"

"Because I haven't lied to you yet. Because I'm the one who's going to get this settled..."

Charlie ignored her. "... And second, *I'll* find my daughter! I'll find that bastard, Rick. When I do... all you'll have to do, Sandy, is call out some guys to clean up the road slick."

"That's the death penalty for you, Charlie. You know that, don't you?"

"Oh, believe me, Gerrard, it'll be worth it! See, Rick's gonna take a long time dyin'."

"And Chelsea? You going to take her father away from her forever?"

"Whad 'ya talkin' about?"

"Think about it, Charlie. You kill Rick, Chelsea's Dad ends up on death row. You know the drill. Rick wins, you lose."

"Fuck you! I better be walkin' outta here in an hour, Gerrard. You got sixty minutes to make it happen."

"I'm workin' on it, Charlie. I promise."

Charlie looked at his watch. "Fifty nine and a half minutes and counting, Gerrard."

Charlie stabbed the disconnect key on his phone.

Sandy looked down at her dead phone and then through the glass wall at Charlie. He stood there grinning at her.

"Damn it!"

Chapter 31

Chelsea

Rick, dressed in fresh slacks and a crisp white shirt, sat on the bed of the casino hotel suite. The view through the half closed drapes was spectacular. From the balcony one could see the white beach below with bright blue umbrellas and chairs in a perfect line. The ocean was an endless deep blue.

A trolley sat to the side of the bed with the remnants of their breakfast. Rick slurped a cup of coffee. He glanced up as Chelsea walked out of the bathroom, fully clothed, her hair still damp from the shower. She looked ridiculously young in cutoff jeans and a peasant blouse.

"Come over here, baby." Rick patted the bed. Chelsea walked over and at the last minute sat down in one of the plush chairs in the room.

"When you gonna let me do more than kiss you, Chels? You know you like it," asked Rick.

Chelsea stared at the floor between her feet.

"Come on, honey, you can tell Uncle Rick what's eatin' ya." Rick cajoled.

"Nothin's eatin' me." Chelsea pouted.

"But, Baby, I know ya love me. Hell, I've loved you for so long I can't remember when I didn't."

"But you said you were takin' me to Atlantic City to see Lady Gaga."

"And we are. Tonight. I got a real special day and evening planned for us. You'll watch me win at Black Jack, then a first class dinner and the show."

He looked at her silently but she wouldn't return his gaze. "What's really wrong, sweetheart?"

Chelsea's eyes filled with tears. She looked up at Rick and one lonely tear slowly streaked down her perfect skin.

"I don't wanna 'do *it*' Rick. I think....it's kinda gross."

Rick's laugh came out as a cough. "Well, damn! That's putting a fine point on it."

"What's that suppose to mean? I can't help how I feel."

"No, you can't. And you have a right to your feelings. But, I thought since we had this terrific vacation planned...well, there's not a whole hell'va lot in it for me."

"There's somethin' else. I'm embarrassed to say it."

"Go on, you know you can tell me anything."

"I don't wanna end up like my Ma."

"My God! I would never let you dance for a livin'."

"It's more than that. I don't want to get tied down to a man; work some minimum pay job and get stuck forever in a one horse town." Chelsea tried to explain.

"Is that how you see you and me?" Rick didn't know whether to be insulted or amused. *Talk about 'out of the mouths of babes'!*

"Noo....Ricky I love ya but I still don't wanna do it."

"Okay, okay, you've made that abundantly clear. We'll just have a nice evening then I'll take you home. Okay?"

"Okay. You're not mad at me are you?"

"No, Chels, I'm not mad." He sighed. "Ya wanna go to the beach for a coupl'a hours?"

Chelsea jumped up from her chair. "Oh! Could we? That would be so cool. Wait 'till I tell my friend

Brittany I swam in the ocean." She ran toward the bathroom, snagging her swimsuit out of her suitcase on her way.

* * *six hours later* * *

Rick and Chelsea sat at a black jack table. The public gambling rooms were opulent with golden columns reaching to a ceiling sixty feet high. The floors were marble with islands of expensive carpet. The casino was really cranking up now. Shouts of despair and triumph were heard around the gambling area.

Hostesses circulated wearing skimpy black costumes which consisted of short skirts with a tiny ruffle in the back. A glimpse of their bottoms flirted into view when they walked. Their braless breasts were barely covered with an off the shoulder top in a peek-a-boo lacy fabric. They walked around the tables with large trays loaded down with drinks.

One of the perks for high rollers was to always have their favorite drink, freshly prepared and instantly available, on the trays.

Rick sat back relaxed with one arm draped across the back of Chelsea's chair. He watched as the dealer dealt a new hand. There was a generous pile of hundred dollar chips in front of him. Without looking up he raised two fingers and one of the waitresses immediately detoured to his table.

"Yes, sir."

"Jack Daniels Black on the rocks, sweetie."

"Right here, Mr. Santana." She said as she deftly selected his drink from the tray and set it down on a coaster.

"And a coke for the lady?" she indicated young Chelsea without batting an eye.

"Yes, please." Chelsea answered.

Rick smiled at the woman and held out a fifty dollar chip. "Thanks, beautiful."

"Thank *you*, Mr. Santana. Just let me know if I can do anything more for you or your daughter."

Chelsea giggled as the hostess walked away. Rick was focused on the new hand being dealt and the comment didn't faze him. Chelsea sipped her drink and glanced around the room.

"Ricky, I'm bored. Can we go pretty soon?"

"Not while I'm winning, we can't. I'm on a roll, baby. Just be patient."

Across the room two men in dark, conservative suits discretely watched Rick and Chelsea.

They had buzz haircuts and wore almost invisible earpieces in their ears. They resembled casino security so no one paid them much attention.

Diagonally from Rick and Chelsea was a lone man in a Hawaiian shirt and khaki shorts. He was standing by a roulette table but not playing. His ear piece crackled and a voice directed him.

"Stand down and let's see what they do."

"Roger that." The Hawaiian shirt said into his wrist watch. He covered his mouth and coughed to cover his actions.

"I would like to take them separately if we can. If she goes to the restroom or something; moves away from the suspect for any reason, then we take both of them immediately."

"If they move off together, we'll see where they go."

"Roger."

Meanwhile Rick had lost the last two hands and Chelsea was fidgeting in her chair.

"Rick...eee, come on let's *do* something else." Chelsea whined.

"Okay." He turned to the dealer. "Guess that's it for me, doll. Last hand." Rick pushed out four one hundred dollar chips.

The dealer smiled and dealt Rick a four of clubs, down, and a ten of diamonds face up. She dealt the house a six of spades and a ten of clubs. She waited for Rick. He was feeling lucky and he signaled for another card.

"Hit me."

The card sailed over to him, face up, and it was a seven of clubs. The dealer dealt herself a card, it was a face card and that busted the house.

"Nicely played, Mr. Santana." She shoved four matching chips over to his bet and he scooped up his winnings.

"Eight hundred bucks. Well hell, Lady Luck is back." He picked up two chips and handed them to Chelsea. "Why don't ya go into one of the shops over there and see if there's somethin' you'd like, Chels?"

Chelsea grabbed the chips and gave Rick a big kiss on the cheek. "Thanks, daddy."

"Buy somethin' pretty. I'll meet ya in half an hour."

Chelsea danced off toward the shops. Rick turned back to the table and pushed another bet forward. He grinned at the dealer.

"Le' see how long the Lady will stick around for me, what'd ya say?"

"I'm here all night, Mr. Santana." The pretty dealer smiled and started a new hand.

Across the room the special agent in charge signaled his men to move.

"Okay, let's take 'em. Jack, wait until she's at the door of one of the stores. Let some distance be gained between her and the suspect."

"Roger." Hawaiian shirt responded.

As Chelsea started into one of the shops, one of the young men in dark suits converged on her. From the other side Hawaiian shirt approached her from the other side. Gently they each took one of her arms.

"Excuse me Miss, Special Agent Craig Wilson." He flashed his badge at her. "Are you Chelsea Baldwin?"

Chelsea, eyes like saucers, looked at each man in turn and nodded.

"We need you to come with us."

"Why?" Chelsea tried to break free of the agent's firm grip on her arm. "Leave me alone. I ain't done nothing wrong."

At the same time the two remaining FBI agents walked casually over to Rick's black jack table.

"Looks like the cards are being real good to you, sir." The agent stood behind Rick's chair. Rick looked up and grinned. The smile died quickly as he identified them. He could spot a cop anywhere, anytime.

"Mr. Santana isn't it?"

"Yeah, so what?" Rick sneered.

"Sooo...the last time I looked it was *very* illegal to transport a minor over a state line. I'd say the young lady you have with you is, oh what?...about sixteen?"

Rick blanched. "I don't know what yer talkin' about. What minor? What young lady? I'm here by myself tryin' to have a good time. Get lost." Rick turned back to his cards.

"Please stand up and turn around, Santana. Cuff him." He directed his partner.

"You have the right to remain silent. Anything you say can and will be used against you in a ......"

As Rick was handcuffed and his rights were read to him, the pretty dealer had backed away from the table, bets and cards forgotten. She signaled her pit boss who immediately walked over.

"Gentlemen, what seems to be the problem? This is one of our best customers. I can vouch for Mr. Santana."

The FBI agents flashed their badges. The pit boss was visibly shaken. "FBI? What's this all about?"

"We have a federal warrant for Mr. Santana's arrest. It would be best if you stood down and let us do this quietly."

"Of course. If I can be of any assistance....." the pit boss said.

"Yeah, we'll need to see whose names Mr. Santana registered under and get a printout from you."

As the agent was saying this, another man in a custom navy blazer with the casino's logo on the breast pocket walked up and overheard the request.

"Good evening, I'm Mr. Gallagher, one of the hotel managers. I can answer your question right now. Mr. Santana registered under his own name with one guest."

Rick glared at the manager and shook his head.

"He was comp'ed one of our executive suites." He smiled reassuring at Rick.

"Oh yeah? And do you know the name of the 'guest'." The special agent asked.

"Yes certainly, his niece, Chelsea..uh...something."

"I'd have to get you her last name."

The agent turned to Rick and threw Rick's words back at him. "*'What minor? 'What young lady?'* Want to change your story, Santana?"

"Fuck you." Rick spat out.

Several yards away the other two agents were trying to escort Chelsea out a side door. Chelsea searched the room with her eyes and finally found Rick standing in the middle of some people. She struggled to break free of the grip the two men had on her.

"Rick!" she cried.

Even though it was clear by the slow flush that stained Rick's neck and ears that he had heard Chelsea's cries, he never turned or looked at her.

The agents were opening the side door where their cars were waiting. As they started out the door, Chelsea tried to turn around to where she had last seen Rick.

"Ricky!" she cried as she was hustled out the doors.

The agents surrounding Rick began to lead him handcuffed, across the casino floor toward the same doors.

"Hey, what about my winnings?" Rick asked.

"You got bigger things to worry about. Let's do this quietly, Santana. You don't want to embarrass yourself anymore than you have." He looked down at Rick, disgust written all over his face. "Sixteen? She's just a kid. You're one sick bastard, Santana."

"Fuck you and the horse you rode in on asshole."

Chapter 32

Sandy, Kitty, Hattie and Alma

A half hour later Sandy was sitting in the visiting room. Charlie stood against the wall with Kitty at his feet.

Joe was pleading once again with Charlie. "Listen, Baldwin, my wife and I; we got four kids waitin' at home. You're a Dad; you understand how worried they must be gettin'. Let my wife out, will ya?"

"No can do, Washington. Everybody stays put until I see that cash and the car."

Hattie reached over and grabbed Joe's arm. She began to cry. "Oh, Joe, make him let me go. My babies is gonna be so scared. What if they sees 'dis here mess on the television?"

"It's gonna be okay, Hattie-girl."

Charlie looked at his watch, ignoring the pleas of Hattie. "Twenty-eight minutes, Gerrard! You know what I think? I think you're full of shit. I think you're stringin' me along. This is takin' too long. I think you been lyin'…about Santana, my daughter, everything."

"I'm not lying to you…they're in Atlantic City for sure…it's just a matter of time before the cops find them and arrest Santana. They'll bring your daughter to you." Sandy assured him.

"What I need to do is show you how serious I am

about gettin' out. Now, let's see, what would convince you? Maybe, I should just do the Duchess, right here."

Charlie pulled the gun from his belt. He reached down and yanked Kitty to her feet by her hair.

Kitty struggled as she tried to rise and keep the pressure off of her hair.

"I got plenty of hostages left. Or no, wait, how 'bout Kowalski?" Charlie pointed the gun at Brad still handcuffed to the table. "Would that convince you, Gerrard?"

Sandy kept her voice quiet and calm. "Wait, Charlie. You don't want to do something rash. We're almost there. The money is almost ready. Don't blow it now."

"Bull shit! You're playin' me. You're tryin' to buy more time."

"No I'm not, Charlie. The car is here and the money is on the way. We had to find a judge to sign off on that kind'a change. I will tell you that we've been trying everything we can to find Chelsea and Rick. I'd like to see this situation resolved another way. By proving to you that Chelsea is safe and convince you to lay down your weapon and give this up before it's too late."

"And why would I do that, Gerrard?"

"Because a little time added onto your sentence is a whole lot better than death row. You kill Rick, it's the needle or a life sentence. Think for a moment, Charlie."

With each of Charlie's words he took a step toward Sandy, holding the gun and aiming it at her head. He punched the air with the gun as he closed in on her.

"Do. You. Have. Any. Idea. How. Sick. I. Am. Of. Your. voice, Gerrard? Blah, blah, blah…Don't you ever get tired of all this talk? Jesus Christ! And to think they pay you to do this."

Sandy held her ground as Charlie got within an inch

of putting the barrel of the weapon to her forehead.

"Twenty-seven minutes left, Gerrard, then the Duchess here…she bleeds. Maybe a little, maybe a lot. Ya just keep talkin' and you'll see how sick I am of your voice."

He glared at Sandy and tapped her forehead, lightly with the barrel. "I want out! Now!"

Suddenly Joe stood and spoke in a loud voice. "Baldwin!!"

"Yeah, wha'd ya want?" Charlie lowered the gun and backed away from Sandy.

"I changed my mind! I…" Joe told him.

"Joe! No!" Hattie screamed. "Lord have mercy, no!"

"I want in. I wanna go with you."

Charlie stared at Joe. "Why? Why the change of heart, *boy?*"

"Family problems… big ones! My wife, she's sick. I need some money."

"Oh, no, Joe! It could be nothin', like I tol' you."

"Hush now, Hattie girl." Joe told her.

"Please, please don't do this…"

"Family problems? Jus' like me, huh, Washington?"

"Thas' right, Baldwin, jus' like you."

"Why should I trust ya, huh?"

"Because I'm a con, like you. And I need the money bad."

"Oh yeah? What for?"

"My wife…she's gotta have some surgery. Now, you gonna let me join ya or not?"

"Washington, you're best left out of this." Sandy warned.

"Hey, Gerrard! Did I ask your opinion?" Charlie snarled.

"Joe, please…" Hattie whispered.

"Well, Baldwin? You want my help with this here jail break or not?"

"Maybe. Let me think about this. Gerrard, go sit at that table over there."

Sandy didn't move. "Do it now, Gerrard."

Sandy stood and backed up to the table that Charlie had indicated.

"Don't get Washington involved, Charlie. He's done nothing wrong, *yet*."

"Shut up and sit down."

Charlie turned back to Joe. "Yer' kinda' changin' your tune, Washington. What's in it for me, if I let you in on this?"

"I know cars. I'm a good man behind the wheel. Besides, how ya gonna drive and keep your eye on all these folks that you plannin' on takin'?"

"Well, ya got a point there." Charlie considered what Joe had said. "Ya say ya know cars…could ya spot it if Gerrard had 'em mess with my car?"

"Yeah, I can."

Charlie glared at Joe long and hard. *I wouldn't trust one of these niggers farther than I could throw one,* Charlie thought to himself. *But, beggars can't be choosy. And like the boy said, I'm not completely sure how I'm gonna manage drivin' and keepin' all these broads under control at the same time.*

"Okay, Washington, I guess I could use ya… sure, sure, the more the merrier! Get over here."

" Joe! Please, no, baby. Oh, my Lord…" Hattie began to cry in earnest.

"Shut up! Shut her up, Washington!"

Joe pulled Hattie up next to him. He placed his arms around Hattie's shoulders and brought her in close, his mouth to her ear.

"Hush now, Hattie. Don't cry. It's gonna be jus' fine. I got a plan. Whatever happens, you jus' 'member that your Joey loves you."

"Oh please God, no…"

Joe turned to Charlie. "Just one thing, Baldwin."

"What's that?"

"I break out with you; you leave my wife outta this. She stays when we go. That's the deal."

"Yeah sure, okay. Your wife stays. Wha'd I need another whiny broad for, anyway? He gave Joe a hard look. "You trading places with her or are ya with me?"

Joe swaggered over to Charlie and slapped him on the shoulder.

"I'm with ya."

Charlie laughed and punched Joe on the arm.

"Welcome to the party, Washington."

Charlie turned to Sandy with a smirk on his face.

"Well, *Sandy,* looks like we're gonna need some more money. You better make a call."

"Mr. Washington, you realize what this means? You realize how many years this is going to add to your sentence, when they catch up with you?" Sandy asked Joe.

"*If* they catch up with us, Ms. Gerrard."

"Shut up, Gerrard. Get on the phone. Washington's gonna need some walkin' around money."

"You certain about this, Mr. Washington?"

"You heard the man. I'll need some money too."

"Joseph, have you lost your mind?" Hattie asked.

"What are you doin'? Please…"

"How much?" Sandy asked.

"Uh…" Joe stumbled.

"Half." Charlie interjected. Yeah, half of what

you're gettin' for me should do it, don'cha think, Washington? Fifty thou'? Ever seen that much green, partner'?"

"Whatever ya say, Baldwin. You the boss. You runnin' this show."

"That's right... I am. Get on the phone, Gerrard."

Sandy took her mobile out of her jacket pocket and quickly dialed. "Yeah, it's me... we've had a development... we're gonna need more money. Yes, that's what I said. Get another fifty...yeah, you heard right... That's the development. Inmate Washington has gone to the other side of the room... yeah, that's what I said...I don't give a damn... get the extra cash..."

Sandy listened to the agent on the other end of the call. Her eyes flashed on Charlie but she quickly regained her composure and looked down. "Roger that."

"And find out where the car is!" Charlie told her.

Sandy repeated Charlie's demand into the phone. "...and find out about the car, will you?"

Sandy disconnected and returned the mobile to her pocket.

"Okay, Charlie, good enough? They're going to call me back and let us know when... and how."

"Negative, Gerrard, just the when. I say how."

"Okay. Tell me about the 'how'."

"Here's the deal...me and Washington, we're gonna walk outta this building with you and the Duchess."

"We're gonna walk straight to the car. Washington, you'll pop the hood and give it a quick check. So, Sandy ya better not mess with my wheels. When I'm satisfied the car and the money is okay, then you, Gerrard will walk away.

You stick to your end of the deal, and give me forty-eight hours to find my girl and Duchess here walks free."

"That's two counts of kidnapping on you, Charlie."

"What 'bout me, Charlie? What'll I do?" Alma suddenly asked.

"You're comin' with me, baby doll."

"But, Charlie, what if Chelsea comes home? Shouldn't I stay here?"

What is Charlie doin'! Alma asked herself. This is all just craziness. Charlie's not violent. At least, I don't think so. What happened to that man I used to know in Reno. The one who loved me better than any woman deserved. The man who never strayed, who changed the dirtiest diaper as if it was a privilege, the one who would always burn my toast in the morning. Who burns toast for heaven sakes? The man who never forgot me or his Mom on mother's day. What am I doing here? And now he expects me to go with him? Like some bad version of Bonnie and Clyde? I don't wanna go nowhere except home. Chels will show up eventually, say she's sorry and probably be a whole lot wiser. Why was Charlie havin' such a fit? He was carrying this whole thing way too far. Rick wouldn't hurt Chels 'cause he'd know that I'd castrate 'em if he did.

"Alma!" Charlie yelled.

"What?!" Alma was snapped back into the now.

"*I said*, ya won't be at home if you stay here."

"But I don't wanna go, Charlie…"

"For Chrissakes, quit arguin' with me, Alma. You're comin' and that's final."

"But, Charlie, I don't like what's goin' on here. And ya know I get car sick…"

Exasperated, Charlie turns to Alma. "God damn it,

Alma, you can sit in front, okay?! Let me think, will ya?"

Distracted Charlie had lowered the gun and it hung at his side. Joe suddenly reached for and grabbed him with both of his hands wrapped around Charlie's wrist. Growling, Charlie repeatedly punched Joe in the side of his head. Joe ignored the hits and doggedly hung onto Charlie's wrist with all his strength.

They continued to struggle for possession of the gun as Charlie punched Joe and in minutes they fell to the floor. Alma ducked under the table and covered her head in fear. Kitty crawled away crying. Hattie fell to her knees and began to pray.

"Let go'a the gun, you bastard." Joe hissed out the words.

Charlie hit Joe again. "Ya son-of'a-bitch! I'll kill ya."

Alma started screaming. "Charlie! Cut it out! Don't shoot! I'll go with you! Don't shoot!"

"Oh, Jesus. Jesus, please make it stop. Please protect us… Oh, God, protect my Joe. Oh, God, who art in heaven..." Hattie murmured.

Joe beat Charlie's gun hand against the back wall causing it to go off. A wild shot hit the soda machines. Sandy ducked behind a chair. She reached down and quietly removed her weapon from its holster. She didn't dare get off a shot while the two men struggled so closely together.

Charlie suddenly lost his grip on the gun and it skidded away across the floor toward Kitty. Joe's hands, free now, returned punch for punch until Charlie grabbed the knife from his belt and, without thought, stabbed Joe in the chest. With a shocked look on his face, Joe grabbed the wound with both hands.

Their eyes met.

"Oh Christ," Charlie said to Joe. "Look at what ya made me do."

Charlie made a grab for Joe but his unconscious weight slipped through his hands and he sank to the floor. Charlie stood up straight while Joe's blood dripped off the end of the knife still in his hand. He stared at Kitty who was holding the gun and aiming it at him. He laughed.

"What're ya goin' do Duchess, shoot me?"

From where he was standing he couldn't see that Sandy was also holding a gun aimed at him.

Oblivious to everyone but Joe, Hattie rushed across the room to Joe's side. "Joe! Joe!" Hattie screamed, sinking to her knees, she tried to lift Joe's body into her lap.

Kitty held the gun in two hands and still couldn't stop it from shaking. Tears ran down her face as she stared at Charlie. Keeping her gun trained on Charlie, Sandy crossed to Kitty's side and spoke calmly to her.

"It's okay now, Mrs. Lancaster. Put the gun down."

Kitty turned her face to Sandy. "What?"

"Everything is under control now. Give me the gun."

"No!" Kitty cried. "He's going to kill me."

Sandy slowly took the gun from Kitty's hand. "It's all right. You can give me the gun now. You're safe."

Keeping her weapon trained on Charlie, Sandy slipped the gun into her pocket.

"Drop it, Baldwin!"

Charlie, with an evil little laugh, started toward Sandy, his knife held in front of him.

Sandy pulled back the hammer on her weapon and fingered the trigger.

"Drop the knife now or I'll blow your head off!"

Charlie stood and stared at Sandy. The air thrummed with death.

"It's over, Charlie. Think about your daughter. Drop it."

Suddenly his body drooped in defeat. Charlie lowered the knife and dropped it on the floor.

"Now, kick it over here." Sandy told him.

Charlie kicked the knife toward Sandy.

"Turn around and face the wall, on your knees, cross your ankles, Charlie. Hands on top of your head. Don't move."

Charlie knelt on the floor and complied with Sandy's directions. Sandy kept her distance, not trusting him. With her free hand she got her mobile out and hit a button.

"Get the EMT's in here, stat! I've got a man down... WHAT!? Yeah, I heard you," she sighed.

Kitty crept over to Hattie, holding an unconscious Joe in her arms and sank down beside her. She ripped off the sleeve of her blouse and folding it, tried to staunch the bleeding.

"JOE!" Hattie kissed Joe's face. "Oh, my God, Joe. Don't die, Joey. Lord have mercy, don't leave me."

EMTs and the prison swat team rushed through the doors. The members of the swat team quickly handcuffed Charlie and stood him on his feet. The medics gently moved Kitty to the side. When they attempted to move Hattie aside, she screamed, "No! No!"

"Come on, Ma'am. Let us do our job. Let us help him."

Kitty crawled over and took Hattie into her arms.

"We'll sit right here together, Hattie. Let them work on Joe."

The medic began CPR and periodically checked Joe's pulse. He looked up into Sandy's eyes and silently shook his head.

Sandy walked over to Charlie and fished the key to Brad's cuffs out of his pocket. She turned and tossed it to Brad.

Hattie moaned and swayed back and forth in Kitty's arms.

"Is' gonna be all right, Joey-boy. Hattie's here right beside ya. Joe? Joe, don't die baby, hang on. Hattie loves ya, Joey-boy. Hattie's here."

Alma got up from under the table and crossed over to the other side of Hattie. She put her arms around Hattie and looked across to her husband.

"Oh, Charlie, look at wha'cha done."

Sandy addressed Charlie. "Well, Charlie, you really screwed this up. I just got word, the Feds are on their way here. They've got your daughter and Santana too. He's been charged with kidnapping."

Charlie raised his head and looked at Sandy.

"And Chelsea?"

"Your daughter's safe. She hasn't been harmed…in *any* way.

Sandy looked over at Joe. "A man is dead and for what?"

"It was worth it, Gerrard. I got you to find my daughter, didn't I?"

"Ah but at what cost, Charlie?"

"Whatever the cost, it's my daughter we're talkin' about."

Their eyes met in a myriad of sadness, disappointment, and in Charlie's case, defiance.

Sandy sighed as she broke eye contact and looked over at Joe's lifeless body.

"This wasn't some old black and white movie, Charlie. In this story the hero dies."

Chapter 33

Alma ~ one year later

Alma sat in the grungy little cubicle waiting for Charlie to appear on his side of the glass. Hanging on the wall next to her was a black telephone receiver, smudged with finger prints.

I hate this, she complained to herself, *not to be able to touch Charlie. Not feel his arms around me if only for the regulation two minutes. What a stupid rule. Like people would start humpin' on the tables if you didn't make rules. And now, the only contact they'll let me have is once a month with a dirty, smudged plastic window between us. All because some guy accidently got killed. It wasn't Charlie's fault. They should'a never pushed him so far. Don't they get that?*

Charlie walked through a door, handcuffed in front and wearing leg shackles. He sat down opposite Alma and reached for the receiver on his side of the window.

Alma grabbed her phone with her left hand and placed her right hand against the window.

"Hi, baby." She said.

"Hey, Lady-bug, how're ya doin'?"

"We're just fine, sweetie."

Alma and Charlie gazed into each other's eyes speaking without words.

"I love ya, Charlie."

"I love you too, baby. You'll never know how much. How's Chelsea?"

"She's just fine, hon. She's doin' so good in school. All A's and B's this year and she seems to have really settled down."

"That's good, babe. How's the new club workin' out?" Charlie asked.

"It's okay. Good tips. I'm able to save some every pay check."

"That's great." Charlie sighed. "I still wish you could work at some other job, Alma."

"Well Charlie honey, you might finally get your wish. Chelsea's got this crazy idea that I should explore my love of decoratin' things. She enrolled me in a decoratin' school on line."

"*You?* Using a computer?" Charlie laughed.

"Yeah. Chelsea's teachin' me."

"And what's this decoratin' school? You goin' be making cakes now?"

"Oh, Charlie, always makin' with the jokes. Chelsea would kill me if she heard me call it 'decoratin'.'"

"What're ya talkin' about babe?" he asked.

Alma straightened her shoulders and lifted her chin. "I'm studying interior design."

"Wow." Charlie couldn't believe it.

"Remember how much you loved my apartment in Reno? You even told me I was quite a decorator. Do you remember?"

"Yeah, I sure do. You did have a flare for it."

"Well, Chelsea convinced me that I *do* have some talent and she showed me how easy it would be for me to learn on line. That way I can work and support us and still learn this stuff."

"Really? Well, I am impressed, Alma. How long is it gonna to take you?"

"Five months on line but I also hav'ta go to the local

community college and do some, what they call, 'practical'. That's where ya have to actually decorate, oops! I mean *design* a room with furniture and accessories and everything."

"Baby, I am so proud of you." Charlie grinned at her. "Just don't tell your future customers what you did in your other life."

"There's a catch." She explained.

"What's that?"

"We'd have to move back to Reno. Then my 'practicals' at the college would be free 'cause I'm a Nevada resident."

"I think that's a good idea, doll. Go home."

"Really? "

"Yeah. Get Chelsea outta here. Fresh start and all that."

"But Charlie, I don't even know if I can finish it. Five months is a long time. And I don't know if I'm any good. I just like to put colors together and it always seems to turn out pretty."

"Now, you listen to me. You can do this. You do have talent. I am so proud of you for tryin'."

"Okay, if you think it's a good idea." Alma's tone was still uncertain. "But I ain't leavin' here until you get your hearing and if you just get extra years, then we're stayin' in Illinois. I can still get my certificate in decoratin'."

Charlie stared through the glass at Alma. He dreaded this part of their conversation. Alma looked back at him closely and frowned.

"Did ya hear something?"

"Yeah, last week."

"And? They reduced the charge right?"

"Naw. The first degree murder charge is stickin'.

Then I submitted a petition for relief to the Board of Pardons and Paroles. It took them less than eight hours to deny it."

"That's not fair!" Alma exclaimed. "Ya didn't mean it. It was kinda self defense. I was there, I saw it. It should'a been manslaughter!"

"Yeah, babe, it *is* fair. There were five witnesses who saw me stab Washington to death."

"But, Charlie that means you'll *never* get outta prison." She cried.

"Now listen, I want you to be brave about this. You gotta be strong for me and for Chelsea. They took me back to court and sentenced me right on the spot. "

"What, Charlie? What're ya talkin' about?"

"They gave me the death penalty, babe."

Alma screamed and then she screamed again. Alma stood up, still screaming and beat at the Plexiglas window with her fists. *Who was that doin' all that screaming?* Alma wondered. *Why doesn't somebody come in and shut her up?* A prison officer came running into the room. He rushed over to her cubicle and grabbed her by the arm.

"Visit's over, lady. Ya gotta leave."

At the same time, an officer came into Charlie's room and taking the phone out of his hand, hauled him to his feet and tried to forcibly drag him through the door. Charlie fought him off and tried to turn so he could see Alma. "Alma, baby, I love you. Go home, ya hear?"

Another prison officer ran in and helped subdue Charlie. Still struggling, he was led from the visiting area.

Alma screamed. "Charlie! Charlie!" She fought the officer's grip on her arm. "Let me go. *Charlie!*"

Chapter 34

Alma ~ two years later

A yellow taxi pulled up to a side door at the state prison. The heavy rain hit the pavement running in small rivers it raced down the sewer drains. Alma, in a dark grey coat and Levis stepped out of the cab. She tried to open a bright pink umbrella and the icy rain hit her in the face while she struggled with it.

Leaning into the open door she told the cabbie, "Wait for me."

"Sure thing, lady. You paying, I'm staying."

"I 'll be about a half hour."

Alma walked quickly up to the door and pressed a large button in the wall. Next to it was a small metal grill. From the grill she heard a loud buzzer. The intercom came alive.

"Yes. Who is it?"

"Alma Gaynor, signing in to see inmate, Charles Baldwin, number 553892." Alma said into the speaker.

"Roger. Ms. Gaynor, as soon as you enter, turn left and face the wall."

She huffed out a strident laugh and sneered, "This ain't my first rodeo, buster."

The door clicked and, opening the heavy door, Alma entered the room, walked to the wall and faced it. She immediately placed her hands, palms down, against the surface and waited.

The prison official took her umbrella and then waved a wand around her body.

"Okay, put any money or keys into the tray and go into the next room through that door."

Alma fished into the pockets of her raincoat and dropped some cash and her small key ring into a plastic tray. She then entered a small room and sat in a chair at a metal table. She waited alone.

Twenty minutes later another guard opened the door in front of her. He motioned to someone in the hall and Charlie walked through the door. He looked older and paler since Alma had seen him six months ago. But his grin was cocky as ever.

The leg shackles made him shuffle but he still was able to manage a little swagger. The guard escorted him to the chair opposite Alma and Charlie sat down. Bolted into the table in front of Charlie was a large steel ring with a short chain that locked. The guard lifted the chain and attached it to Charlie's handcuffs, securing his wrists to the metal ring.

Alma reached across the table with both hands, and held Charlie's shackled hands. They silently smiled at each other as the guard moved over by the door to give them a molecule of privacy.

"God it's good to see ya. You're as beautiful as ever. How ya doin', doll?" Charlie asked.

"I'm okay, hon." Alma smiled.

"How was your flight?"

"Long."

"Looks like this is it, baby. Shane ain't ridin' back into town anytime soon."

"Charlie, how can you make jokes at a time like this."

"It's all I got left, baby. Besides I love to see your smile. How's Chelsea?"

"She's still pissed at me for moving us back to Reno, but what's new? Other than that she's fine, baby. She got a full scholarship to Nevada State. Can you believe that?"

"Yeah, I can. She's a smart cookie."

"Well, I for one almost fell over when she showed me the letter. All we got to worry about is books and food."

Charlie leaned down awkwardly and kissed Alma's hands. "So we're on the same page. You're not gonna tell her about this, not until she's older. For now just let her believe I got life. Okay?"

"If that's what you want, Charlie-baby."

"I don't want to mess up her head. She's doin' so good. And when you do tell her, if she gives you grief for lyin' you tell her that her Dad wanted it this way."

"Okay, hon." Alma swallowed a sob. "You gettin' her letters?"

"Yeah."

They were quiet for several long moments, gazing into each other's eyes....remembering.

"Listen, Alma, about tonight. I don't want you there. It's no way for you to see me."

"Fuck that!" Alma cried.

"Alma Jean! I've never heard a single swear word come outta your mouth and the first time you cuss that's the one you pick?"

"Yeah and you'll hear a lot more where that come from if you say I can't be there with you tonight. For once in your life, *you* listen to *me*."

Charlie grinned but said nothing.

"When they…." Alma swallowed hard. "…strap you down, I want you to look at me, only me, through the glass. While they work on you, ya know… puttin' the needle in, you stay on me. Don't look nowheres else. I'll be talkin' to you through the glass. I'll be tellin' you how much I've loved only you through everything. The last thing you're gonna see is me and my love for you. Understand?"

Charlie's eyes filled and he smiled sadly. "Yeah, doll, I got it. And Alma…?"

"What?"

"Thanks for all the years. Thank you for giving me such a beautiful daughter. Thanks for all the time you sat in that miserable visiting room with me."

"Ah, baby, where else would I be? I love you. I always have."

The prison guard glanced at his watch and straightened up off the wall. "Time's up."

Alma squeezed Charlie's hands tight, "Baby, I want you to remember all the good times we had. Remember that first weekend when you came home and found me dancin' at the club? God, I wish you could'a seen your face." She laughed. "Remember that first weekend, baby? We never got outta bed. Remember when Chels was a baby and we'd drive the neighborhood late at night 'cause that's the only way she would stop cryin' and sleep?"

"Visitin' time is up, lady." The guard said as he unlocked Charlie's cuffs from the table. Charlie and Alma stood.

"You just keep remembering all those happy times. Promise me, Charlie?"

"I will babe. I love you."

Alma turned to the guard. "Can I kiss my husband?"

"Yeah, sure." The guard stepped away.

Charlie stood there as Alma wrapped her arms around his neck and kissed him on the lips.

Alma looked deeply into Charlie's eyes. "I have loved you since I was a kid. That's never gonna change no matter what they do to us."

Alma stood there as the guard led Charlie from the room.

Chapter 35

Alma

Charlie walked, unaided, between the six burly guards. He was followed by the warden and the prison chaplain.

'Dead Man Walking' Charlie grinned to himself. *Never thought that would apply to me. What a great flick with that sexy redhead all stripped down plain to look like a nun. A waste of a beautiful woman that's what that was. It sure ain't an oldie but I liked it anyway. Here's my chance to see how close to real life the movie was. Me and Sean Penn, checkin' out like real men.*

Charlie chuckled out loud. The guards glanced down at Charlie and then back at the warden. Shrugging his shoulders, the warden indicated that they should keep walking.

Let them wonder what's so funny, Charlie thought. *Never let them see you sweat, that's my motto. They probably think I'm crazy laughing as I go to my own execution. Dumb shits. Let them wonder.*

They came to a door at the end of the hall. Beyond it was what the inmates called the 'death room'. One of the guards opened it for Charlie and all eight of the men escorted him into the notorious room. Charlie was surprised at how small it was. A square box twelve by twelve feet with a low ceiling and a permanent metal bed affixed to the floor in the center. The bed, adorned in clean white sheets filled the room.

One of the guards led Charlie to the side of the bed and he sat on the edge of the bed. As the guards took charge, there was little conversation as each man knew his job. This was the last stop in the justice system's express lane to hell.

Charlie's body was secured with thick leather straps; one around his chest, midsection, groin, thighs and calves. The men then strapped his arms onto boards jutting out at a 45 degree angle from the bed.

While they methodically worked Charlie closed his eyes and took his thoughts back to the movie. *Yeah, the movie was right on the mark. Wonder how they found out all this stuff? Probably brought in some expert consultant like a warden moonlightin' for Hollywood. At the end of the movie you really liked Penn even though he was a very bad ass.*

A whiff of alcohol made Charlie's eyes fly open. An orderly was leaning over his right arm and swabbed it with antiseptic.

"Gotta stick you, Baldwin, find a vein. Both arms. You understand?"

"It's thoughtful of you to swab my arm first to prevent infection." Charlie laughed.

The warden stood to one side at the foot of the bed. Charlie could see two identical windows sealed off by curtains. *Is Alma sitting there now?* He wondered. *Will I see her when they pull those curtains back? God! I hope so...I can get through this if I can just see her face.*

* * * *

The witnesses were escorted into the viewing room. The room was divided by a seven foot wall separating the victim and perpetrator's families. Each room held three rows of metal folding chairs. Three walls were concrete cinder block. The fourth wall had two large glass windows and on the other side a closed curtain blocked their view.

The turnout was small. The victim's side was eerily empty and silent. Alma was dimly aware that one of the observers in her room was Sandra Gerrard.

What the hell was she doin' here? Alma wondered. *Oh, well, guess it don't matter who's here. Not to me anyway, just as long as Charlie knows I'm here.* Sighing, Alma sat in the first row, in the center where Charlie could easily see her. She wore a black coat and jeans. Her hair was tucked up under a baseball cap. She had on dark glasses.

Slowly the curtains started to draw back. On the other side of the glass was a gurney holding Charlie, his body strapped down to the bed. Behind the head rest was a control panel with tubes and lights. All the lights were red. A chaplain stood at Charlie's side. An orderly stood at the control panel behind Charlie's head. The warden stood at Charlie's feet.

"Mr. Baldwin, do you have any last words?" the warden asked as he pulled a microphone down from the ceiling.

"Yeah, I do."

As Charlie spoke he turned his head to the glass window and found his wife. Alma took off her baseball cap and shook out her fiery-red hair. She removed the dark glasses.

"Alma, when you tell my daughter about this tell her that I loved her more than life. Tell her that I'm sorry."

Charlie casually looked to see who else was in the room with his wife. When he saw Sandy Gerrard sitting there, several seats away from Alma, his eyebrows rose in surprise.

"Hey Gerrard! Did ya bring the pizza and beer?"

Sandy gave him a small, sickly smile.

"No hard feelings, Gerrard." Sandy stared at him through the window. Charlie grinned at her one last time.

"Oh… and Sandy? I don't care what the hell you think, Shane was just wounded," he said with a laugh.

Charlie's eyes found Alma again, "I love you, Lady Bug. Always have, always will. Only you."

He looked at the warden. "Let's get this show on the road, Warden. Time's awastin'."

"Do you wish to pray, Mr. Baldwin?" the chaplain asked.

Charlie laughed. "Not much use for prayers where I'm goin', preacher."

Charlie turned back to the window. Alma leaned forward and with her eyes, she silently commanded Charlie to stay locked on her face.

Out of the corner of her eye she saw one of the lights change from red to gold. She saw the first tube fill and then the gold light went to green. She mouthed the words to Charlie, "I love you more than anything in this world. I always have."

As the green light on the panel glowed Charlie smiled in response to her words. His eyes flickered, closed briefly then snapped open again. The boldness was still there but now there was a glimmer of panic.

He stared intently into Alma's eyes one last time.

"Alma, I love you."

Alma inhaled on a sob. She smiled and nodded to Charlie. His eyes flickered again and closed forever.

Epilogue

Hattie and Kitty

Kitty was sitting in a winged back chair with a cup of Earl Grey in her hand and the morning edition of the Chicago Tribune in her lap.

The morning room was one of Kitty's favorites in the whole house. Pale green silk wallpaper covered three walls, with cream colored wainscoting. The furnishings were upholstered in a pale green palm frond design with various shades of the green on the walls. One whole wall was glass with French doors that led out on a large, well tended flower garden. The window treatments were a soft gold and cream stripe and held back by cords with heavy gold tassels. The deep Persian carpet was gold and green.

"Auntie Kit!" The door from the foyer burst open and Stella ran across the room and threw herself into Kitty's lap, causing Kitty to juggle the cup of liquid. Newspaper pages flew everywhere.

"My stars, child, let me set this down before you cause me to scald both of us," she laughed as she placed the teacup and saucer on the side table.

Stella looked up into Kitty's face, her eyes bright with excitement. "Guess what? Bet you can't guess where I'm goin'!"

Kitty hugged her close and then gave her an expression of intense concentration.

"Let's see...the moon?"

Stella giggled, "No."

"No? All right. China? I've always wanted to see China."

"Uh-uh."Stella giggled more.

"A dude ranch?"

Stella burst into bright laughter. "No, I don't even know what a 'dude ranch' is."

"All right, then I give up." Kitty teased.

"The Zoo!" Stella crowed. "Mommy says tomorrow is her day off and her and me are going; just the two of us. She said it's a 'mommy-daughter date'."

"'She and I' ". Kitty automatically corrected Stella.

"Yes'm. 'She and I' are having a mommy-daughter date."

"That's wonderful, Stella. I believe I read in the paper that there's a new baby giraffe."

"Really? Do you think that they'll let me pet it?"

"Well, about that I'm not certain, but you surely will be able to see it."

From out in the hallway, Hattie's voice could be heard calling. "Stella! Where'd that chil' get off to now."

"We're in here, Hattie," Kitty called.

Hattie walked into the room with a scowl on her face. "Stella-girl, wha'd I be tellin' ya about botherin' Miss Kitty all the time?"

Stella jumped out of Kitty's lap and stood with head hung low.

"I'm sorry, Miss Kitty, but she drawn to you like a little ol' bee to honey."

Kitty laughed and pulling Stella in close, kissed her cheek.

"And I adore this little ol' bee, don't I Stella."

"What does 'adore' mean, Auntie Kit?" Stella asked.

"Scoops of hugs and kisses with lots of love on top!" exclaimed Kitty.

Stella looked up at her mother with her big, solemn brown eyes and said, "Yep, Mommy, we adore each other."

Not being able to resist Stella's seriousness, both Hattie and Kitty burst out laughing.

"Go on, chil', Miss Kitty and me, we gots to discuss the finances of this fine house. Go find your sister. Lunch be ready in about an hour."

"Okay, Mommy." Stella turned to Kitty. "See ya later alligator."

"After while, crocodile," Kitty laughingly answered.

Stella ran from the room while Kitty continued to chuckle and Hattie stood shaking her head.

"Miss Kitty, if it's convenient, I got the ledger here for the house expenses for ya'll to look over," Hattie told Kitty.

Kitty held out her hand for the book and Hattie pulled up a chair near her. Kitty opened the ledger and studied it for a few minutes.

"My word, Hattie, these numbers can't be right," Kitty exclaimed.

Hattie leaned over and scowled at the page. "Whas' wrong, where is my mistake? I went over the arith-a-ma-tic three times, Miss Kitty."

"Oh, I didn't mean your math was wrong, Hattie. The thing is I am quite surprised at the money you have saved this quarter. Can this be correct?"

Shyly and with great pride, Hattie said, "Yes'm, we had us a good quarter."

"You know you can save a lotta money goin' to the Farmers' market on Saturdays. And I buy in quantity at the price club. It all adds up, Miss Kitty."

"Well, you're the first house manager and cook that I've ever had that tried to save *me* money," Kitty beamed at Hattie. "I am so lucky to have you and the children here. Edward will be home soon and I can't wait for him to meet the kids."

"You still thinkin' that Mr. Lancaster gonna be alright with us bein' here?"

"No question in my mind. Now, Hattie, there is something else I think you should know."

"Whas' that, Miss Kitty?"

"The newspaper had an article about Charles Baldwin and Joe, this morning."

"Lord-a-mercy, what them vultures got to say now?" Hattie sighed.

"All the appeals and requests for leniency have been exhausted. Baldwin's execution is scheduled for next week."

"I feel sorry for Miss Alma and her chil', Miss Kitty. I truly do."

"This is difficult for me to ask but I wasn't certain if you knew your rights as the victim's wife. You have the right to be there."

"Wha'cha mean? Be where?" Hattie asked.

"You are allowed to witness the execution."

Hattie looked shocked. "God in heaven! There been enough grief around that white boy without there bein' an audience in his final moments. I never heard'a such a thing!"

"I wanted to let you know that I would go with you if you wanted to be there."

"I appreciate that Miss Kitty, but no. We moved on, that's what Joey would'a wanted."

"Well, then we won't speak of it again." Kitty paused. "Hattie, are you happy here?"

"Oh, Miss Kitty, we so happy living here with you." Hattie's eyes sparkled with tears. "When my Joe passed I was scare't how my chil'un was goin' to be taken care of. And the house you gave us is so cozy and *safe* and close to my kitchen. Lordy, those projects we done lived in got to be downright dangerous. I miss my Joe and my heart is in pieces, but yes Ma'am I am very happy here. I can' thank ya'll enough for all ya done."

Kitty rose and crossed to Hattie. She knelt down and took her rough, callused hands in hers.

"Hattie, you and the children will always have a home here. And I'm the one who's grateful. Your husband, '*your Joe*', saved my life and probably the lives of others on that terrible day. As I explained to you before, you could live here for free. The house I gave you belongs to you. You don't need to work for me."

"Oh, no, Ma'am, I needs to work. I needs to be needed. And carin' for this beautiful ol' house ain't no work, a'tall. I love takin' care of it *and* you."

Alma

In the main bar area Alma took her long time customer by the hand and led him through the tables to one of the VIP rooms in the back. *My last half-shift and my last customer.* She sighed. *An easy one; all Jake will want is a private dance and some conversation. And he tips me like money is water.* She looked over her shoulder, squeezed his hand and flashed him her mega-watt smile.

"Come with Alma, baby. I got a new dance especially for you."

Jake followed her with a stupid puppy smile on his ugly face. *He's far from pretty*, Alma reflected, *but he's polite and courteous to all the girls and the money is good...very good.*

There were three VIP rooms with lights above the doors. Two lights were red but Alma saw, by the green glowing above, that one of them was free. She opened the door and led Jake in.

"Ya want me to dance first, Jake or shall we talk?"

"Ah, hell Alma I had a bitch of a day and I'm tired. Let's just have us a drink and a chat."

"If that's what will make you happy, honey, that's what we'll do." She said as she sauntered over to the mini-bar. Without having to ask, she poured Jake his whiskey and water, two cubes. She poured herself a coke with a lime that all her clients believed was a rum and coke. The customers were uncomfortable if the girls didn't drink with them.

Jake eased into one of the deep plush chairs and sighed with relief. He toed his loafers off and leaned back. Alma walked back with the two glasses and set them on a side table. She posed in front of Jake and waited.

"God, you are so beautiful, Alma. I so look forward to seeing you and talking."

Alma started to sit on his lap which is where she usually perched while they chatted.

"Take a load off, honey. Sit here next to me." Jake patted the twin chair next to his.

"Wow." Alma said. "You must be tired."

"I'm exhausted. The corporate guys were in town last night so we were out *very* late. I'm too old to be getting' in at half past three in the morning. Then today was filled with meeting after meeting."

"I'm sorry, baby. You want a massage?"

"Oh God, that would be great." Jake sighed.

Alma got up and walked behind Jake's chair. She gently began massaging his temples and hair line.

"Ah…" Jake sighed. "That feels like heaven. I almost didn't come tonight 'cause I've got this bitch of a headache and now….your fingers are chasin' it away."

"I'm glad, hon."

They were quiet for several minutes. Alma slowly rubbed his temples and then began massaging his scalp. *I love this guy,* she thought to herself. *This is all he ever wants and someone to talk to. Never pressures me for anything more."*

"Jake, honey, I got some news."

"Oh yeah, what's that?"

"This is my last night."

Jake's eyes flew open. "What? What'd ya mean?"

"I gave Pete my notice."

"Are ya moving away again?"

"No. Remember I told ya a few months back that I was going to school part time?"

"Yeah."

"Well, I got my license for interior design."

"Wow, doll, you surprise me."

As they talked Alma continued massaging Jake's shoulders and neck.

"And I been savin' money 'till I get a client or two. I got a small job already so I let Pete know this is my last night."

"Alma, that's terrific. What's the small job?"

"I'm going to stage two model homes for this contractor I know. He just finished building two subdivisions out north of town and he wants me to do the models."

"Good for you, baby. What's 'staging' mean exactly?" Jake asked.

"I decorate the rooms, only with rental furniture and accessories. To show buyers what their homes could look like if they bought in the subdivision."

"I'm happy for you. But, I gotta ask, Alma, what am *I* gonna do…. without you?"

"I'm gonna introduce you to a new girl we just hired. Her name's Samantha, Sam for short. I handpicked her for you, Jake. She knows you like to just relax and talk and have a private dance once in a awhile. And guess what? She's a massage therapist. So she can work on your headaches the way I do."

"I'm sure gonna miss you, Alma."

"Don't worry, Jake, Reno's a small town. I'll see ya on bingo night at the casino. Get your girls to give me a free drink." She laughed.

"That's a deal." He looked at her thoughtfully. "But I got a better idea."

He reached back and gently took her hands and brought her around to sit back down.

"What's this?" She smiled and sat next to him.

"Well, I got a design job for you. I been wanting me one of them home movie theater rooms with the big leather loungers and all? It's an addition on my house. How about I hire you to design and decorate it for me. You will have one hundred percent decision making. All I ask is that you don't turn it into a French bordello; no flocked wallpaper!"

They both laughed.

"Are you serious, Jake? For real? You want to hire me?"

"For real, Alma. And I want a combination bar and concession stand for when my adult friends or my grandkids come over."

"Don'cha want to know what I charge?"

"I figure about seventy-five dollars an hour so let's make it a hundred. And there's no budget; just buy nice stuff for me. I've already hired an architect. I got a resource for state-of-the-art high-def TV but you'll need to find the geeks to hook everything up. I want stereo surround sound."

"Jake I don't know what to say. My first real job as an interior designer and it's gonna be for the owner of one of the biggest casinos in town."

"When can you start? I'll want you and my architect to meet to get the ball rollin'."

"How would Monday be?" Alma held her breath for his answer.

"Great! Whatever you say, doll. What do you need from me?"

"I'll take a look at your architect's drawings and incorporate anything that I think you will want. And then, if you have time, I'd like to sit down with you fairly soon and discuss colors. Get a feel for what you like and really dislike."

"How 'bout one o'clock in the afternoon, before the high rollers wake up. I'll arrange for a credit card for you for when you start buying stuff for me."

Alma tried to contain her glee with a professional game-face but totally failed. She grinned and jumping up grabbed Jake's head and landed a big kiss on his forehead.

"Jake, you are the best! How can I ever thank you?"

"Just give me a wonderful movie room and a snazzy bar. The works! I'll be happy."

He leaned over and extracted his wallet from his back pocket. Opening it he took out ten one-hundred dollar bills.

"That's an advance on the job." He told her. And then taking out five more bills, he said, "And that's for tonight." He handed her the money.

Alma's eyes filled with joyful tears. "Jake, how did I ever deserve you?"

"Words right outta my mouth, honey, how did I ever deserve *you*?"

Trisha Sugarek, author, playwright, and poet has been writing for four decades. Until recently her work focused on play writing that ranged from prison stories to children's fables.

She has expanded her body of work to include two books of poetry, *HAIKU, A Collection of Haiku poetry and Sumi-e ink-Art* and **Butterflies and Bullets,** a collection of her poetry and free verse. Also a group of children's books, entitled the "*Fabled Forest Series.*" This is her debut novel.

She has enjoyed a thirty year career in theatre as an actor and director. Originally from Seattle, she has worked in theatres from coast to coast. Her plays have been produced across the country and Samuel French/Bakers Plays has published four of them.

Trisha lives in Savannah, Georgia with her three golden retrievers. Her plays and books can be found on line and at your favorite book store. Visit her web site at **www.writeratplay.com.** She loves to hear from her readers.

10041340R00189

Made in the USA
Charleston, SC
02 November 2011